# DEATH SCENE

*Recent Titles by Jane A. Adams from Severn House*

*The Henry Johnstone Mysteries*

THE MURDER BOOK
DEATH SCENE

*The Naomi Blake Mysteries*

MOURNING THE LITTLE DEAD
TOUCHING THE DARK
HEATWAVE
KILLING A STRANGER
LEGACY OF LIES
SECRETS
GREGORY'S GAME
PAYING THE FERRYMAN
A MURDEROUS MIND

*The Rina Martin Mysteries*

A REASON TO KILL
FRAGILE LIVES
THE POWER OF ONE
RESOLUTIONS
THE DEAD OF WINTER
CAUSE OF DEATH
FORGOTTEN VOICES

# DEATH SCENE

*A Henry Johnstone Mystery*

## Jane A. Adams

This first world edition published 2017
in Great Britain and the USA by
SEVERN HOUSE PUBLISHERS LTD of
Eardley House, 4 Uxbridge Street, London W8 7SY.
Trade paperback edition first published
in Great Britain and the USA 2018 by
SEVERN HOUSE PUBLISHERS LTD.

British Library Cataloguing in Publication Data
A CIP catalogue record for this title is available from the British Library.

ISBN-13: 978-0-7278-8703-0 (cased)
ISBN-13: 978-1-84751-808-8 (trade paper)
ISBN-13: 978-1-78010-872-8 (e-book)

Typeset by Palimpsest Book Production Ltd.,
Falkirk, Stirlingshire, Scotland.

# PROLOGUE

I t should, she thought, have been a lovely evening and indeed the play had been enjoyable and the conversation lively and cheerful.

If it hadn't been for one small thing, it would have been a perfect time.

That one thing, though; that had played on her mind throughout and Cissie had been unable truly to relax.

The evening had been warm and, although it was late, Cissie laid her coat down on the red armchair and went back outside on to the veranda. The night air felt cooler as it drifted in off the ocean, reminding her that it would soon be autumn and, she noted, the scent was changing. It was still salt-tanged and sharp and pungent with the smell of seaweed but with an underlying mellowness that predicted harvest and falling leaves.

She stepped down on to the shingle beach, pebbles crunching beneath her feet as she wandered down towards the sea. It was only when she stopped and her own feet ceased to crunch on the pebble beach that she became aware of other footsteps.

Cissie turned in surprise. 'Oh,' she said. 'It's you. I thought you'd gone home.'

'I thought we should talk.'

She sighed and then shook her head. 'There's nothing to say. I promised to keep quiet and asked you to promise to leave me alone.'

'It's not as simple as that.'

She had turned her back on him, hoping that he would take that as a hint to go.

'Really not as simple as that, my dear.'

The blow felled her. Cissie crumpled, dropping to the sand and pebbles without making a sound.

Her assailant tucked the blackjack into his pocket and slid

his hands beneath her arms. He dragged her up the beach and
back on to the veranda, then inside the little wooden house
that had been Cissie's home for the past three years.

After hauling her up on to the bed he then went back to
close the door, shutting out the cool night air, the fresh breeze,
the soothing wash of the ocean.

'You lied to me,' he said as he stood over her. 'You lied to
me and caused me trouble. You can't just promise to keep
your mouth shut and hope that will be enough.'

A quick search uncovered what he wanted, and she was
coming round by the time he returned to the bedroom. He
was glad that he'd not had to wait too long – though he'd
brought smelling salts with him in case he needed to wake
her more quickly. He wanted her awake; he wanted her afraid.
He had suffered; why shouldn't she do the same?

He took the pillow from beneath her and laid it on the chair.
Unfolded the paper that wrapped the powder, filled the glass
from the covered jug she kept on her bedside table.

She opened her eyes – 'What . . .?' – trying hard to focus
on him, fear suffusing her features as she remembered what
had happened on the beach.

'I told you,' she whispered. 'I wouldn't tell. Not ever.'

'No,' he said quietly. 'You won't. Not ever.'

# ONE

'**C**issie, darling. Cissie, I did knock but I suppose you didn't hear me. I'm just off to the . . .'

She paused, standing in the centre of the living room rug, oddly concerned to see Cissie's coat still lying on the back of the chair. She called out again and then realized that it was more than the coat that was bothering her. It was the smell, and the sound. The smell was not strong, but it was definitely there, as was the buzz of flies.

'Cissie? Are you there?'

She crossed the room and pushed the bedroom door and the first thing that registered was that Cissie was still wearing the pink dress she had worn two nights before, when they had all gone to the theatre. The second was that Cissie's stockings were wrinkled at the ankles – and Cissie's stockings were *never* allowed to be wrinkled at the ankles. The third was: why did she still have her shoes on when she was lying on the bed?

Muriel's fourth reaction was to scream, and scream very loudly. Her friend was dead, there could be no doubt about that, and the most shocking thing was that she had probably lain there since their evening at the show two nights before and had not even had time to change out of her favourite dress.

Constable Prentice had been summoned, as had Dr Arnold, and the two of them arrived at pretty much the same time.

'A suicide,' Dr Arnold said, pointing at the glass and the opened paper (which had evidently contained powder of some sort) lying on the bedside table. 'You say she was an actress?'

His tone of voice let Constable Prentice know that Arnold considered actresses particularly prone to such deaths. 'Apparently so,' he replied, though whether he was agreeing that Cissie Rowe had been an actress or that she had committed suicide was open to debate.

The two men crossed the room and stood on either side
of the bed. The eyes were still slightly open, the lids having
receded after death, and the flies had taken advantage, crawling
into the damp places of the nose and slightly open mouth.
Arnold waved them away and they shifted briefly before settling
back. 'Blasted creatures,' he said.

'Don't touch the glass, please, sir,' Prentice advised as the
doctor reached out for it. 'Just in case it's not as it first seems.'

Dr Arnold scowled at him. 'I know a suicide when I see
one. Or possibly an accident,' he conceded. But he left the
glass and the paper alone anyway. 'No doubt she was in
the habit of taking a sleeping draft and then took more than
her stated dose. I've seen this many times, Constable. Too
many theatrical types round here. Too many would-be actors
and actresses. Temperamental types who find themselves in
dire straits when they hope for stardom.'

'Perhaps so, sir.' Constable Prentice nodded but continued
his examination of the room. He remembered what Muriel
Owens had said when she had told him about finding the body
of her friend. *She had her shoes on. Why would she keep her
shoes on when she was lying on the bed?*

It was an odd question but the sort of odd question that
Constable Prentice knew he should take notice of. Muriel
Owens had known the dead woman; he and the doctor had
not.

The bed was made and the sheets turned back over a blue
counterpane. The body lay full-length, stretched out on top
with the head slightly propped atop two pillows. The hands
had fallen by her sides, lying one palm up and one palm down
on the counterpane.

Constable Prentice stepped back to examine the shoes. One
foot was wedged against the pine rail at the foot of the bed,
the other twisted a little to the side. He peered at Cissie Rowe's
feet and spent so long in silent consideration that Dr Arnold
became annoyed.

'For goodness' sake, man. Let's get the poor woman
covered up and out of here.'

'I don't think we can do that, sir,' Constable Prentice said.
'I think we should get out of here and leave the scene alone.'

'For goodness' sake, man,' Arnold said again. 'It's a simple case of suicide – or an accidental overdose, if you want to be kind. Tragic and all that, but . . .'

Constable Prentice was shaking his head. 'I think you're wrong, Doctor. I think you're very wrong indeed. I think what we have here may well be a murder.'

Detective Chief Inspector Henry Johnstone was so used to his own capacity for silence that he often failed to register it in others, even those for whom silence was an uncharacteristic trait. It was therefore some time before he realized that his sergeant had barely spoken since they had left London.

For Mickey Hitchens this was a state of affairs bordering upon the unique and Henry finally decided that he should ask the reason for it.

'She was one of the wife's favourite actresses,' Mickey said. 'Oh, she was never a big star, not like we reckon she should have been, but she was a real tragedian, if you know what I mean. Played the discarded ingénue beautifully, broke your heart so it did.' He looked speculatively at his boss. 'Not that it would have broken yours, I am most fully aware of that, but for those of us lesser mortals who like to get involved with our fictional characters . . .'

Henry nodded. He glanced up briefly as the door to their compartment opened and two people, a man and a woman, glanced in, presumably looking for a place to sit. They closed the door again and went on their way and Henry reflected that the sight of himself and Mickey often had that effect.

Henry himself, tall and whip thin. Austere, some might have said. And Mickey, smaller and more solid but with the face of an experienced boxer.

Neither of them, Henry thought, looked like men who would either offer or invite convivial company on a lengthy journey.

Dismissing the would-be interlopers from his mind he wondered instead about the current state of Mickey Hitchens' marriage, but didn't like to ask. Mickey and his wife seemed to have an interesting arrangement; sometimes they lived together, sometimes they lived apart. Sometimes very much apart, though as far as Henry could make out this was never because of arguments between them but rather because Mrs Hitchens was a woman of very independent mind and liked to go her own way. Many of Sergeant Hitchens' superiors considered this to be a scandalous state of affairs, though even they had to admit that it never impinged on his work. Henry, being a man who hated others probing into his personal life, afforded his sergeant the same respect that he himself would expect to receive and usually refrained from asking for details.

He had been better acquainted with Sergeant Hitchens' mother, another formidable and independent woman, whose pearls of wisdom were often quoted by her son and whose presence was still pervasive even eighteen months after her death.

'So tell me what you know about her,' Henry said, settling back into his seat and allowing the rhythm of the train to sooth his nerves. He had been sleeping badly again but had declined his doctor's offer of more Veronal. He was too painfully reminded of how quickly he had become dependent on the stuff the last time he had been through one of these episodes of prolonged insomnia. 'And tell me about this place we're going to. I've read about it in the newspapers, but I'm no great fan of the cinema so know relatively little about our film industry.'

'You enjoy it enough when that sister of yours drags you along,' Mickey observed wryly, and Henry nodded, conceding the point.

'Well, you know perhaps that the south coast has proved a fruitful space for our own film industry to grow and thrive, and the little town of Shoreham-by-Sea has its own studio. The light is very good, so I'm told. I forget who it was, but one of the companies built a great glasshouse on the seashore so that they could film for more of the year. That, I believe, is still standing but the main studio complex suffered a fire a few years back – 1923, I believe, in the winter of that year. The producer Stanley Mumford and his brother had been editing film when they spotted the fire. Fortunately for them they managed to get themselves out, and also the boxes of silver nitrate film the silly buggers had been storing under their beds. You know how that stuff goes up?'

Henry nodded. 'Anyone hurt?'

'Not that I recall, but the Mumford brothers brought one of the film cameras out with them and filmed the whole shebang. I remember seeing it all on the newsreels only a day or two later.'

'But the studio survives?'

'The glasshouse was largely untouched. The rest, I believe, has been rebuilt. I think it's fair to say that the high times may have passed, but they still produce films there and the little spit of strand that is our destination still houses a fair few theatrical types. Like our poor Miss Rowe.'

A police car collected them from the station. Their route looped out of town and then back towards the sea, crossing the River Adur by the road bridge. There was access by a footbridge too and there was also a ferry, Henry was told. Bungalow Town, as this part of Shoreham Beach was known, was a narrow strand separated from the main town by the River Adur. About a mile and a half long and perhaps half a mile wide at its widest stretch, it was marked at one end by the film studio and the Church of the Good Shepherd and at the other by the old Palmerston Fort, built to guard the mouth of Shoreham harbour. Across the river mouth lay another finger of shingle which protected the harbour itself. They were driven along a track that the constable accompanying them said was called Old Fort Road, sea on one side of them and a line of wooden bungalows along the other.

The day was bright, a polished blue to the sky, and even the sea looked determinedly azure and summer calm. The screech of sea birds filled the air as Henry got out and surveyed the scene.

'That's the bungalow, sir,' the constable told him, pointing – perhaps unnecessarily – to the little wooden dwelling outside which another constable stood. 'Will you be wanting me to wait, sir?'

'I think we'll walk back,' Mickey told him, glancing at his boss and receiving a nod of approval. 'We can get the lay of the land better that way.'

The constable nodded, turned his car with some difficulty

on the narrow track and the rough shingle and then drove away, sand and dry earth puffing up around the tyres.

A dry season, Henry thought. Dry and bright and far too blue. He turned then and followed Mickey Hitchens inside.

Cissie Rowe had been twenty-eight at the time of her death; she had been born only two days after the new century had begun. She was small, blonde, of slight build, and from the pictures that adorned her walls had been elfinly beautiful. Now two days of heat, flies and the onset of putrefaction had mottled her skin and bloated the delicate features.

Constable Prentice was eager to show them what had alerted him to a possible crime. 'The friend that found her, sir, she commented on the fact that the lady still had her shoes on, even though she was lying down on the bed. She reckoned that was out of character. She was a fastidious lady, so her friend told me. So that got me to thinking. And so I looked at her shoes, and you can see on the backs of the shoes and on the heel . . .'

He pointed, and Henry took hold of the woman's ankle and gently raised the leg so that he could clearly see the scuff marks on the dark leather. The bedroom floor was timber, with rugs only at the bedside. But it was smooth and would not have done the damage that he could now observe.

'She was dragged,' he said. 'But not just across this floor. And it looks as though the right shoe started to come off. It's been pushed back on but not seated on the heel.' He nodded at Constable Prentice.

'Good observation,' Mickey Hitchens approved. He looked hard at his boss, reminding him that the compliment should also be given by the inspector.

'Yes indeed.' Chief Inspector Johnstone nodded again. 'Very solid observation.'

Constable Prentice preened.

'There are marks on the face and neck that look like bruising.' Mickey was staring hard at the young woman's face. 'See, they've likely developed *post mortem*, but it looks to me like someone's had hold of her just close to the jaw.' He glanced across at the water glass and folded paper lying on the bedside table. 'Maybe she was less than eager to drink her sleeping draft.'

'It's possible,' Henry conceded. 'Best not to speculate yet, I think.' He turned back to Constable Prentice and steered him gently towards the door. 'You said she was found at ten this morning?'

'Yes, by Mrs Owens. She lives down the beach. In Blue Horizons.'

'Blue Horizons?'

'Yes, sir. All the bungalows have names, not numbers. She's in another one of the originals, like this one, built from the railway carriages.'

Henry nodded. He'd noted the odd construction of the building. The bedroom was an old railway carriage and, from what he'd seen, the kitchen on the other side of the main room was similarly constructed. The middle room formed a square space in between.

'I'd like you to go there now,' he said. 'Tell her that my sergeant and I will be along shortly to ask some questions.'

'Prepare her, like.' Mickey Hitchens nodded encouragingly at the younger officer. 'I'm sure it's all been a bit of a shock for her, so a familiar face will be reassurance, you know? And if you stay with her, make sure she doesn't go gabbing to anyone else.'

Constable Prentice nodded. 'Might be a bit late for that, sir, but I'll do what I can.' He looked pleased with himself as he left and Henry closed the door behind him.

'Show me these finger marks.'

'Sorry, shouldn't have said anything with the boy here, he's bound to gossip. Too pleased with himself not to.'

'He's hardly a boy, Mickey. He's a police officer and seemed sharp enough.'

'And is probably fifteen years my junior, so he's a boy to me.'

Henry looked curiously at his sergeant and wondered, not for the first time, if Mickey felt that he'd been passed over for promotion. There were many who had entered the service at the same time as him and were now inspectors, but Mickey Hitchens had shown no sign of wanting to move onward and upward. Henry thought again about the conversation on the train and about Mrs Hitchens and of her . . . odd habits. Perhaps this did have something to do with Mickey's lack of advancement.

'Look, here, and here. Like someone's grasped her face with his thumb on this side and his fingers on that. Maybe forced her mouth open, poured in the sleeping draft and forced her to swallow.'

'And then sat back calmly and waited for her to go to sleep?'

'And then taken this pillow and pressed it down upon her face.' Mickey indicated the second pillow beneath the dead woman's head. 'The angle is all wrong. No one would lie like that.'

Henry nodded. Mickey was an expert at reading a scene and Henry could see nothing here to invalidate his preliminary conclusions. 'And so hope to stage it as suicide. No note, though, so far as we can see. Though not everyone leaves a note. And I would add one coda to your conclusions. At some point she was dragged, possibly across the beach, though not far or she would have lost the shoes completely. If she'd been conscious she would have screamed and struggled and the bungalows are not so far apart that her cries could have been ignored. My guess is that she was unconscious when he laid her out on the bed, barely conscious when he forced her to drink and able to put up very little resistance.'

Outside, they heard a vehicle pull up on the gravel of the Old Fort Road and moments later there was a quiet knock on the door. Mickey crossed the room to greet the mortuary ambulance driver and told him to wait a moment more.

Gently, he and Henry turned the body on to its side. On the back of the head were signs of bruising and a little blood.

'So she arrives home, someone's waiting for her, bashes her on the head.' Mickey frowned pensively and Henry knew what he was thinking. 'You're wondering why he drags her in here, why he—'

'Didn't pick her up and carry her,' Henry said. 'She's a tiny little thing and weighs nothing.'

He rolled her body a little further. The skirt of the dress

was stained with dried urine, as was the counterpane. It was quite common for the body to void both faeces and urine after death but that wasn't what Henry was thinking.

'It is only a guess, but perhaps she was frightened enough to lose control of her bladder. Perhaps whoever killed her needed to stay clean. There would also be the risk of getting blood on his clothes though there is not a lot of it in her hair.'

'No, but head wounds do bleed, often profusely. There might well have been more blood when he first hit her.' Mickey paused, frowning. 'If we follow that line of speculation then whoever it was fully expected to be seen by someone who would be close enough to notice any transfer on to his clothes.'

'So perhaps someone who only had a short walk home.'

Mickey nodded, and then told the ambulance driver that he could come in and collect the body.

While Mickey supervised the mortuary collection Henry wandered out on to the veranda in front of the little bungalow. The beach was stony and dotted here and there with wild plants like marguerites and sea kale. It looked out upon the open ocean. Looking between the bungalows, Henry could see the stretch of water that separated this narrow peninsula from the main town of Shoreham-by-Sea and the South Downs beyond. The day was still calm and blue and even the gulls were silent now, replaced by a more melodic call which Henry thought might be skylarks.

He took out his cigarette case, rubbing his thumb, as he habitually did, across the engraved letters cut into the brass, the letters A and G, somewhat crudely fashioned. The case was smooth with handling from the decade or more that Henry had owned it and carried it in his pocket.

He wasn't sure he wanted a cigarette but he removed one anyway and lit it with the Dunhill lighter that had been a gift from his sister on his last birthday. That too was engraved but it had Henry's own initials on it.

A clump of boots on wood and then on gravel alerted him to the removal of the body and Henry turned to watch as the two men struggled across the pebble beach and on to the little road where they had left the ambulance.

Mickey Hitchens joined him on the veranda. 'They're transporting her back to London,' he said. 'I thought it best to hand her over to our experts. If the local pathologist is as inept as that Dr Arnold was I'd as soon not risk leaving her here.'

'A little harsh, Mickey,' Henry said.

'The man saw what he was looking for, not what was there. He passed judgement before he had the information he needed to make it.'

Henry nodded and offered Mickey a cigarette. Mickey lit it with Henry's lighter. 'It's a pretty spot,' Mickey said.

'It is if you like the sea.'

'I take it you're not sleeping again.'

Henry frowned. 'And what leads you to that conclusion?'

'You're dreaming about the sea.'

'I never said that.'

'You didn't need to. Shall we be getting on, then?'

The two of them went back inside. The murder bag and other bits and pieces of paraphernalia had been left just inside the front door and Mickey retrieved them now. 'I took her fingerprints,' Mickey said, 'but we need to do a better job back at the lab. What I've got will do for comparison for now, and I took some pictures before they moved the body.'

'So where should we start, do you think? He must have handled the glass and probably touched things in the bedroom at the very least, but the likelihood is he wore gloves. I suggest we start in the living room; that's the most public of spaces so we're most likely to get prints of friends and neighbours. Then we can start with the woman who found her, take comparison prints for elimination and fingerprint anyone who came to the cottage – sorry, bungalow – on a regular basis. That will give us our call for analysis.'

'Right you are,' Mickey said. 'The camera's there if you want to make a start. With the bedroom, perhaps, then we'll not get in each other's way. When I'm ready to photograph prints, I'll give you a shout.'

Henry picked up the camera and returned to the room where they'd first seen the body. It looked oddly empty now that Cissie Rowe had gone. He spent a little time looking at the photographs on the wall. There were, inevitably, quite a few of her professional life but there were others too of a child aged perhaps twelve or thirteen, obviously Cissie in her younger days, standing with an older woman. There were tall stone buildings in the background, and a Ferris wheel. Henry wondered where the photograph had been taken. He moved methodically around the room, working across the walls and then down towards the floor. It was a method that used a lot of film but since the camera and other equipment were Henry's own he felt that he was answerable to no one in this regard and his method meant that they would have a very complete picture of both the scene and the background.

From the other room he could hear Mickey moving about, the slow shuffle of steps and the occasional shifting of furniture or equipment. They worked well together, were well used to one another and needed little discussion. After a while, Henry returned to the living room and, knowing Mickey's methods, began to photograph those areas that his sergeant had finished with. A light dusting of fingerprint powder identified where pictures additional to the contextual shots would be required. Mickey would already have photographed what he could with the fixed lens fingerprint camera that was part of their kit when working away from their base. The fixed lens camera was an improvement on the half size plate camera, heavier and more cumbersome, that they had previously used.

Mickey glanced up. 'I've photographed what I can. There are a few items I'll be packing up and sending back to London and a few more prints I'll have to try lifting. I'd rather not ship a complete door up to the bureau if it can be helped. Our Mr Cherrill and his people wouldn't thank me for that.'

'And they can't be photographed?'

'They can, but the angle's awkward and I'd as soon have a contingency plan. There are also partials I'll use the dactyloscopic foil to pick up, then I'll photograph them here before I ship them off.'

Henry nodded. The lifting of prints was a little hit and miss.

The dactyloscopic tape worked with the black powder that Mickey was using on the lighter coloured objects he had fingerprinting. The darker furniture and the door would have to be printed with the paler grey 'light' powder which did not respond well to lifting.

'When I'm done with this, I'll go down and talk to the Owens woman,' Henry said. 'If you can head back up the beach towards the road, knock on a few doors. I'll send Prentice back to look after the scene and the equipment so you can leave it here.'

'You're assuming he'll have followed instructions and still be at the Owens bungalow, then?' Mickey grinned.

'I'm assuming this is the most exciting thing ever to have happened to that young man,' Henry said. 'He and the Owenses will be picking over the bones for every scrap. Which may or may not be a good thing.'

'It'll be a case of who wants to tell you the story first,' Mickey said. 'Young Prentice or the woman who was actually in here.'

'So I listen to both, and see what tallies.' Henry flashed a rare smile at his sergeant. 'I think we should work on the basis that the murderer is local, at least for the time being. That he knew Cissie Rowe's habits and knew that she'd been out that night and when she was likely to be back. I also think he waited outside, just in case Mrs Owens came in with her. He didn't want to be surprised by two women, perhaps with a husband in tow. I think he wanted to be sure that Miss Rowe was alone.'

'It seems likely that he also enticed her outside after she'd arrived home. She'd had time to come in, drop her coat on the back of the chair and then perhaps go back outside to meet her death.'

Henry glanced over at the coat and nodded; that seemed logical. 'Whatever happened, it took her by surprise. Someone was able to get close enough to her without her suspecting anything – so we start with friends and neighbours and we move on to her work.'

Mickey nodded and turned back to his fingerprints. 'I'm going to have to mix up some more of the grey powder,' he said. 'The humidity is getting to it and it's clumping badly. I keep having to regrind before I brush.' The grey powder was a mix of two parts prepared chalk to one part (by weight) organic mercury. Mickey mixed it, in small quantities, as it was required. It had a grave tendency to absorb moisture.

Henry took a last look around before setting off to interview the finder of the body. So far he was satisfied with the day's work. He and Mickey both knew the drill and needed no instruction and at least, this time, the body had been left undisturbed thanks to the vigilance of a very young constable. There was nothing more frustrating than arriving at a scene to find that the body had already been moved and the scene tidied up.

'There was one thing I noticed,' Mickey said as Henry stood in the doorway. 'Might be nothing. But a photograph or something's been moved from that table over there.' He pointed to a small, round table set in the corner of the room. The top was carved and Henry recognized it as Anglo-Indian. It was placed on a stand that could be folded down and put away and on it two photographs had been set in wooden frames side by side. The bungalow was kept very clean but even so, if you looked closely it was possible to see a faint line in the very fine coating of dust that had settled on the table top. The carved surface made it even more difficult to discern but Henry could see that Mickey was right. Something had been moved and from the length of the line in the dust it looked as though it had probably been a photograph frame, probably of the same size and shape as the other two.

'I'll ask the Owens woman,' Henry said. 'It seems she's familiar enough with the place to be popping in and out uninvited so the likelihood is she would remember what was there.'

He picked up his hat and, with a final nod to Mickey, stepped out on to the veranda.

It was almost noon and the day was getting hotter by the minute. Henry stripped off his jacket and wandered along the beach in just his shirt and waistcoat. The strand was shingle with a lot of flint, softly saturated by slow-moving water at the edge of the inlet. Further along the beach he could see

girls with baskets picking up stones and he recollected vaguely
that flint was still gathered here for building work. It was
probably something his sister, Cynthia, had told him; she and
her husband had a house just along the coast that they used
during the summer season. In amongst the shingle wild plants
proliferated; he could identify marguerites and sea kale and
here and there pink pom-poms of thrift. The line of bungalows
stretched along the beachfront and, he could see, also along
the road that ran at the rear of Cissie Rowe's little home. What
he took to be the older buildings had small gardens fenced off
around them; the newer ones were crowded a little closer
together. Many had verandas, most painted and well cared for.
Blue Horizons, home of Mrs Owens who had found the body,
was five bungalows down. Constable Prentice had obviously
been looking out for him because the door opened immediately
and he was ushered inside with barely time to put his jacket
back on and make himself decent.

Prentice proudly made the introductions. Mrs Owens rose
to greet him. She was a small woman dressed in dark blue
and with tightly waved grey hair. Spectacles hung on a chain
around her neck and she wore a longer chain that ended in a
blue bauble just below her waist. When she shook Henry's
hand her grip was so slight that he was barely aware she had
even touched him. She introduced her husband, a taller man
who stepped forward and shook hands with a much firmer
grip. Henry considered that he was probably trying to make
a point.

'Will you sit down, Inspector?' Mr Owens indicated a chair.
It was red leather, armless and very upright, the sort that
might be brought out for visitors that were not particularly
welcome.

'That's . . . um . . . Chief Inspector,' Constable Prentice
corrected.

Henry waved the objection aside. 'I understand you must
be very upset,' he said. 'I will try and make this as easy as
possible.'

'How can it possibly be easy?' Mrs Owens said. She dabbed
at her eyes with a little lace handkerchief and Henry found
himself hoping that she would not need to use it in earnest

since there were only about two square inches of fabric at the centre of the lace.

'Please,' he said, 'sit down and tell me what happened this morning. Take your time.'

Mrs Owens sat on the blue loveseat and her husband took his place beside her. He reached out and grasped one nervous hand, leaving the other free to dab at the eyes with the little handkerchief. Henry could see that the woman had been crying and that her grief was genuine. He could also see that she was a little overwhelmed by the sense of occasion; having a policeman, a *senior* policeman, in your house was not something that happened every day and although you could be thankful for that, when it did happen you wanted to be prepared.

'Tea,' she said suddenly, and started to rise. 'I must get you some tea.'

'Please.' Henry waved her back into her seat. 'It really isn't necessary.'

Constable Prentice was hovering, watching Inspector Johnstone intently, and Henry noticed a slight flush brightening the younger man's cheeks.

'Constable, if you could go back and assist my sergeant? When he's finished up at the bungalow he needs to go and interview the neighbours and would be grateful if you would guard our belongings and equipment while he does that.'

For a second or two disappointment clouded the constable's face as it became clear he was going to be excluded from this conversation, but then he nodded enthusiastically and replaced his helmet. 'Yes, sir, of course, Inspector,' and he disappeared out of the front door.

The Owenses gazed after him as though watching an old friend depart, one they might not see again.

Henry glanced around the small room. It was comfortably furnished – a little over-furnished – with a heavy sideboard and a set of bookshelves laden down with what looked like a lifetime of memories. Inside the bungalow it was possible to discern that it had indeed been built from two railway carriages placed on either side of this middle room. The carriage doors were still extant and one, partly open, led into the kitchen; he assumed the other must be the bedroom.

Mrs Owens was following his observation. 'The carriages were being sold off cheaply,' she said, 'so many people took advantage of that and had them towed down here. The wheels were taken off of course and the carriages were floated across the river and then dragged up on shore by teams of horses. It was a quite marvellous sight. And then we got the local builders and carpenters to build between them and fix the roof.'

Henry, knowing that compliment was expected, rummaged in his mind for something that Mickey might say in the circumstances. 'It has made a beautiful home,' he said, and was rewarded by an attempt at a smile from Mrs Owens.

'We have been very comfortable here,' she said. 'And of course it's perfect for work, so close to the studio.'

She sat up a little straighter then, and Henry guessed that work was very important to her. He could hear Mickey's voice in his head telling him that he needed to ask her about her acting career before he dived into the dreadful events of the morning, so dutifully he said, 'Do you work at the studio?'

She no longer dabbed at her eyes with the tiny handkerchief; instead she fanned herself coquettishly. 'I did in my day, yes. Only small roles, you understand, I never rose to the heights that Cissie would have done, but they were happy times, and now I assist the wardrobe mistress and sometime chaperone the younger performers. I enjoy my work, Detective Inspector.'

Henry nodded. 'And is Mr Owens also employed by the film industry down here?'

'Cameraman,' the man said briefly. He was looking intently at Henry Johnstone. It was clear that he was more interested in dealing with this interview and getting rid of this intruder than in discussing his participation in the theatrical profession.

'And so you went to see Cissie Rowe this morning and . . .'

Mrs Owens took a deep breath and went back to dabbing her eyes. 'It was strange, you see. We usually see her out and about even if we don't speak every day. She likes to walk along the beach and when she passes she always waves. So I thought I'd go and see if everything was all right; she had not quite been herself out at the theatre two nights ago. She seemed distracted, somehow.'

'She seemed lively enough to me,' her husband objected. 'Muriel, I think the inspector needs the facts as they were at the time, not the way they might seem in hindsight.'

Mrs Owens frowned at her husband. 'She *did* seem upset, just a little anyway. She was such a sensitive soul.'

'And so, not having seen your friend since your visit to the theatre you thought you ought to check that all was well.'

She was on firmer ground now. 'Exactly that,' she said. 'I knocked at the door. I wanted to see if she needed anything fetching from the shop. I was going to the Bungalow Stores down on Ferry Road, you see. Not that they have a great deal, but they do stock the everyday essentials and I thought that Cissie might . . . I thought that Cissie might need something, even want to walk down with me. She often did, you see.'

'But you didn't get a reply.'

'No, I did not. So I opened the door and went inside and called for her. No one ever locks their doors along here.'

I imagine they will now, Henry thought.

'So I went inside and I saw that her coat was still lying on the back of the chair. Cissie never did that, she took care of her clothes. She'd take off her coat, brush it down and then hang it up. Same with the rest of her things, she told me that. Neat as a new pin was Cissie. Never a stain or a wrinkle. "Muriel," she used to say to me. We were close, you see, though she always called me Mrs Owens when we were out in public. She was proper like that. But "Muriel," she used to say to me, "I've worked hard for everything I have. It wouldn't make sense for me not to take care of it."'

'Such a pretty voice she had. Not like some of them; the studio said she would have no problems in the talking films – that's if they catch on, of course, though there's already great excitement within the industry, as you can imagine.'

Henry nodded. 'I'm sure there is.'

'Some of them will have to have such a lot of voice coaching. You would not believe. Pretty as a picture they look, but open their mouths . . .' She waved her handkerchief dismissively. 'Of course, it may well turn out to be so much pie in the sky. You'll have heard all about *The Jazz Singer*, of course? But one film . . . I ask you, is the success of one film really enough to warrant such radical change? Enough to cause a whole industry to change?'

Henry sought to bring the conversation back to the business in hand.

'And so this morning you went into the bungalow and you called out but there was no answer. So what made you go into the bedroom?'

Mrs Owens' look shot daggers at him. She looked away briefly, dabbing again at her eyes, and her nose and mouth this time. 'I knew something was wrong. I saw her coat, and then . . . and then I heard the buzzing and I smelt the smell and I knew something was wrong. There were never flies or smells in Cissie's bungalow. Clean. Always clean. Spotless.'

'Was the door open, the door to the bedroom?'

She thought for a moment and then nodded. 'Not all the way, but it must have been open, mustn't it, for me to have heard them? The flies, I mean. I know I didn't turn the handle, I know I just pushed the door. And there she was lying on the bed.

'At first I couldn't take it in. I thought she must have fallen asleep but then I saw that she had her shoes on and her stockings were wrinkled and she was still wearing the pink dress. She would never have lain down in her pink dress. She loved that pink dress. So I went closer to the bed and I looked at her and I realized that she was dead.'

'And what did you do then?' Henry asked.

'Why, then I screamed, of course. What else would you expect me to do?'

Henry wondered if it was inappropriate to find that funny. He decided it was.

'And then she came running back here.' It was the first time her husband had intervened in the narrative. 'I went back with her to Everdene – that's Cissie's bungalow, you know the older ones all have names, not numbers?'

'I do, yes.'

'I realized that Muriel was right, Cissie was in fact dead, so I knocked on the door of Elizabeth – that's the next bungalow down – and Mrs Clark sent one of the boys to fetch the policeman and the doctor. Her husband is a doctor, but he only comes down for the weekends, otherwise . . . anyway, and the rest you know.'

'Did you notice anything unusual about the bungalow, about Everdene? Was anything missing?'

Mrs Owens' eyes widened. 'I didn't even think to look,' she said.

Henry glanced at Mr Owens, who also shook his head. 'I'm sorry, Inspector, I think the shock of seeing the body drove everything else from our minds. The place was tidy as always. We would have noticed had it been otherwise.'

Henry nodded and jotted a few more details down in his notebook. 'Did Miss Rowe own Everdene?'

'Oh, no, no, no, she rented it. I think she was hoping to raise enough money eventually, and the Clarks – those are the people who *do* own it, they live in Elizabeth, next door to Everdene – they had said that she could have first refusal should they decide to sell. But no, she rented it from them, had been renting it for the last two or three years. We managed to buy this place, of course. We had it built specifically for us and we've never regretted it, not for one moment.'

'Thank you.' Henry nodded. 'Mrs Owens, in the corner of the living room at Everdene there is a little round table, do you know it?'

'Oh yes, with three little photographs set out on it.'

'One appears to be missing,' Henry said. 'Two remain, sitting side by side. One is of Miss Rowe herself, sitting on the veranda, I presume, of her bungalow. A second shows a group of three young women. Could you tell me what was depicted in the third?'

She closed her eyes as though thinking deeply and trying to recall, though Henry guessed that she knew immediately but just wanted to be seen making an effort. 'It was a picture of Cissie's parents,' she said. 'Or maybe it was an uncle and aunt, an older couple anyway. The three girls are three of our young performers, our young actresses; they were Cissie's friends. That photograph and the photograph of Cissie on the veranda were taken on the same day, last summer.'

'But you remember less about the other photograph?'

Mr Owens spoke. 'I remember that it was of an older couple,

middle aged, I suppose standing outside a rather severe looking house. There's a boy in the picture too, perhaps eleven or twelve years old. It's a little faded and tattered, as though before it was put in the frame it had been carried around without protection. Perhaps in someone's pocket or wallet.'

His wife looked at him, eyebrows delicately raised. 'Why would you take so much notice of a tattered old thing like that?'

He shrugged. 'I suppose because it stood out against the rest. The other photographs in that room are all of friends she had now, places she liked to visit, the sets and the studio. I suppose I noticed it because it was different.'

'She had other old photographs on her bedroom wall.' Mrs Owens nodded to herself. 'Quite a number of them, thinking about it.'

'But I don't imagine Mr Owens would have been in a position to see those,' Inspector Johnstone observed. 'So I can understand why that photograph must've stood out for him.' It would, Henry thought, be the kind of thing he would have noticed too.

He checked back through the notes he had been taking and decided that there was little else to be asked at present, in fact just three more things, standard questions that would be asked during any investigation.

'Can you think of anyone that would wish to harm Cissie Rowe? Any argument she might have had or professional disagreements or rivalries?'

The Owenses looked at one another and heads were shaken. 'No one, nothing,' Mrs Owens said. 'She was popular.'

'And did she have a particular young man that she might have been seeing? A gentleman friend?'

Mrs Owens smiled at his circumspection. 'Cissie had many admirers,' she said, 'but she took none of them very seriously. She was intent on her career.'

And the last question. 'Have you noticed any strangers in the area in the past few days? People you didn't recognize or who were behaving oddly?'

'There are always a few tourists who wander down here but mostly people come to visit the bungalows and are on their way to see someone specific. We are not on the beaten track here, Inspector. You must either take the ferry or cross the bridge so there is little to draw strangers to Bungalow Town, as the locals call this area, and I can't recall seeing anyone in the past few days who caused any discomfort or drew our attention.' Mr Owens looked at his wife for confirmation and she nodded, then shook her head.

Henry took that as agreement with her husband. Having nothing further to say or to ask, he rose and took his leave. 'There may well be other questions later,' he said.

'We understand that,' Mr Owens said. He escorted Inspector Johnstone to the door and Henry was aware that he stood watching him as he walked back along the shingle beach towards Everdene. He suspected that there was something on Mr Owens' mind but that the man had not yet decided whether it might be important, or whether he wanted to say it in front of his wife. He felt that Mickey might be able to shake whatever it was loose, and made a mental note to send his sergeant to have another conversation with Mr Owens – preferably alone.

Constable Prentice had brought a chair out on to the veranda and was sitting, staring out to sea. He jumped to his feet as soon as he spotted the inspector.

'Sir, I was just—'

'Being sensible,' Henry said. 'There is nothing to be gained by standing in the hot sun when you can sit in the shade. Sergeant Hitchens?'

'Oh.' Prentice looked flustered. This was evidently not the response he had expected. 'He's talked to the Clarks and the two bungalows on from theirs and he said to tell you that he's finished in here and maybe you could come and find him.'

Henry thanked him. The shade of the veranda looked very inviting. The shingle reflected the sun back and he could feel the heat even through the soles of his shoes. He glanced out towards the water, squinting against the glare. The girls were still moving up and down the beach putting stones into baskets, and he pointed at them. 'What are they doing?'

'Collecting flint, sir. Not many of them do it now but twenty years ago, so I've been told, there were girls up and down the

beach in all weathers, all day long, filling up their baskets.
Miserable work, sir. Some of the locals used to knit gloves
for them because their hands would get ripped to shreds from
the sharp stones and they'd get chilled to the bone in cold
weather.'

'For building work?'

'Used to be. Not so many do it now, there's no demand,
but some people still like the flint for decorative work.'

'And the girls are here most days?'

'Mostly in the summer now. There are very few who carry
it on through the winter months.'

'So if there have been strangers around, the girls are likely
to have seen them.'

'I know them, sir. Most likely they'd answer questions
for me.'

That made sense, Henry thought, and it meant that he could
sit in the shade for a few moments instead of having to walk
down closer to the water. 'Go and talk to them, Constable,'
he said. 'But remember, you are not there to gossip about the
death. An officer needs to learn discretion.'

Constable Prentice coloured slightly and then nodded
his head and strode off down the beach. Henry dropped
gratefully into the chair, pushing it right back into the shade.
What, he thought, would possess anyone to live this close to
the sea?

For the moment he closed his eyes and almost felt that he
could doze. It had been ten days since he'd had anything
approaching a good night's sleep and if this followed its usual
pattern there would be a few days more before exhaustion
eventually overcame whatever his brain was doing and allowed
him to rest. These episodes happened less frequently now,
perhaps three or four times in the past year, and he was
uncertain what had triggered them.

He listened to the sound of the water. He could feel the
warmth on his skin and reminded himself that this was a
bright sunny day, but his mind told him otherwise. In his
head this was a cold December day, and he could hear the
screams of men and women and horses and remember
the panic after the water had closed over his head and he

could no longer grasp which way was surface and which led down into the depths.

Henry opened his eyes and stood up. He went back into the bungalow and, standing just over the threshold, looked around again. He was tempted to pack everything and take it back to London, but to do so would take time and effort that might be wasted. Until he knew a little more about the dead woman it would be difficult to decide what was relevant and what was not.

He knew that Mickey would already have done a basic search of drawers and cupboards and would have packed anything that he immediately saw as important so he was unsurprised, when he opened the murder bag, to find that Mickey had taken the photographs from the bedroom wall and those in the living room, removed them from their frames and packed them carefully into a large manila envelope. There was also a collection of letters and some other paperwork.

Henry went from room to room tracking the work that his sergeant had done and looking to see if there was anything he might wish to add to this stash of possible evidentiary material but, as he expected, Mickey Hitchens had already done a thorough job.

In the bedroom was a small wardrobe and when Henry opened the door he was struck by the neatness of the clothes on their hangers. The wardrobe smelt of lavender and rose petals and Cissie's winter coat had been draped in an old sheet to protect it from dust. The smell of mothballs led him to the pockets; there were a few in each pocket, carefully wrapped in tissue paper so that they would protect but not stain. She had not owned a lot of clothes but Henry had the feeling that each item had been chosen with care and they seemed to be of good quality. He knew that Mickey would have checked pockets but he checked them again out of habit. Empty.

A three drawer chest held stockings and underwear and nightclothes and a few small items of jewellery, none of which initially looked valuable. A painted cardboard box held a wristwatch with a small face and slender leather strap, a brooch set with a paste amethyst, a red beaded necklace and a coral bangle.

In a second box Henry found something which Mickey had missed and which to Henry's eyes jarred with everything else in the bungalow. This was no cheap piece of costume jewellery, neither was it the sort of thing that a young woman with a modest income might conceivably have saved for – as she had for her clothes.

Henry looked thoughtfully at the gold bracelet, shaped like a snake biting its own tail, the snake's jaws forming the clasp. His sister had something similar, though Cynthia's had been bought in Bond Street and had ruby eyes; he thought that this snake might have eyes of garnet and gold of lower quality. But it was still gold.

The sort of thing an admirer might have bought for her, Henry wondered? Mrs Owens had been of the opinion that Cissie didn't take any of her admirers particularly seriously and yet it seemed to Henry that this was a serious piece of jewellery indicating, perhaps, a more serious intent, at least on the part of the giver. He took both boxes out of the drawer and put them with the rest of the evidence in the bag.

Footsteps on the veranda, footsteps that he did not recognize as Mickey's, suggested that Constable Prentice had returned.

'In here,' Henry said, and Prentice stuck his head round the door.

He watched curiously as Henry packed the jewellery boxes into the leather bag, obviously wondering what he had discovered.

'Had the girls seen anything?'

'A few tourists hanging around, nothing much. But they did see Miss Rowe talking to a man a few days ago. Said they seemed to be arguing.'

'Did they hear what they were saying?'

The constable shook his head. 'No, they were down on the strand and Miss Rowe and the man were near the bungalow. The girls said they looked like they were arguing, the man was waving his arms around, and when Miss Rowe tried to walk away from him he grabbed her arm. She shook him away and he stormed off. That's all they saw.'

'And when was this?'

'They think two or maybe three days ago. They can't be sure. But they know it was her.'

'And did they say what this man looked like?'

'Tall, they said. They said taller than Miss Rowe, but that don't mean a lot, she was only a little lady.'

Henry Johnstone nodded. He doubted she stood more than five feet tall and she was very slightly built. Henry thanked the constable, commended him for his efforts and asked him to stand guard again while he went to find his sergeant.

Constable Prentice, satisfied with himself now, took his place on the veranda and Henry set off in search of Mickey Hitchens.

He found his sergeant chatting to an old lady with a very small pug dog. The woman wore a purple hat decorated with many, many white daisies and the pug a purple collar, also decorated with daisies. The pug looked glum.

Mickey Hitchens spotted his boss and began to take leave of the old woman, backing away still talking, the lady following him with the pug in tow. Henry heard Mickey say 'I really have to go, Mrs Willberry' before hurrying over to where the inspector stood. Henry, taking the hints, turned and headed back in the other direction.

'Local gossip?'

'Yes, but unfortunately not a proper local gossip, only a visiting one. Her sister lives in Eveyline, that bungalow back there. She spotted me, decided I needed to be challenged and asked what business I had sniffing round here. When she found out I was a policeman, well, I thought I'd be there till teatime. Speaking of which, I'm sloshing with cups of tea and stuffed with home-made Madeira cake, chocolate cake and anything else that the fine ladies of this area decided to push my way, but when was the last time you ate or drank?'

'I suppose that would be this morning, before we got on the train.'

Mickey Hitchens shook his head. 'So,' he said, 'are we heading back to London or along the coast?'

'Cynthia is sending the car for us. Or a car anyway, Lord knows she has enough to choose from. We need to check in with the locals, make sure a guard is posted on the bungalow – we can't leave Constable Prentice there all afternoon and all night – and then we can come back first thing. It will be quicker than heading down from London and more comfortable than finding ourselves a boarding house.'

Sergeant Hitchens nodded enthusiastically. 'Better food too,' he said.

# TWO

They had walked back across the footbridge into Shoreham old town and gone on to the police station.

Now that the death was officially a murder inquiry they were able to mobilize the local force and by the time they left a couple of hours later Henry was satisfied that troops had been called in from Hove and Bournemouth to supplement the rather scant resources they had at Shoreham-by-Sea.

They had phoned in their report to the central office at Scotland Yard and arranged for a courier to take the prints that Mickey had lifted at the scene and the movable objects he had selected back to the fingerprint bureau. Neither Mickey nor Henry Johnstone was hopeful of anything turning up from this; the prints would probably be from friends and neighbours of the dead woman. They doubted that the murderer had been careless enough to leave anything as incriminating behind, but you never knew. Stranger things happened.

When they finally left it was a little after five p.m. Cynthia's car was parked outside the police station and attracting quite a bit of attention. She had sent the Bentley, much to Mickey's satisfaction and Henry's discomfort. Having a sister who was married to a rich industrialist had its advantages, but there were also moments when Henry wished she could be a little more discreet. Mickey never had those worries; he enjoyed himself when Cynthia decided to spread her largesse around, especially since it frequently came his way. Cynthia had a soft spot for her brother's sergeant.

Henry was quiet as they drove along the coast road and said very little until the car had pulled up outside Cynthia's town-house in Worthing. The butler welcomed them and the maid attempted to take their bags.

'Thank you, my dear,' Mickey said, 'but I'll hang on to that one if you don't mind. It's official, like.'

She looked suitably awed. 'The mistress said to tell you

that your usual rooms have been prepared,' she said, 'and that you'll be dining at seven. She will be returning shortly.'

Henry thanked her and he and Mickey made their way to their designated rooms. Neither were strangers here. Twice now they had used Cynthia's house as their base when work had brought them to this part of the coast and Henry was a frequent social visitor. Mickey had been known to join him on some of those occasions; a small curiosity for the gentlemen and their ladies to enjoy.

When Cynthia returned, Henry and Mickey were in the library drinking rather good whiskey and discussing the day's events. They had checked in again with the central office and also with the local police force, who had assured them that guard would be kept all night, though it was likely just to be a single officer. The Clarks, who owned the bungalow, had agreed to a hasp and staple and padlock being put on the front door for added security and this would be done as speedily as possible.

House-to-house enquiries had been continuing into the evening but so far there was nothing to report. Miss Cissie Rowe was a familiar figure in the area and seemed to be well liked.

'No one had a bad word for her,' Henry had been told, but he did not find this surprising. In his experience, people rarely spoke ill of the dead.

Cynthia and the children piled into the library and Cynthia flopped down in one of the big leather chairs. 'Lord, but I'm tired. You wouldn't believe, Henry, how tiring it is prancing up and down on a beach all day. Especially with these three in tow.'

'These three' were two boys and a little girl, Henry's nephews and niece. The two boys dived on to the sofa next to Mickey and demanded to be told what he'd been doing. Melissa, the middle child, came over to Henry, kissed him on the cheek and then settled herself in his lap.

'Hello, Uncle Henry. How are you?'

'I'm very well, thank you, Melissa. And how are you? And how are you enjoying your holiday?'

'I would be enjoying it more if I didn't have brothers,' she said.

'Brothers can be a trial,' Henry agreed.

Cynthia watched, amused. 'Time for the three of you to go upstairs and find Nanny,' she said. 'Go and have your supper. We're late already and Nanny will be hungry and Cook will be cross because the food will be spoilt.'

They watched the children leave and then Cynthia regarded the two men thoughtfully. 'I take it we're not dressing for dinner.'

'Not unless Albert has spare clothing in very tall and very square,' Henry said.

His sister laughed. 'So how are you, darling? And how are you, Mickey? Still doing this ghastly job, then?'

It was something Cynthia always said despite the fact that Henry knew she was very proud of him and the job he did. Cynthia was his older sister by only two years but to hear her speak you would think it was more like a decade. Older sister was a role she took very seriously.

'So what brings you both here? I heard there's a dead actress down Bungalow Town?'

Henry nodded. 'A young woman by the name of Cissie Rowe. Have you heard of her?'

Cynthia gaped at him. 'Heard of her! My goodness, Henry, she is one of the rising stars. Or was. Poor, poor thing. What happened to her?'

'As yet we're not sure,' Mickey said. 'But definitely foul play and likely someone she knew.'

'Oh no, that makes it worse somehow, doesn't it? It's bad enough if it's some random stranger, but to think that someone she knew could want to kill her! Well, not just want, actually do it.'

She got up and crossed to the sideboard spread with decanters, poured herself a whiskey and offered Mickey and Henry top-ups.

'Whiskey before supper, Cyn,' Henry commented. 'That's not like you.'

'And it's not every day I hear about a murder. Sherry is just not up to that kind of news. So, will you be down here for a few days then? You know you can both stay as long as you like. Albert won't mind, it brings a little excitement into his otherwise very mundane business life.'

'Will he be dining with us?'

'Probably not. I'm not expecting him till after nine, so I'll get Cook to leave him some sandwiches. But he's promised to take a few days next week to spend with the children before they have to go back to school. He's looking forward to that. He's a bigger child than they are. They all play cricket on the beach, it's a lovely thing to see.'

Henry nodded. Their own father would never play cricket or anything else. It was rare for him even to notice they were around, not that they ever tried very hard to attract his attention. That was usually bad news. Albert, Henry thought, was actually a very nice man.

Conversation was general at the dinner table. Servants drifted silently in and out of the dining room delivering courses and removing plates, and Henry was reluctant to discuss anything of importance where others might hear. It was not until they withdrew to Cynthia's own little sitting room and coffee had been brought that Henry brought out the snake bangle and asked his sister's opinion. After a quick examination she left them and went to fetch her own.

Cynthia laid her own bangle down on the table and picked up the one that had belonged to Cissie Rowe. 'It's not a cheap thing,' she said. 'I've seen some very pretty ones just made in rolled gold. This one has Birmingham hallmarks and I think I recognize the maker – Smith and Pepper. They make some very pretty toys and I've a recollection that this is their mark. It's a very popular design, very fashionable.' She looked more closely at the marks. 'This is nine carat gold. Mine is twenty-two, but you'd expect that considering what Albert paid for it. Not the sort of thing a girl like Cissie Rowe would have bought for herself, I wouldn't think. No, I think you're right, Henry, some gentleman friend of hers must've bought it for her, but I don't think you're looking for a particularly upmarket admirer, if you see what I mean.'

'So, not an Albert, then.' Henry smiled.

Cynthia grinned back at her brother and stuck out her tongue and for a moment Mickey, watching them, caught a glimpse of the children they had once been.

'She could have stolen it, of course. But she'd need to be clever to do that. It's not exactly the sort of article that lends itself to casual shoplifting, is it? But perhaps she could have stolen it from someone?'

'Possible, of course,' Henry agreed.

'And Cynthia is right, of course, not something that a shoplifter would be able to take, but it's not unusual for an attractive young woman to be used as a decoy for more expert thieves.'

'Male thieves, no doubt.' Cynthia rolled her eyes. 'Heaven forefend that a woman should operate at such a high level of thievery. Or a group of women, even.'

'It's true,' Mickey said casually. 'Women rarely make it to the status of master criminal—'

'Sergeant Hitchens! Are you suggesting that women don't have the brains for it?'

She looked to her brother for support, only to realize that Mickey was deliberately winding her up. 'What about that German woman? Bertha . . . something. She ran a whole gang of housebreakers and fences, didn't she? And, from what I remember, ran the lot of you ragged for months before you could get sufficient evidence.'

'Ah, yes.' Mickey sat back and raised his glass as though in a toast. 'Bertha Welner.'

'But my dear girl, you are going right back to something like 1901 to find your example,' Henry goaded gently.

'I remember reading about her in our father's newspaper. It made a big impression at the time.'

'It must have done, you can't have been more than ten or eleven.'

'I have an excellent memory. And I'm willing to bet that if I did turn to a life of crime, brother dear, you'd not catch me as easily as most of the men you chase down.'

'If Mickey and I were to be the ones after you then your crime would most likely be murder. And if you are planning on becoming a widow or disposing of some of Albert's more unprepossessing relatives, then perhaps it might not be the brightest idea to announce the fact beforehand.'

'Not Albert,' she said. 'I'm fond of Albert. His cousin Harvey, though. Now I might be disposed to be rid of him.'

'Then keep it simple,' Mickey advised. 'Take him for a walk on the cliffs and give him a good shove.'

She nodded. 'We do get some terribly strong winds along the coast. Thank you, Mickey. I'll bear that in mind. You don't hear of many murderesses, do you? Perhaps that's because they are more careful than their male counterparts and don't get caught as often.'

'It's true that the female mind is more devious,' Mickey agreed.

'But those we do know about don't plan as well as they might,' Henry argued. 'What about Mrs Thompson, back in the autumn of Twenty-two? Plotted with her would-be lover to have her husband bumped off as they walked home from the theatre. Oh, the incident itself was well enough planned: an attack in a side street, a woman who acted out her shock and distress with great aplomb. But she had also been stupid enough to write to her lover about earlier attempts that she had made on her husband's life. Attempted poisoning and on more than one occasion putting broken glass into the poor man's food.'

'You could also argue that it was the stupidity of the lover . . . Bywaters, wasn't it? A sailor, or something of the sort, wasn't he? Anyway, his stupidity in keeping the letters. Silly man. Why couldn't he have just thrown them overboard? He must have realized they'd come back to bite him.'

'Apparently not,' Henry said. 'Cyn, I've no doubt you'd make a better fist of it than they did, but do me a favour and wait until you are elsewhere. Monaco or Argentina or wherever you and Albert are trotting off to next. I'd rather not have to arrest my own sister.'

'I promise you, Henry. Should I ever consider such a deed and should there be no convenient cliffs in the vicinity, I shall cover my tracks so well that even you will not be able to prove my guilt. Another drink, either of you?'

Henry watched her thoughtfully as she refreshed their drinks. He knew that Cynthia took a keen interest in his work, avidly reading accounts of what the media termed the 'murder squad' and their activities and even some of the text books that Henry collected on forensic and psychological practice.

He acknowledged also that she was one of the most intelligent people – of either sex – that it was his privilege to know.

Cynthia set their glasses down and turned her attention to the other jewellery that Henry had found at the bungalow. 'It reminds me of the sort of thing Mother used to wear,' she said. 'A little old-fashioned. The brooch is like the mourning jewellery the old Queen made popular, and the coral bracelet . . .' She paused for a moment, considering. 'It's probably been around since before Cissie was born. Looking at the style, I would have said 1890, before the war anyway.'

Henry nodded; that had been his feeling too. Inherited jewellery, probably. He would ask Muriel Owens if she had ever seen Cissie wearing any of it or if she knew who had given her the snake bangle. Henry would not be surprised if Mrs Owens did not even know of its existence.

'I can tell you a little bit about her, though,' Cynthia said. 'Melissa has taken over my old scrapbooks – you remember the ones I used to have with the postcards and pictures in them about all the starlets and the stage shows we would have liked to see but never quite managed to?'

Henry nodded solemnly. His sister was evidently trying to make light of what had been something of an obsession in her teenage years and even well into her twenties. Life had been somewhat humdrum and Cynthia had escaped by compiling scrapbooks of newspaper clippings and magazine articles and pictures of stage actors at first, and then Hollywood starlets and British film stars.

'Well, Cissie Rowe is one of the . . . or *was* one of the up-and-coming names. So far she had only played small parts but the prediction was that she would take over from Joan Morgan. You know that she was the daughter of Sidney Morgan, who was a producer at the Shoreham studio? Well, anyway, Cissie had something of the same look, though she was older, of course. Joan Morgan was starring in her father's films from when she was about sixteen, I believe.

I don't think Cissie Rowe even started until she was in her twenties.'

'We'll be looking into her background but anything you can tell us is useful,' Mickey said.

'Well, she's not British, you know that, I suppose? She was born Cécile Rolland and she came over here in about 1917 as a refugee.' She paused thoughtfully. 'I think she came from Amiens, though I may be wrong about that, but you can imagine what the poor girl must have gone through in her early days.'

She looked cautiously at her brother and at Mickey Hitchens, knowing that they could do more than imagine.

'The story is that she was working as a shop girl and was discovered, but I very much doubt that's how it happened. I imagine she was among all of the other young hopefuls who turn up for auditions. But it seems she was luckier than most. She had a good future ahead of her.'

'Had,' Mickey said heavily. 'That gives us another direction to look in, I suppose. Someone from her past? Admittedly it seems unlikely, the girl had been over here for eleven years, give or take, so it's much more likely to have been someone she had encountered in the last two or three, I would have thought.'

'Perhaps whoever gave her the bracelet,' Cynthia commented. 'Perhaps she was not as willing as he thought.'

'Perhaps not. We need to know a great deal more before we can make those sorts of decisions or observations,' Henry said. 'We will know more when the post-mortem has been done. We are presently making assumptions about the cause of death and they may be proved wrong.'

He thanked his sister, and further conversation was interrupted by Albert's return home. The next hour, while Albert ate his sandwiches and drank his brandy, was taken up with discussions on the achievements of Tich Freeman and his three hundred wickets. Henry, not a particular cricket fan, tuned them out.

'Thank you for your help,' he told Cynthia. 'And it's very good of you to put up with the pair of us, landing ourselves on you at such short notice.'

She smiled at him. 'Darling, you never need to give me notice, you know that. Through thick and thin, Henry, and Lord knows we've been through both.'

Henry woke. The house was very quiet and his room seemed very dark. It took him a moment to remember where he was. He slipped his watch off the bedside table and squinted at the face. It was a little after two a.m., so he had slept for nearly three hours, which was better than he'd managed for quite some time.

Knowing that there was nothing to be gained by lying in bed he put on his borrowed dressing gown and padded back down the stairs and into Albert's library to find something to read.

Examining the bookshelves he came across two familiar volumes, albums of photographs from Cynthia's wedding. It had been an extraordinarily glamorous affair despite it being 1915 and the country being at war. Henry had managed to get a forty-eight hour pass so he could attend – he suspected Albert of pulling strings to make that happen, but he had never asked. He smiled as he took the albums from the shelf and sat down with them on the sofa. Cynthia had been married for almost thirteen years and Albert had been in pursuit of her for almost two years before that.

'I'm taking my guidance from Anne Boleyn,' she had told Henry, 'but hopefully without the bloody, beheading bit. She kept Henry the Eighth waiting for years, refusing to become his mistress and settling for nothing less than wife.'

'And you plan to do the same?'

'Absolutely, but I shall just manage matters better post matrimony. Albert is used to the girls in the office giving in to his pestering, and he's been lucky not to have been caught out and got any of them pregnant. Or if he has, then Mummy and Daddy have paid them off and made them discreetly disappear, I suppose.'

'Cynthia, I believe you are getting cynical.'

'Getting? Henry, my love, I have been cynical for a very long time. Anyway, I prefer to call it realistic.'

'But you love him?'

'I like him. He's a good friend and he respects me and my abilities. I love him enough to know that I can make a good wife. Henry, I don't expect more than that. To have a marriage based on friendship, that I can live with.'

Henry turned the pages of the album, remembering the conversation that had taken place about six months before the wedding. Albert, as predicted, had finally proposed. The wedding had been organized with military precision and Cynthia had continued to organize Albert with the same precision ever since. Albert, if he noticed at all, didn't seem to object.

Tucked between the pages were other photographs, and these were rarer. Henry's father had owned the camera but had seldom used it, at least not to photograph his family. But there was a picture of Henry, Cynthia and their mother, taken, he recalled, a few months before their mother had died. They were standing in the garden with ash trees behind them, marking where the wood began. The woodland had been a refuge for the child Henry, who had learned early that out of sight really was out of mind as far as his father was concerned and that out of mind was where it was safest to be.

Henry studied the picture. He thought about the pictures on Cissie Rowe's walls and on the little table. For those that could afford it, he reflected, photographs were now a vital part of identity. In some ways they were still status symbols too but a photograph somehow validated and verified existence, relationships, memories that might otherwise give way to imagination. Something Henry loved about photography was the way that it fixed things absolutely in time and context, allowed for no interpretation; it simply recorded.

The photograph of Cynthia brought to mind another memory. Cynthia had been fifteen years old and he remembered how she had taken off the borrowed black hat and shaken out the long brown hair that she could never keep pinned as neatly as their father required, that always had a mind of its own.

Henry had been thirteen, and they had just returned from their father's funeral. Neighbours and the few remaining friends his father had maintained had come together to give this one time respected country doctor a reasonable send-off, but now the two of them were alone and Henry had spent the day when, so custom told him, he should have been recalling his father's worth wondering what on earth they were to do now.

The vicar had spoken about the stresses and strains of life bringing about a premature end and of course no one had directly mentioned that the man had drunk himself to death, though some spoke of grief following his wife's demise.

The adult Henry reached back in time and recalled that he had looked at his sister in expectation that she would sort things out. Cynthia always sorted things out.

She had stood for a moment in the narrow hallway and then, hanging the unwanted hat on the wall stand with the comment that she must return it in the morning, she had looked at Henry and said, 'Well, this will never do, will it?'

'Cynthia?' He had needed to say no more.

She had placed her hands on his shoulders and looked intently at him. 'We will survive, little brother, and we will prosper. I promise you that.'

'How? The landlord says we have to be out by the end of the week because father was so far behind with the rent. We have nowhere to go, Cyn, and no money, and —'

She shook him gently. Then she pointed to the basket at her feet. Neighbours, not wanting to seem uncharitable, had provisioned the wake and then packed the leftover food for the children to take back with them. Both Cynthia and Henry were wise enough to realize that this was the only help they would be getting locally.

'Right now, we eat. And then we sit down and we make a plan. I already have the outline of such a plan in my head.' She picked up the basket and strode along the hall to the kitchen, Henry trailing behind.

As she filled the kettle she said, 'Tonight we try to get a good night's sleep. Tomorrow I return Mrs Webb's hat and I speak to the landlord and see if we can get an extension of a few more days. Then we sell everything. Father's books, Mother's jewellery and dresses, the furniture, the rugs, the lot. We pay debts that we absolutely have to pay or give a little on account and then we take what is left and we go and find Uncle Derek.'

'Uncle Derek? What use will he be? He didn't even come to Mother's funeral.'

'Which gives us an immense amount of ammunition for emotional blackmail, don't you think? Henry, he's our only living relative and he has rooms over that bookshop that are never used for anything but storage, so my thought is that he can spare us one. Once we have a roof over our heads, and an address, we can find work. Henry, we need to work and we need to educate ourselves. Between us we have brains and nerve and we have survived this far without breaking into little pieces. We can get through this.'

Henry was never quite sure how Cynthia had persuaded the landlord. She had probably shamed him; Cynthia was good at shaming people when she had to. But he had granted them another week and in that time they'd held a series of sales and cleared out everything that their parents had ever owned. Henry knew that they had sold things at a pittance and he recognized the pain in Cynthia's eyes when their mother's brooches had been carried off in triumph by a neighbour, but his sister had added a few shillings to the ever-growing purse and looked triumphant for Henry's benefit and, he realized, for her own.

Henry closed the album. His prediction had been right and Uncle Derek had been of very little use but he had allowed them to take up lodgings in his attic and that, as Cynthia had said, at least gave them a roof over their heads and an address.

By the time Albert had encountered Cynthia she was twenty-seven and had been working as personal secretary to his father, having worked her way up from the post room. Albert's father, himself having come from trade and begun with very little, appreciated Cynthia's enterprise. When Albert declared that he was going to marry his father's secretary it caused a few ripples of shock but Cynthia completed her transformation to fine lady with skill and aplomb and by the time the pair had been married for six months, society seemed to have forgotten her origins as it had forgotten and forgiven her father-in-law's. Except in the eyes of the old, aristocratic families, money had a way of bestowing class, Henry thought, and even they were bowing to the inevitable and marrying selectively into the families of the newly wealthy.

He placed the album back on the shelf and found himself a novel to occupy the rest of the night. On the way across the hall a small sound attracted his attention. The door leading down to the kitchen opened and Mickey Hitchens, shoes in one hand and the murder bag in the other, tiptoed out.

'Mickey?'

'Trying not to wake the house,' Mickey said. He lifted up the bag he held. 'I borrowed the rear scullery to process the photographs of the scene. I couldn't start until everyone was in bed so I grabbed a couple of hours' sleep and went down just after midnight. Now I plan to get a couple of hours more. I've rigged a line above the sink and borrowed pegs, left the prints drying. I'll get down there before the scullery maid in the morning, otherwise I think the poor girl will get a nasty shock.'

'I hope you've left a sign on the door to keep curiosity out,' Henry said.

'I've left a sign but I doubt curiosity will take any notice. If they see what they shouldn't see that's their problem. Now I'm off to bed and you should be too.'

Henry nodded, though he doubted he'd get more sleep that night. It was now a little after three a.m.

He returned to his room and lay down intending to read by the light of the bedside lamp, but to his surprise the next thing he knew was the morning light streaming in through a tiny gap in the curtains and a tray being placed on the chair by his bedside with tea and breakfast.

# THREE

Jimmy Cottee was an early riser, always had been. He liked to stand on the steps outside the railway carriage that he'd lived in for the past five years and look out across the water, watch the sun sparkle on the ripples and the darkness lift.

Jimmy Cottee knew he was a romantic – Cissie was always telling him so, anyway – but he could never quite break himself of the habit.

This morning he was awake when he heard the footsteps on the shingle, puzzled when he became aware of the heavy tread on his step. He set his cup down on the table and got up from his seat. Was standing when they burst through his door, but a second later lying on his back staring up at the ceiling, a man's boot heavy on his chest.

'Where is it? We know she gave it to you.'

'It? Who? Where is what?' Jimmy's brain couldn't comprehend what the man was asking him. He understood only that two others stood close by and that they meant to do him harm.

'I don't have anything. Look about you, please. You can see I don't have nothing.'

The boot lifted from his chest and Jimmy knew a brief moment of relief before the foot was drawn back and then the heavy boot launched with full force into his side.

They dragged him to his feet and then slammed him into a chair. A face leered, close to his own. Hot breath that stank of tobacco. 'Where did you put it? We know she gave it to you.'

'Gave what to me? Who? I don't understand.'

Jimmy Cottee was not a big man. He was neither tall nor solid and when the man grabbed him again and swung him from the chair, hurling him against the wall, Jimmy could do nothing to defend himself. He struck out once, felt his nails rake across skin, heard a grunt that was part pain but mostly anger, felt the hand around his throat and the life ebbing from him.

Someone spoke and the hand released its grip.

'Now, where is it?' the voice was asking him again and Jimmy, breath knocked from his body, throat tight as though the hand still pressed against his windpipe, could hardly get the words out.

'What? Don't know.'

So they beat him again.

Jimmy Cottee was regaining consciousness when they put the rope around his neck. He was thrashing in panic as they threw the rope around a bracket in the carriage ceiling. He still had no idea why he was about to die.

Henry stretched, enjoying the moment. It was almost seven and he had slept for another three hours since encountering Mickey on the stairs. More sleep than he'd had in weeks. Perhaps this bout of insomnia was not going to be so bad after all.

Retrieving his breakfast tray, Henry realized that Cynthia had also had one of the scrapbooks she had mentioned sent up to him. She had marked a page with a slip of paper and while he ate breakfast and drank his morning tea Henry examined the pictures of Cissie Rowe. He knew that she was twenty-eight but she looked much younger in these images and he wondered if they had been taken recently or if they had simply been styled to flatter. Someone had once told him that photographers smeared a tiny amount of Vaseline on their lenses to create a softer focus on their subject. Henry sometimes wished you could do that with real life. Real life was all knees and elbows, far too sharp, prodding and intrusive.

He thought about his sister's children. It had always seemed to Henry that it was the most extreme expression of optimism that anyone should choose to have children though, he supposed, Cynthia's would be protected from the worst shocks that life had to offer. Or at least he hoped so.

He washed and dressed and took himself downstairs. His sergeant, he was told, was collecting his photographs and his sister had already gone out.

'Mrs Garrett-Smyth enjoys an early walk along the promenade

when the household is in residence down here,' he was told. Henry decided that he would follow.

The morning air was fresh, the wind coming in off the sea and whipping the waves into froth as they hit the pebble beach. He spotted Cynthia leaning against the railing of the promenade, her coat collar pulled up and her shoulders hunched. When he reached her Henry noticed that her cheeks were flushed and reddened by the morning chill and her eyes were bright. She smiled at him. 'And how are you this morning? Did you sleep?'

The question was never *Did you sleep well?*

'I woke and went downstairs for a while, made use of Albert's library. I found the old photograph albums of your wedding.'

'Ah,' she said. 'So no doubt you saw the other pictures as well. I'd almost forgotten I still had them. They were packed away in an old box. I remembered how you didn't like to see them, so I tucked them out of sight.'

'I was glad to see them,' Henry said. 'We have come a long way since then, Cynthia. You especially have.'

'That,' she agreed, 'is certainly true.' She stepped back from the promenade rail and looked down at the fur-trimmed coat and the Cuban-heeled shoes she was wearing. 'Look at me, Henry. Did you ever see the like?'

'Our father would have been scandalized,' Henry agreed. 'He was a great believer in women knowing their place, and you have certainly stepped out of yours. I'm glad of that, Cynthia. And you seem to be happy?'

'I'm content,' she said. 'And you know, Henry, I've come to realize that in many ways contentment is a better emotion to feel. It is more consistent, more reliable. I am married to a man I like, and even love in my own way. If you are looking for me to be passionate about my husband then you are looking at the wrong woman.'

'And is there another woman? One who is passionate?'

'Not recently, I am happy to say. There have been two or three and I never expected otherwise. He is a rich man and there are many pretty women in the world. Whenever his preoccupations become obvious, then I remind him of his obligations and he steps back into line. Compared to the way some husbands behave, Henry, I have no complaints. Albert is my friend and he respects me as an equal in terms of intellect and thought. He listens to me and he is a very good father.'

'Cynthia . . .'

Smiling, she touched a finger to his lips. 'Henry, I was never one for romantic love. My life has always been ruled by practicality, you know that. And I love my children and I have to say, darling, that in general I love my life. I am desperately aware of my good fortune. Henry, I have freedom to act, to make my own decisions, to become involved in my husband's business in a way that he values. I would not trade that for schoolgirl romance, I promise you.'

She slipped her arm through his and they strolled slowly back to the house. Her car was out at the front and Mickey was waiting in the hall. Time to leave.

'I may not see you tonight; we are going up to town to the theatre and will probably stay over. But the servants know you'll be returning and meals will be prepared, and you know that you are both very welcome.'

She kissed her brother gently on the cheek and shook Mickey Hitchens' hand and then went on up the stairs, unfastening her coat as she went. Like Cissie Rowe's, Henry thought, Cynthia's clothes were hung and put away as soon as she took them off.

In the car on the way to Shoreham, Henry wrote in his journal.

*I do not agree with Dr Freud that we should be constantly probing our dreams for meaning. I have no wish to sit or lie on a psychiatrist's couch and recall the moments of my history that cause me pain. Frankly, if I found myself capable of forgetting, of hiding the truth, then I would do so. I am afraid that in this – and probably only in this – regard I am in agreement with Nietzsche that those who stare into the abyss should beware In case the abyss should stare back.*

*I once asked Cynthia what she does with those bad memories we share and, I suspect, many bad memories that are hers alone. She seems so solid, so sound, and I wondered how she managed that. She told me that she imagined the tartan biscuit tin that had held Christmas shortbread. It sat on the pantry shelf in our mother's kitchen. She told me that whenever a memory grew too big or too vivid she would imagine that tin, open it and put the memory inside.*

*I laughed, but I suspect she was serious.*

*I also suspect that Cynthia would have no truck with the abyss. That it would not dare to stare back at her.*

He found himself smiling at the thought.

# FOUR

*Ten days earlier*

She had been standing on the rocks beside the old fort looking out to sea and he had taken her by surprise. More than surprise when he had called her by her old, half forgotten name.

'Cécile,' he said 'Cécile Rolland.'

And she had turned, shocked to look at the young man and to recognize who he was.

Cécile's hand rose to her lips and she stared at him in disbelief. 'Philippe? Can it truly be you? I never thought I would see you, not ever again. How are you here? How did you find me?'

He laughed. 'Finding you was easy. Your photograph is in the newspapers, you appear on the cinema screen. Cécile, you may have changed your name but nothing else about you is altered in the slightest jot.'

Philippe, she remembered, had always had a good command of English and his accent was soft, nothing like the faux French accents that her theatrical friends liked to practise for the stage. All *zis* and *zat* and *oh monsieur!*

Her own accent had been largely eradicated in the eleven years that she had been in England. She had listened to the native speakers around her and carefully contrived to shorten her vowels and harden her consonants. The slight accent that remained was considered exotic but still within the parameters of acceptability. She had done her best to become in real life the Englishwoman that she portrayed on screen.

'I never thought to see you again,' she repeated. 'Philippe, this is wonderful, but I don't understand. What brings you here? When I left you said—'

'You left at a time of war. I had no hope of either of us surviving. Our families did not. And I had no belief that there would be a time when it was safe for me to find you. But times change, Cécile.'

He spread his arms as though encompassing Cécile, the fort, the rocks, the River Adur, and not quite believing any of it. 'Look at you,' he said. 'Look at how splendid you have become.'

She laughed with him. 'I must go back. Filming will begin again in less than half an hour and I must not be late.'

He nodded, then followed as she picked her way back across the rocks trying hard not to trap the kitten heels of her shoes in the cracks and crevices.

'Hardly suitable for scrambling on the rocks,' he said, and Cissie laughed.

'No,' she agreed. 'Philippe, I must work now. But we must talk, later. Tell me how I can meet you. We must celebrate this reunion.'

He told her where he was staying and suggested a restaurant where they could meet for an evening meal, and she agreed.

Cissie, once the girl called Cécile Rolland, had walked away from Philippe with her head held high and a smile on her lips, but the young woman with the camera whom neither of them had observed but who had been happily photographing the pair could not help but note that it was one that didn't quite reach her eyes.

They were in the car on the way back to Shoreham-by-Sea, Mickey driving Cynthia's Ford Tudor sedan that she'd had shipped back from the States after their last visit.

Henry examined the photographs that Mickey had taken the previous day. He had borrowed one of the postcards from Cynthia's scrapbook and he held it up now to compare with the images of the dead woman, fixing in his mind the way she had looked before someone had chosen to take her life away and the ravages of early decomposition had reshaped her features, caused the eyes to sink back in their sockets and drained the lips of colour.

He handed the postcard to Mickey. 'Victim,' he said.

'She looks like a child in this picture,' Mickey observed. He flipped the card over and found a date on the back, written in Cynthia's hand. 'Taken only a year ago, but presumably there was a little camera trickery and a great deal of cosmetic intervention. She was getting a little old to be the ingénue. Even the wife commented on that the last time we saw her on the screen.'

'The film industry likes to keep actresses young, I suppose. Youth in love or in peril presumably has more appeal to the cinemagoers than would middle age.'

'Not so different from real life then,' Mickey observed. 'A young person goes missing and the newspapers have an attractive photograph to slap on to their front pages, and the world is in outcry. My advice to would-be victims is to be either very young or very, very old. Either way you will elicit sympathy, but to be somewhere in the middle is to be forgotten and neglected.'

'Unless you are rich,' Henry corrected him.

'Unless that,' Mickey agreed. 'So, our tasks for the day are?'

'Interview her friends, go to this film studio and speak again, I think, to Mr Owens. Try to have that discussion when his wife's not present.'

'You think he knows more than he's prepared to say in front of her?'

'I think he observes things that his wife does not, that perhaps she chooses not to see. Though what those might be I can only guess.'

'And that guess would be?'

'That Cissie Rowe had some young man in tow that Mrs Owens would not have approved of. That her husband might've seen Cissie Rowe become, shall we say, more involved with one of her admirers than his wife believed.'

Mickey nodded. 'Your sister could have a point,' he said. 'It's possible our young victim was a thief and that bracelet was stolen.'

'So we follow that line of enquiry, but I think it the less likely of the two. A young woman who chooses to steal either needs a receiver for her stolen goods, in which case she needs connections, or she steals something she can wear openly that would cause no comment. The bangle seems elaborate, obvious, something to be noticed. So we need to find out whether she wore it and whether, if anyone noticed it, she had any explanation for it.

'And we keep an open mind; I would not like to predict where this case might lead. The manner of her death, from what we have seen so far, suggests to me that there was rage there. That, had he used a knife, there would have been multiple wounds. It is one thing to strike someone in temper but quite another to follow this up by carrying them into their home, forcing poison or a sleeping draft down their throat and then finishing them with asphyxia.'

'We are making assumptions,' said Mickey. 'Until the post-mortem is complete you cannot be sure of any of those things.'

Henry nodded solemnly. 'So I'll wait for the post-mortem to confirm it then,' he said. 'You're not telling me that she went gently.'

'No, I will not try and tell you that.'

# FIVE

*Ten days earlier*

I n the corner of Cissie's bungalow was a little table and on
the table were three photographs. The subject of one of the
photographs was a couple then in their forties and a young
boy. Philippe, Cissie thought, would have been eleven or twelve
when this picture was taken and she recalled the day with
sharp intensity. She had been eight years old and the sun had
been shining. The two of them had paddled in the brook and
then run home through her aunt's orchard where the greengages
had been ripening and the mirabelle plums were almost ready
to drop from the trees.

Cissie remembered being as happy on that day as she could
ever recall being in her entire life. Her uncle had brought
out his little camera, placed the heavy box in her hands,
reminded her how to crank the handle to wind on the film and
trusted her to take a picture of the three of them. Himself, his
wife and their son Philippe. Other pictures had been taken,
but this one Cissie had been allowed to keep and she had
cherished it even through the darkest days. It was like a
talisman, and she had cleaved to the belief that if she kept this
image safe, kept the memory alive and perfect in her mind,
she could survive the worst the world had to throw at her. She
had that one bright moment, that remembrance of pure,
unadulterated happiness.

And now Philippe had returned to her and Cissie was not
sure how she felt about that. He was not twelve years old any
more and she was not eight and the world was not the same.
Her aunt and uncle were now dead, as were her own parents,
and the places they had cherished were churned to mud and
ruin, blasted out of existence by the war she had fled not so
many years after this picture had been taken. She had then
been almost seventeen and Philippe had been twenty and she

had expected, as had he, that this would be a final farewell. She had adjusted her mind to it, to the fact that her past was gone and ruined and utterly spoilt – apart from the memory of that one day which now stood as a symbol for everything else in her first sixteen years of existence. Cissie could rarely bear to think of the rest. The loss, the sense of isolation became too acute if she did.

She should have rejoiced that Philippe had come back into her life and yet, standing in her little bungalow, surrounded by all the things that symbolized the life she had now, the person she had become, Cissie could not bring herself to rejoice. Instead she felt vaguely afraid. It was as though Philippe had packed all of that first sixteen years of life into his valise and brought it with him, opened it like some leather-clasped Pandora's box and released all the ills of the world to settle on her shoulders.

Cissie picked the photograph up and peered closely at it. The truth was that she was a little short-sighted and she often wore spectacles in the privacy of her own home – though rarely outside it. She looked into the face of the boy Philippe had been, smiling and open and trusting that the world would always be as wonderful as this. She had known his voice, of course, when he had first spoken her name and brought the memories crashing over her. And no doubt she would have recognized his face. It was familiar once she was able to look closely at him, though, she realized with shock, this young man she had once loved could have passed her in the street and she would not have picked him out from the crowd.

'What is he doing here?' Cissie asked herself. She sighed. If she were to be truthful with herself she probably knew the answer to that, and knew that it was not going to end well.

Henry and Sergeant Hitchens had been given a quick tour of the studio and introduced to 'the people that matter' by one of the senior cameramen. They had spotted Mrs Owens in a lean-to space that she proudly announced was 'the wardrobe' and Mr Owens in the glasshouse talking to someone about light and whether the cloud cover was likely to increase in the afternoon.

Mickey was dispatched to go and speak with him. Henry was told that the local police had already interviewed most of Cissie's friends but that, of course, he and his sergeant should have free rein. He was asked to remember that this was a working studio and that time was money. Henry promised to try and keep out of the way and in turn reminded his guide that this was a murder inquiry.

Mickey Hitchens looked around with interest. The main studio building was indeed a giant glasshouse. Their guide had told them that the Shoreham Film Studio had been taken over by Progress Films in the early 1920s and the studio had been one of the first to make use of custom-made, functional sets. Progress had built a joiners' shop for producing the sets and a small preview theatre and also accommodation for actors – a sparse but functional building called Studio Rest. There had been a fire in 1923 that had damaged part of the studio site but the glasshouse itself had escaped with only a few cracked panes of glass.

It was an impressive building, Mickey thought, and the current set, a flight of very convincing stairs leading to a very convincing landing, could have found a place in any grand house.

Mickey caught Fred Owens' attention and beckoned him across. 'You have a moment or two?' he asked politely.

Fred Owens excused himself from his colleague and came over.

'Sergeant Hitchens, sir. You spoke to my boss yesterday. I believe your poor wife was unfortunate enough to find Miss Rowe dead?'

Fred Owens nodded, his expression a picture of sadness. 'She was a lovely young lady,' he said. 'It's a real tragedy, Sergeant. I'm finding it impossible to believe. Who would want to hurt poor Cissie?'

Mickey was a man who believed in coming straight to the point. 'My boss left with the impression that you wanted to tell him something, but didn't want to speak in front of the wife,' he said. 'He thought that it was perhaps something of a personal nature that you know about Miss Rowe but that you didn't think suitable to . . . speak of in feminine company, shall we say. We all know that ladies can be a little sensitive about such issues, especially when they relate to a friend.'

Fred Owens pursed his lips as though he disapproved of Mickey even introducing the subject. 'I'm sorry that the Inspector gained that impression,' he said. 'Miss Rowe, as I said, was a lovely young lady. Never did any harm to anyone. And certainly does not deserve to be gossiped about.'

'No young lady who's met her death in such an unfortunate manner deserves to be gossiped about,' Mickey agreed. 'But it's a sad fact, sir, that not everyone in the world is as gentle as Miss Rowe. Not everyone in the world is as blameless. And if your Miss Rowe brushed up against one of these . . . others, shall we call them – through no fault of her own, you under-stand – then we should know about it. If we are to catch the perpetrator of this sad and terrible act then things need to be spoken of, even those things that a gentleman such as yourself would not usually wish to mention.'

That he had read his man right was confirmed for Mickey when Fred Owens straightened himself up and squared his shoulders decisively.

'No,' Fred Owens said. 'Of course you are right. Needs must. You understand I would not wish to speak ill of the dead – anyone dead, and certainly not someone of the calibre of Miss Rowe. But even such young women can make misjudgements and I believe she did. My wife was of the opinion that although she had admirers, she took none of them seriously.'

'But you think different,' Mickey prompted, afraid that the man was about to clam up again.

'I'm afraid I do. There were two young men, one who worked on the set here and another who was an outsider. Both made something of a play for Cissie in the last few months. And she treated both equally. Going to the cinema with one on one week and perhaps for a walk along the beach with the other. You must understand that she was always careful to maintain proprieties and that each young man knew about the other. But of late . . .' He paused.

'Of late?' Mickey prompted.

'Of late, the other young man, the outsider, he had been

a little . . . shall we say impatient? He put pressure on Cissie
to make up her mind, and to make it up in his favour. He
and the other young man, on one occasion, almost came to
blows.'

'You understand I shall need names and addresses for both
of these young gentlemen?' Mickey said. 'If not from you, Mr
Owens, then I am bound to get them from someone who is
perhaps less discreet and less caring of Miss Rowe's reputation
than you are. You understand that?'

Fred Owens nodded regretfully. 'Unfortunately, Sergeant, I
do realize that. And I should have spoken to your inspector
yesterday.'

'The chief inspector is always discreet, sir. In fact you can
depend on both of us, as far as it is possible in a case like
this. You understand that things will be said, that things will
come out, especially when the press become involved. The
death of an actress always attracts the headlines.'

'Indeed,' Fred Owens said heavily. 'I take it you've seen
this morning's . . . I cannot call them newspapers. Rags, I
call them. And I would not credit the perpetrators with words
like journalist.'

Mickey, who had in fact only had a chance to glance at the
more upmarket papers that Cynthia and her husband had delivered every morning and had had little opportunity for gossip
with servants or a glimpse at the papers that they would have
bought, was a little at a disadvantage here.

'It's a sorry story,' he agreed. 'Best I hear the truth from
someone who knew her, don't you think?'

Fred Owens nodded reluctantly and gave Mickey the names
and, as far as he knew them, the addresses of the two young
men involved.

'In fact, I'm surprised young Jimmy Cottee isn't here this
morning. He should have been in an hour ago. But we all
assume he's heard the news and is too grief-stricken.'

Mickey nodded. 'Well, we'll get someone to speak to him
as soon as we can,' he said. 'Mr Owens, one of the things I
wanted to ask you about was, would either of these young
men have been likely to give Miss Rowe presents? I mean
nothing by it, you understand, no impropriety is suggested.

But it is not unusual for a young gentleman who is fond of a young lady to give little gifts.'

Fred Owens frowned, and then he smiled as though remembering something pleasant after all. 'Jimmy would always arrive with flowers,' he said. 'I don't mean florist flowers, not big bouquets and that sort of nonsense. You may have noticed down on the beach there's always something pretty growing. Marguerites and sea thrift and the like. He would make a little posy for her. And sometimes he would buy her chocolates. He is a sweet lad, is Jimmy. Not the brightest or most polished pebble on the beach, but he works hard and as I say is a sweet lad.'

Mickey mentally crossed him off the list as the giver of the snake bangle. 'And the other?'

'The other was undoubtedly more, shall we say, favoured in his income. He worked in a bank, I believe, and we all thought that he was just after a touch of glamour, you know how it is. Humdrum days and a little excitement on the Sunday. As to whether he gave her gifts, I really wouldn't know. Jimmy is open about that kind of thing and Cissie was open in her pleasure at receiving them but as to the other, I'm sorry, Sergeant, but I've really no idea.'

'Just one more thing. I know I said I'd finished, but I just thought of this,' Mickey dissembled. 'We found some little bits of jewellery among her things; most look like the kind of thing a girl might have inherited from her mother or grandmother. Was she fond of jewellery, was there a piece that she wore more often than others?'

'You mean there might have been a theft as well as the murder? Oh, dear Lord. You know we did talk about this, but we decided that Cissie didn't have anything worth stealing. She kept a little bit of money in the house, perhaps five pounds or so, but nothing significant. Poor lamb, she might have been an up-and-coming star, but up-and-coming was where she was at the moment. She certainly hadn't reached her destination in terms of income or anything else.'

He frowned, thinking about jewellery, and then said, 'there was a little amethyst paste she was fond of, a brooch. Old-fashioned looking, but she said it belonged to an aunt, I believe. Oh, and there was a coral bangle, but she wore that only rarely, on special occasions. She said it was getting a little fragile and she didn't want it to be ruined. I think that had a similar provenance.'

'You never saw her wearing a gold bangle in the shape of a snake? One biting its own tail with an ornate clasp and little red eyes that look like rubies, though I think they must be garnets.'

Fred Owens looked at him as if he'd gone mad. 'She never owned anything like that. Where would she get the money for anything like that?' Then understanding dawned. 'Oh,' he said. 'The gift you were talking about.' He shook his head. 'Jimmy would never have been able to afford anything like that. If it didn't come from Woolworths she wouldn't have got it from him. And I don't see Mr Selwyn Croft being able to afford anything on that scale. He's a respectable enough young man, with what seems to be a good job, but gold bangles? No, no, never anything like that. That's the kind of gift a man makes if . . . if he's expecting . . . if he's expecting a woman to become his wife.'

Or something with as many obligations and fewer of the advantages, Mickey thought. He nodded.

'Well, thank you, Mr Owens. But what I don't understand is why you could not have spoken of these two men yesterday. You've told me nothing that is scandalous and nothing that would not be known to most of the people who worked with Miss Rowe, I would have thought?'

For the first time Fred Owens looked embarrassed and awkward.

Ah, we are coming to it now, Mickey thought.

'She was a very beautiful young woman, you understand.'

'I have seen her pictures and must agree that she was.' Mickey paused and then he said, 'Though after death, of course, much of that beauty had fled. The hands of the assassin are not kind.'

He saw the other man shake his head and momentarily close his eyes. Then Mr Owens spoke. 'Recently, I saw her returning late. There are nights when I cannot sleep and I go for a walk. Once I saw her on the footbridge, late at night.

She was with a man I didn't recognize and seemed to be hurrying and I was anxious for her. So I made my way to this end of the footbridge and she was so shocked to see me. She asked me not to mention it to anyone, that I had seen her or that she'd been in company. There was a moment when I thought the man might offer me out and I didn't trust myself against his fists, I can tell you. He was tall and quite broad and he was in evening dress and Cissie was wearing a pretty pink thing that she kept for special occasions. She had saved for it, you know, that pink dress. Paid for it a little every week until it was hers.'

'And did you see this person again?'

'The first time was about three months ago. I glimpsed him again perhaps two weeks since. He was driving through the town, though I couldn't tell you what kind of car it was, it was a glimpse only. But I think I would know him again. It was late, but the moon was full and there was light enough to see his face.

'I warned her, I said, "Cissie, don't let some racy young fellow with a lot of cash to splash take advantage of you" and she just laughed and said, "I know my way around, Fred. Don't you worry about me."'

'And she told you nothing more than this?'

'Nothing. I tried to broach the subject on occasion because it was obvious that she had a little more cash than usual and there was also a small change in her, in her attitude. I told you before that she was on the road to stardom but had not yet attained it and I had the feeling that she was becoming impatient with the wait. That the journey was becoming too much of a burden and that she wanted more and she wanted it right away, not at some future time. In this business you see that often and I can't blame the young women who feel that way. They are often years waiting on the sidelines for their break to come and often it does not. They see others who are younger and fresher and considered more appealing taking the place that they feel should have been theirs, and many of them become embittered.'

And, I'm guessing, you married one such, Mickey thought.

'I worried for her, but what could I do? She made me

promise not to tell Muriel what I had seen because, she said, she didn't want to be diminished in the eyes of Mrs Owens, a woman she respected. And so I stayed silent – in truth there was very little I could tell, and I had said my piece to Cissie herself, warned her to take care. I never dreamt anything as terrible as this might happen.'

Mickey nodded his understanding. 'I wonder if I could just ask something else,' he said. 'Not strictly to do with the investigation, you understand?'

Mr Owens looked a little puzzled. 'Of course,' he said. 'But I'm not sure . . .'

'Oh, it's just a little personal question. We . . . that is, I was wondering, you know, how Miss Rowe was first discovered. Who recognized that she might have talent? I know the stories, but . . .'

'Ah.' Mr Owens almost laughed. 'Oh, well that I can tell you. It's the practice, or was, in slack times, to send us cameramen out on to the streets to shoot a little stock footage. Crowd scenes, traffic, even more dramatic moments that might come our way. I remember one time being close to where a traffic accident was occurring so, naturally, I captured what I could of it on film. And while we were out we'd also be looking for any likely face that would look good as a bit player, or could be entered on to the postcard list, if they lived a little further out.'

'Postcard list?'

'Oh, let me explain. If a particular actor or even a particular type of actor were required and they were not part of our usual local talent, then they'd be sent a postcard telling them to report for filming, usually with a couple of days' notice. There was always the need either for attractive background talent or for character parts, you know.'

'And Cissie was found on one of these random trawls?'

'I believe so, yes. Not by me, unfortunately. That would have been rather splendid, but, you know, some of the young people trying to break into the industry, they knew if they were hanging around when we were out and about they'd be likely to be called on. Maybe even earn a little bit of money, you know.'

Mickey nodded. 'And she made a point of hanging around until someone noticed her.'

'That's what I'm given to understand.'

Mickey nodded, oddly satisfied by the idea that Cissie Rowe had in fact been picked out from the crowd. Discovered, as it were.

'A very lovely young woman,' Mr Owens said sadly. 'Very lovely indeed.'

Henry Johnstone had been interviewing the stage manager, Herbert Hood, a man more guaranteed to notice the comings and goings than most. He had already spoken to some of Cissie's friends and it was clear that they were all extremely upset. She seemed to have been genuinely popular and was described as kind and caring and funny. He had asked about male friends, about young men who might have had a romantic involvement with Cissie Rowe, and a few had been named, including Jimmy Cottee and Selwyn Croft, and others who had come and gone and for a brief time attracted her attention or affection.

'I don't want you to think that she was fickle,' a young woman by the name of Violet Smith told him. 'Indeed by the standards of many young actresses she was positively – well, cautious, one might say. But she was very beautiful and she did attract a great deal of attention.'

'And any of the wrong kind of attention?'

'What woman doesn't?' She shrugged. 'She'd have to be as ugly as sin not to attract some man or another. It's just the way of the world, isn't it?'

Henry was left to consider that. Only one piece of information appeared to be particularly relevant and that was an observation from the stage manager himself.

'We don't like to encourage outsiders on the set but occasionally a few turn up as guests of whoever happens to be working that day and so long as they keep out of the way we can turn a blind eye. And there was one day when Cissie had someone. The young man, he stood well back, didn't speak to anyone much. He was in here for about half an hour right at the end of the day, as though he'd come to collect

her. He wasn't local, I do know that much. I think she called
him Philip or' – he paused to think – 'no, it wasn't Philip,
it was more like Philippe, and when he spoke to her he had
a bit of an accent. French, I suppose. She didn't introduce
him to anyone and we thought that was a little strange, but
they rushed off and I assume they had an appointment
somewhere.'

'Miss Rowe came from Amiens, I believe?'

'Well, she certainly lived there for a time. I believe she was
born in some little village somewhere. I remember her
mentioning an aunt and uncle – in fact I believe there is a
photograph of them in her bungalow. There was a group of
us down the beach one day talking about family and' – he
paused, thinking again – 'Cissie said something about not
having family now, about losing them in the war. And Mrs
Owens commented that Cissie at least had remembrances of
them, family photographs and that sort of thing, so that was
meant to be compensation.' He waved a hand dismissively.
'I suppose people say all sorts of things when they're trying
to fill the silence – and Mrs Owens, I have to say, likes to fill
silences.'

'Do you remember where her family came from?'

'Sorry, no I don't. She said something about a country house,
a farmhouse maybe, and an orchard but, as I say, there was a
group of us and I can't pretend I was really listening all that
closely.'

'So it's very possible that this young man, the one on set,
was someone from her past before she came here.'

'I sort of assumed that, but I did think it strange that if
someone had come all this way, from France or Belgium or
wherever, she didn't introduce him to us.' He shrugged. 'But
then I forgot about it until you caused me to call it to mind
just now.'

'Would anyone else have seen him or spoken to him?'

'In passing, maybe. Given him directions or something, I
suppose. But as I say we were all working; there is no room
for anyone hanging around chatting. And when we're filming
it's usually either a closed set or we demand absolute silence.
We can't afford the film stock to be constantly reshooting and

we're still very reliant on natural light down here. We do have electric lamps now, of course, but we try to keep their use to the minimum. Perhaps you know that's why the studio was based here? The light is so good?'

'So I've been told,' Henry said.

He thanked the man and then went off to find Mickey, but on the way was waylaid by Mrs Owens, who had spotted him and wanted to know what progress was being made.

As yet very little, Henry told her, and then he asked about the snake bangle and whether she had ever seen her young friend wearing it.

Muriel Owens stared at him. 'Cissie owned nothing like that,' she said. 'Where would a girl like Cissie get something like a gold bangle? I know the kind you mean, very fashionable. I keep saying to my Frederick I would love one of those bangles. So clever.' She shook her head angrily. 'I don't like what you're assuming, Inspector.'

'And what am I assuming?' he asked her.

'Not assuming, perhaps. Inferring. You are inferring that someone made a gift of this bracelet to our Cissie. That someone . . . someone may have expected something in return.'

'What someone might have expected and what someone received are two different things,' Henry said quietly. 'And expectations of that kind can lead to violence, you know.'

Muriel Owens was genuinely shocked, he could see that.

'I never saw her with anything of that kind. And I'm sure she would have shown it to me.'

'Unless,' Henry pushed the idea home, 'she knew you wouldn't approve of whoever had given it to her or how she had acquired it. If she held your opinion in regard, then she may have been very cautious about what she told you. She might have feared your disapproval or disapprobation and, since I'm sure she valued you as a friend, that might have been something she did not wish to risk.'

Muriel Owens nodded. 'Quite so,' she said. 'You can understand, Inspector, that it hurts me to think that Cissie might have been in trouble and could not confide in me. That upsets me a great deal.'

'I can understand that,' Henry assured her. 'Thank you, Mrs Owens, I've no doubt we will be in touch again.'

Henry had spotted Mickey Hitchens walking towards them and he now disengaged himself from Muriel Owens and went to meet his sergeant. He was interrupted by a female voice. 'Take your picture, Inspector?'

Henry turned, frowning. A young woman stood off to his right, a Kodak camera very like his own clasped in her hands.

'Sophie Mars,' she said. 'Freelance photographer and journalist.'

She spoke brightly and confidently but wilted a little under Henry's glare.

'I take pictures of the actors, mainly,' she added. 'Write little snippets. Review the occasional film for the local papers.' She smiled suddenly, as though gathering her confidence again. 'Take the picture of handsome detectives going about their work?'

She must have realized at once that this was the wrong thing to say. Her cheeks flushed and she looked away.

Henry turned his back on her and strode off towards where Mickey Hitchens, clearly amused, waited for him.

'Nothing funny,' Henry said.

'Oh, I don't know. It's not every day an attractive woman accuses you of being handsome.'

Henry's scowl deepened. He glanced back and saw that Sophie Mars was standing where he had left her, camera still between her hands.

'I spotted her earlier. She hangs around taking pictures. They put up with her because she's local and knows how to keep out of the way, never takes anything racy or too outrageous. A girl has the right to earn a little extra cash. You'd not turn a hair if young Sophie Mars was called Samuel and wore a Norfolk jacket.'

'I'm not against women working,' Henry argued. 'I just have reservations about certain professions and being a so-called journalist is one of them.'

Mickey grinned at him but knew when to leave the conversation alone.

They walked some distance away from the studio, down towards the Church of the Good Shepherd, and, finding a bench in the churchyard, sat down to exchange the intelligence they had received.

'So,' Mickey said, 'several young men in the frame, then.'

'All of whom may be completely innocent, but the one she was seeing secretly does interest me, as does this Philippe. Jimmy Cottee is the closest and most easily available, so I suggest we begin with him. Then we find out which bank this Selwyn Croft works for and we make him our next port of call. And we search the bungalow for any trace of this Philippe. I'm intrigued by the fact that the only missing object would seem to be the photograph of her French or Belgian relatives. Why take that? Why take nothing else?'

Mickey glanced at his watch, tugging it out of his waistcoat pocket and stroking it lovingly before he put it away again. It was of old and battered brass and of no value except that it belonged to Mickey's father and he loved it.

'It's approaching noon,' he said. 'I suggest we find a local pub and adjourn for some refreshment and to get directions to where this Jimmy Cottee lives. I don't know about you but I'm parched. It's either feast or famine round here. You go from house to house and come out awash with tea; obviously a film studio doesn't have the same level of hospitality.'

'For once, I agree. For once I confess to being thirsty and a little hungry.'

'Miracle of miracles,' Mickey said wryly. 'I take it you slept better then, after I met you on the stairs last night.'

'I slept a little before and a little after, so yes, better.'

'Good,' Mickey said, and in that single word managed to convey an entire vocabulary of relief.

They had been told that Jimmy Cottee lived further along the beach in a railway carriage parked on the shingle, supported by the now familiar concrete slab beneath. Three wooden steps led down from the door directly on to the beach and there was no pretence at garden or enclosure around it. A much poorer construction, Henry thought, than the one he had previously seen and set somewhat apart from the more affluent bungalows. He noticed that there were several such structures close by, with water tanks behind fed from guttering on the roof, as Mrs Owens had told them was still commonplace.

They knocked on the carriage door but received no answer. Local enquiries had told them that Jimmy Cottee was twenty-six years old and had lived alone since his mother had died five years before. She had once shared the railway carriage with him and he had supported them both; she had been ill for a long time. 'A nice boy,' they had been told. 'Does odd jobs at the studio and fills in with odd jobs elsewhere.' Someone else had told them, 'He was soft on that young actress what got killed, followed her around like a little puppy.'

They knocked again but no one came to the door.

Henry, remembering what Mrs Owens had said about no one locking their doors, pulled it open and they both stepped inside. Mickey called out. 'Jimmy, Jimmy Cottee! You home, lad? It's the police, got a few questions for you.'

'Something's not right here,' Henry said, saying aloud what they had both felt since they had first stood on the doorstep.

The carriage appeared to be divided into two living areas, with a little kitchenette in the corner and a day bed under the window and what must be a bedroom separated by a thin stud wall. Presumably that had been the mother's room and was now Jimmy's. Henry opened the door.

'God,' he said. 'He's hanged himself.'

Mickey Hitchens pushed past. The chair lay overturned on the floor and the young man with a rope around his neck was suspended from what seemed to be a bracket, structural to the carriage itself. Mickey reached out a hand and touched the dead man's. 'Cold,' he said. 'He's long gone, nothing to be done for him now.'

'Guilt, or sorrow?' Henry wondered. 'You look in there for any sign of a note and I will check the other room.'

It didn't take long and moments later they were standing on the steps outside the railway carriage. 'Nothing that resembles a note,' Mickey said. 'Poor little sod must have had it bad, though.'

'But bad enough to kill her, or just himself? Mickey, I'll wait here. Will you go and summon a constable? I'll take another look around inside but I doubt we'll find much.'

Mickey nodded and tramped off across the shingle.

# SIX

Henry was careful not to touch anything. He and Mickey would work the scene together later but for now he just needed to assess the space.

The railway carriage was sparsely furnished but neat and clean. The day bed beneath the window had a hand crocheted afghan along its back and two rather faded red cushions. There were two chairs and a scrubbed pine table. Cooking would be done on a double burner. Pans had been suspended from the ceiling above it and shelves stocked with jars holding flour and dried fruit and sugar were set against the wall. Butter was stored in a contraption the like of which Henry hadn't seen for quite some time, though his grandmother had owned one. A shallow glazed dish sat beneath an unglazed terracotta plate. The glazed dish held water and the butter was placed in the terracotta plate and covered with another dome of unglazed terracotta. It was a little chipped and had obviously seen a great deal of use but slow evaporation kept the butter fresh. Beneath a second, similar cover, he found cheese.

A threadbare rug covered the lino and Henry noticed that it was set at an angle as though kicked off-square. He bent down and lifted a corner, paused and then let it drop back.

Blood. There was blood on the floor. Someone had made an attempt to clean it up but a streak remained. Jimmy Cottee's blood?

Alerted now, Henry chastised himself for being satisfied with the immediate option of suicide. He should have been more cautious in his appraisal. He had rushed to judgement in the same way as Dr Arnold. Looking closely this time he spotted more traces on the doorframe and spotting on the bedroom floor.

In the bedroom the body turned slightly. The rope was tight around the neck and the knot crude. One look at the young man's face told Henry that he had been strangled rather than had his neck broken. Death had not been quick; it could take minutes to die that way and looking at his hands Henry thought that he could see blood beneath the nails and guessed there would probably be matching scratches on the throat. It was not uncommon for suicides, suddenly faced with the realities of asphyxiation, to scrabble for relief and tear at their throats in the attempt to loosen the rope. He had never known them to succeed. Jimmy Cottee had been alive and conscious when he'd been strung up and Henry no longer believed that his death was caused by suicide.

The bed was narrow, carefully and neatly made up and the boards were scrubbed and covered with a scrap of rug.

'So, perhaps neither guilt nor sorrow?' Henry mused, but whatever the cause, Jimmy Cottee was now dead and this matter was getting deeper by the second.

Henry wandered out on to the steps. He examined them carefully before sitting down but there was no sign of blood and no footprints to be wary of. The steps were narrow and steep, settling on the beach at a level about a foot lower than the concrete slab. He guessed that in the winter, storms must scour out the shingle from around these concrete supports, perhaps even undermining them. This spit of land might be a pleasant enough place in the summer – if you liked that sort of thing – but he imagined it would be a bleak kind of hole during the winter months.

He took out his pen and his journal. Mickey always referred to this as his 'murder book', though in truth he used it to record many other events as well.

Now, though, his thoughts were very much on Jimmy Cottee and how the young man had met his demise. Henry wrote,

> So, what had he done to bring down this degree of violence on his head? To judge from the condition of the body, rigor has set in and not yet passed. The nights have been warm so the body will have been slow to cool. My initial guess is that he has been dead perhaps a day, and less than two. So, after Cissie Rowe was murdered.
>
> Did she name him? Did she make some accusation? Did he even know that she had died? It seems possible,

*given that Miss Rowe's body was discovered only yesterday morning and the news would spread like wildfire within this small and close community.*

*If we had come to see him yesterday – if we had known then that this young man even existed – what would he have been able to tell us? Someone evidently believed that he knew something or had something or could lead them to something.*

*Most murders have the same depressing themes in common. Greed, passion, fear. Too often all three. He evidently worshipped Miss Rowe and we are told that she was pleasant to him. I suppose she meant to be kind, but in my view it is sometimes kinder to be honest rather than to give false hope. Or is that, as Cynthia and Mickey would both tell me, simply the view of a dried and hardened cynic?*

Henry was alone close on an hour, time enough to mull over the previous day's events in his mind, before Mickey returned with a train of officers in tow and the murder bag clasped firmly in his hand. Henry quickly dispatched the constables on house-to-house duties and brought one inside to assist in cutting the dead man down.

'Make sure you cut well above the knot,' Henry instructed. 'We need to keep the knot intact. It's no longer so certain that this poor soul did for himself; it may be more likely that someone helped him on his way.'

Mickey gave him a sharp look, but held his curiosity in check until the two of them should be alone.

'Right, that's right,' Henry instructed. 'I've got the weight of the legs; you keep your arm around his chest. That's it, don't be squeamish, he's past hurting you or you hurting him, just put your arm around his chest and cradle his body against yours. Then you can lower him down to us.'

The constable did as he was bid, albeit rather reluctantly, and Henry took over the weight of the man's upper torso as soon as he had lowered it enough. Together he and Mickey carried Jimmy Cottee through to the other room and laid the young man out on the table so they could take a better look.

The constable departed to join his fellows in speaking to the neighbours.

Carefully, Henry pulled the shirt from the trousers and exposed the trunk. The signs of the kicking and beating he had received were obvious.

'Someone beat seven shades out of him,' Mickey observed.

'There's blood on the floor beneath that rug and a smear or two on the doorframe that probably came from his hands. My guess is he grabbed at the frame as they carried him through.'

'And the blood on the floor came from his lips or ears,' said Mickey. 'Now we can see properly, there's cuts and splits on both.'

'His death was not as simple as it first appeared,' Henry said. 'We were in danger of jumping to the same conclusions as our Dr Arnold did.'

'Constable Prentice is trying to find us a boat to come up the River Adur and then be pulled up on shore. He considered it might be simpler and swifter than summoning an ambulance. They tell me the river is shallow here so it has to be something that has very little draft but there are boats enough to be had in Shoreham. Prentice will find something.'

'Did you summon a doctor? We must still have death declared.'

'I've put Prentice in charge of that too though he reckons the only one that might be available at such short notice is our old friend Dr Arnold. I think we should take the lad back up to London, get the post-mortem on this one done alongside that of Miss Rowe.'

Henry examined the knot and then took a look at Jimmy Cottee's hands. He was unsurprised to find the scratches on the neck and the blood beneath the fingernails as he had predicted.

'Tried to free himself,' Mickey observed.

'I think it's more of a reflex than any conscious thought,' Henry said. 'I think it would take great determination not to fight for life in those final instants. And I don't believe that most people who actively seek to use this way out understand what they're getting into. They think they can just take a length of rope and a chair and that it will be easy. You and I both know how hard it goes. And this poor young man didn't make that choice.'

Mickey Hitchens searched the dead man's pockets but they were empty. His jacket hung on the back of a chair in the bedroom. A cheap wallet was lodged in one pocket, small change and cigarettes in the others. Also a key, which when Henry tried it fitted the door to the railway carriage, or rather fitted the hasp and staple and padlock that from the look of it had rarely been used. 'No one locks their doors around here,' he said quietly.

'And we were looking for a local man. That someone helped him on his way doesn't let him off the hook on the murder. It's still possible that Jimmy Cottee's death was a reprisal for the girl. It's possible he killed his girl in a fit of temper and then some other returned the favour.'

'It is. But I don't see it. However, we must keep all thoughts in mind.'

'I'll start to process in the bedroom,' Mickey said. 'Then when the doctor arrives he can do his business in this room here without either of us getting in the other's way.'

'I'll get started with the camera, photograph the body and we'll see where we go from there.'

It was a further hour before the doctor arrived – Dr Arnold as predicted, who seemed a little cowed by the presence of the chief inspector and his sergeant but relieved that his verdict could be directed with a fair degree of confidence this time.

'Was the young man known to you?' Henry asked.

'Good Lord no, he couldn't have afforded me,' Dr Arnold said.

Henry glanced at Dr Arnold, noticing the cut of his jacket and the quality of the cloth, and he nodded. Henry doubted that the likes of Jimmy Cottee could have afforded his father's services either. 'Thank you, Doctor,' he said. 'I'm sorry I can't offer you transport back into town.'

If Dr Arnold noted the insincerity in that comment he showed no sign of it. Instead, he took himself off back down the shingle strand and it was only later that Henry realized that he had borrowed a constable to carry his bag for him.

Constable Prentice had managed to secure a boat and by four in the afternoon the body was on board together with the boatman and Mickey. They had wrapped Jimmy Cottee in a blanket from his bed and Henry had locked the door with the key from the young man's pocket and then he and the constables, who had re-adjourned at the railway carriage, set off down the beach. They had learned very little. A neighbour said that Jimmy Cottee had heard the news of Cissie Rowe's death and had been distraught. Another said that he was 'daft after the girl'.

No one seemed surprised at the news that he had hanged himself. It was, to quote a third, 'just one more rough deal in a lifetime of bad deals'.

Henry gained the impression that Cissie Rowe was perhaps the one fine thing to have come into Jimmy Cottee's life, and whatever the relationship had been she had definitely brightened it. But was he a man to have taken rejection hard? Had he lain in wait for her, knowing, perhaps, that she favoured another man above himself? Had he then taken his revenge?

It was possible, Henry thought, but it felt so unlikely. Jimmy Cottee had cared deeply for Cissie Rowe. Henry could not believe that he would have harmed her. Neither could he believe that Jimmy's death was an act of revenge. Typically someone angry enough to want revenge would hit out, would attack, would do what was felt necessary and apt with swiftness and heat. Jimmy's death had been a slow, deliberate and painful one and Henry found that it angered him deeply.

# SEVEN

It had been decided that Mickey Hitchens should go back to London with the body of Jimmy Cottee and Henry should remain behind. It made sense that his sergeant should go and check in with the central office, see if anything had arisen regarding fingerprints and look at the records relating to the status of Cissie Rowe, Cécile Rolland as she had been, as a foreign national.

Henry would return to London the following afternoon when the post-mortem of Cissie Rowe was scheduled and it was hoped that Jimmy Cottee's body would be dealt with on that same afternoon.

In the meantime Henry made his way back to Cissie Rowe's bungalow with the intention of looking now for anything that might relate to this mysterious Philippe. Although he and Mickey had already gathered together papers and photographs that looked relevant, it was entirely possible that now he was looking afresh, and with a fragment more intelligence about the woman's life, he might notice something that he had disregarded before.

When he arrived at the bungalow he was surprised and somewhat annoyed to find that there was no one on duty outside. He was even more annoyed to find that the door had been left open. Thinking that the constable might have gone inside for some reason, Henry pushed it wider and called out but it was clear from the moment he stepped over the threshold that something was very wrong.

The bungalow, which they had left tidy and almost un-touched despite their examination, was now a mess. Cissie's possessions had been strewn on the floor, across the sofa, everywhere. Whoever had set about the place had been not just searching for something but wrecking and attacking any sense of order.

Henry could see from where he stood that the bedroom had

been similarly attacked, even the mattress turned from the bed, and a constable was nowhere in sight.

Furious, Henry went back outside hoping that he could recall one of the officers who had walked back with him from Jimmy Cottee's house. They were about to leave the beach and return to the Old Fort Road and were almost out of sight, but Henry bellowed at them. They turned as one and all three headed back in his direction.

'Where the devil is the constable I left here?' Henry demanded. He pointed at one of the constables. 'You, Evans, go and rouse him from wherever it is he's hiding. Pratt, get back to the police station and report that Miss Rowe's bungalow has been vandalized.'

'Vandalized, sir?'

'Someone's been in and searched the place and has not been very careful doing it. Your colleague is nowhere to be found.'

'Prentice, you're with me.' Henry turned on his heel and back inside. Prentice joined him by the door.

'Oh,' Prentice said.

'Quite.'

Henry was glad that he'd kept the murder bag with him. He hadn't thought he would need it when Mickey went back to London that night, and had hung on to it only because it would give him the opportunity to re-examine the photographs he had taken.

Prentice voiced what Henry was thinking. 'Where do we start, sir?'

'Good question, Constable.'

Henry bent down and checked the bag, removing the camera to see what film he had remaining. There had been no chance to restock so he would have to go carefully with it. 'We start with pictures, so we can compare what we have now to what was here before. As far as that is possible, given the mess.'

'What would they have been looking for?'

'Right now, Constable, I have about as much of an idea as you do.'

A clatter of boots on boards caused Henry to swing around as the errant constable appeared in the doorway. He was carrying his helmet and his face was bright red. He halted in astonishment at the sight of the room and of Henry. Then he swore loudly.

'And where the devil did you get to?' Henry demanded.

'There was a boy, sir.'

'A boy?'

'Yes, a boy, sir. Sent to fetch me and Dr Clark. He lives next door . . .'

'I know where he lives. What boy? Fetch you? Why?'

'He said, sir, that there was a kiddie in the water. Little girl. Some fishermen were trying to drag her out but they needed the doctor and he said I was to come too, because . . .'

'Because?' Henry wasn't ready to let him off the hook yet.

The constable shrugged awkwardly as though the reasons were self-explanatory.

'And so you and Dr Clark went with this boy? And when you got to the scene?'

'Little bastard, begging your pardon, sir, he ran off, sir. Well, me and Dr Clark, we hung around looking up and down the beach, just in case it was real, just in case there was a little girl in the water, but . . . Then we came back here, sir.'

'And as you will see, someone took advantage of your absence.' Henry indicated the chaos and devastation in the little bungalow. 'How long were you gone?'

The constable looked blank, then shook his head. 'Ten minutes? No more than that. I'm sure of it.'

'Ten minutes too long,' Henry said flatly.

The constable's gaze travelled guiltily around the room and then back to Henry. He looked utterly shamefaced but also defiant. 'What else could I do, sir? I've lived around the water all my life, I know the currents, I know the deep pools, I thought I could be of help. If I had *not* gone and there *had* been a little kiddie in the water, and I might have helped, well, I don't think I could have lived with myself.'

Henry glared at him and then allowed his expression to soften. He knew he would have done the same himself so how could he blame the constable for reacting with natural compassion?

'So what do I do now, sir?' the constable asked nervously.

'Did you know the boy?'

'No, sir. But he won't be that hard to find. And when I do . . .'

'And when you do you'll lock him in the cells for an hour or two, just as a warning, and you'll find out who sent him on his errand. In the meantime you'd better take up your post outside and record everything you can remember in your notebook. Then you can make a proper statement when you get back to the station. Understood? And then you're going next door to talk to Dr Clark and take a proper statement from that gentleman. Understood?'

The constable nodded. 'Yes, sir. Thank you, Inspector, sir. If I could just trouble you for a drink of water, sir?' he asked, pointing towards the kitchen.

Henry closed his eyes in exasperation. 'This,' he said heavily, 'is an active crime scene. One that has been left unprotected. One that I now have to assess anew. Constable, I suggest if you need refreshment you should go next door and speak with your Dr Clark, take his statement and see if you are fortunate enough to be offered a cup of tea.'

The constable disappeared with great alacrity and Henry sighed.

'What would you like me to do, sir?' Constable Prentice asked. He had maintained a diplomatic silence throughout.

Henry studied the scene carefully, not quite sure what should be done.

'Assist me with the photographs; we need some sense of what has been moved and disturbed and what might have been taken. Touch nothing. I imagine our perpetrator wore gloves but we'll need to fingerprint anything he might have been in contact with. But for now, the day grows late, as does my patience.' And, though it was still bright outside, the sun had shifted round and the interior of the bungalow was now in shadow. He was reluctant to find and light the paraffin lamps because the smell of paraffin in the room was very strong. He suspected they had been knocked over and the spirit perhaps soaked into the floor or the furniture. He had no wish to start a fire. He had a torch and guessed that Constable Prentice would have one too and others could be borrowed, but even so, the thought of embarking on any attempts to untangle things just by torchlight did not appeal. They would be lucky if they got the photographs finished before the light became too weak.

Henry examined the bag again and discovered that there was a small stock of flashbulbs so they could make use of those if necessary. He preferred not to; the flash could distort.

'We photograph what we can; we draw any conclusions that we might as to what the perpetrator might have touched. We note this down. Then you, Constable Prentice, will stand guard while I return to the police station and arrange not only for your relief but also for a locksmith to be found, something that should already have been done. Something that I was assured would already have been seen to. And someone to board up the windows temporarily. We can have no repetition of this.'

'You think he'll come back?'

'I think we can't be sure he found what he was looking for. If the officer is to be believed, then he was away for no more than ten minutes. Let's say fifteen; he is certain to have sought to limit the damage by underestimating the time that he was absent. In ten or fifteen minutes this was done, which suggests to me that the perpetrator either did not know what to look for or did not know where to find it. That being so, we cannot be sure that he achieved his aim.'

Prentice nodded and looked a little unsure of himself. Henry realized the boy was thinking about being left alone outside the bungalow. He hastened to reassure him. 'I think two officers might be better than one. One to stand and one to patrol and good locks on the door will slow anyone down.'

'I'm sure it will, sir. Did you think to check the water tank?'

Henry nodded. Most of the water used by the residents in the bungalows was rainwater, caught in large butts and tanks outside. He understood that fresh water could be bought from the bungalow stores but that they relied on this natural source for washing and cooking.

'Sergeant Hitchens examined it,' he said. 'But it would not hurt to have a closer look. I will leave that task to you, Constable Prentice, when we have finished with the photographs.'

It was almost an hour and a half later that Henry set off back. He had already sent word back to the police station, making use of one of Dr Clark's boys to carry the message and giving him a shilling for his reward.

The locksmith, he was told, was now on his way. A second constable had been sent to keep Prentice company and another would relieve him as soon as possible.

Henry had to be satisfied with that. He made a telephone call to Mickey Hitchens in London and relayed the day's events to his sergeant.

'Nothing so far on the fingerprints,' Mickey told him. 'The post-mortems have both been scheduled for tomorrow afternoon, starting somewhere after two. Shall I remain here and wait for you?'

Henry told him that would be the best idea and he would catch the train from Worthing the following morning. He planned to process the new photographs at his sister's house that night, he told Mickey.

'You'll be running a bit fly on the chemicals,' Mickey told him.

'I'll do what I can; the rest may have to wait until I return to London, but I would prefer to examine them tonight.'

Cynthia had sent a car, but not the Bentley this time. Her own little Ford sedan was waiting outside and the driver told him that his sister had 'gone up to town, to the theatre, sir. She said to tell you that the master would be in later, and if there was anything you needed or wanted you should just ask.'

Henry thanked him and spent the journey back to his sister's house in quiet reverie. It had been an eventful day but not one on which the events were in any way satisfying.

# EIGHT

'Hello, old chap. You still up?' Albert came into his study and headed straight for the drinks cabinet, poured himself rather more than two fingers of Scotch, added a splash of soda from the tall glass siphon and waved a glass in Henry's direction. 'Can I get you a top-up?'

Henry thanked him and said he would indeed like another drink. He made to gather the photographs that were spread all across Albert's desk and on the floor, but Albert gestured that he should leave them. Henry's brother-in-law peered curiously at the pictures. 'What sort of a day have you had, then, old man?'

'Frustrating. A damnably frustrating one,' Henry told him. 'And yourself?'

'More boring than frustrating, if I'm honest. I had a lot of business to clear out of the way, today. Although it is only Thursday, I have taken tomorrow off, and next week I have promised Cynthia absolutely nothing will disturb us. So if I am to have an undisturbed week I must have a very disturbed Thursday.'

Albert threw himself down on the small sofa and gestured at the photographs once more.

'Local press is buzzing with it. I picked up some of the papers on my way home. *Glamorous Actress Done to Death in Her Own Home*, you know the sort of thing. It's a damnable shame, though. What a ghastly thing to happen to a beautiful young woman.'

Henry thought it was a pretty ghastly thing to happen to anyone but he didn't bother saying so. He knew that Albert meant no harm by the comment. 'And so,' he said, 'how is the world of business?'

'More complicated than I'd like, if I'm honest.'

'How so?' Henry asked, sensing that his brother-in-law would like to talk about it. Henry wasn't at all sure that he wanted to talk about his own day so he was glad of the distraction.

How was business, Henry had asked him, and Albert said that it was sound, and expanding. 'But we don't want to expand too far or too fast,' he said. 'To be frank, Henry, I don't trust the times. I keep looking to Europe and more especially to Germany and what do I see? Hyperinflation and demoralization and a disturbing rise in the more extreme politics. There'll be trouble from that quarter again, you mark my words.'

'I thought the idea was that a weakened Germany would insure against that,' Henry commented.

'A weakened Germany, yes. Now, politically I'm all in favour of that. But you start to push the ordinary people too far and one day they will start to push back. And I, for one, don't like what I'm seeing.'

'You've been there recently, I believe.'

'I have. They are desperate for stable currency. If you have dollars or sterling you can buy yourself anything. But there's a desperation, Henry, a sense of injustice that you can't escape. It worries me. I'd had the thought to open a factory there, a spot just outside Münster that I could have bought for a song. Labour is cheap and people are desperate for jobs but . . .'

'But you decided against.'

'I did, but I can give you no sound business reason. Sometimes, Henry, you just have to trust your gut and mine is telling me to leave well alone.'

Henry nodded. It seemed strange to him that a scant decade after the end of the war, Albert should have been considering such a venture anyway.

'So, I came back from Münster and I discussed matters with my board and also with your sister. We have made the decision to consolidate rather than expand, and are keen to try and insure our business against shocks. Cynthia has proposed, and I agree, that we should begin to move money out of stocks and shares and into more concrete products. Our business was always focused around commodities and this has stood us in good stead in the past. We have been considering our options and are thinking to put the capital that we managed to liberate from the sale of our stocks and bonds into property. Good quality property. That rarely loses value in the long term and we need to secure the future for the children, whatever happens in the business world.'

'That would seem a sensible course of action,' Henry approved.

'To my mind, yes. Many of my fellow men of business disagree, of course, and the board took convincing, I can tell you. But fortunately, I have always retained a casting vote. They see this as a safe, slow option in a world that is no longer safe and slow. They think we should be taking more risks, expanding more swiftly and, of course, there are still those who believe I listen to my wife more assiduously than is good for me, but I worry about the volatility of the markets. I worry about some of the trends that I'm seeing and I would rather be slow and safe and have a steady investment in the years to come than strive to make pots of money now only to lose it all when the markets turn. It's happened before and it will happen again, Henry. Mark my words.'

Henry Johnstone nodded. It occurred to him that he could almost hear his sister's voice in what Albert was saying. He was glad that she had such influence and also glad that Albert gave her some credit for it. 'I would take my sister's opinion over that of most men I know,' he said. 'She has always been a source of great good sense.'

The conversation turned to cinema and the prospect of talking films becoming a widespread phenomenon.

'Cynthia is very enthused about that new film *The Jazz Singer*; apparently it will be reaching London in late September. I imagine there will be queues around the block at every cinema. You think it will catch on, old man?'

'From what I have heard in the last couple of days, those involved with the industry certainly think it will,' Henry told him. 'I imagine it will be good news for the voice coaches and the elocutionists. I'm told there will be many actors and actresses who will not make the grade because their voices are inadequate to the task.'

'Well, there were many whose acting was not up to the task, but that never seemed to stop them.' Albert laughed at his own joke. 'It strikes me that all the young women ever had to do was stand there and look glamorous. However, I do find it an exciting prospect. Sound on films! I was reading the other day about that experiment with television. I'll find the article for you if you like; I know you're interested in such things.'

'You mean the transmission in colour?' Henry asked him. 'Yes, Sergeant Hitchens was telling me something about it. His reading matter is surprisingly broad, you know.'

'So I'd noticed. He is a good chap, all told.' Albert nodded as though to affirm his opinion and got up to get himself another drink. Henry declined.

The clock in the hall struck midnight and Albert announced he was going to bed. He'd been up since five trying to get business out of the way.

'I expect I'll see you at breakfast. And I hope your day goes better tomorrow. With fewer frustrations and a little more progress.'

Henry thanked him and his brother-in-law took himself off to bed, a glass of whiskey in one hand and the latest P.G. Wodehouse, *Money for Nothing*, in the other.

Henry sat for a little longer, still sipping his whiskey. Both his sister and brother-in-law drank quite heavily, as did most of their set, but Henry himself was more restrained. He did not like the way that alcohol dulled his thoughts – though, he supposed, for a lot of people that was the whole point of it.

His mind wandered through the events of the day but he was no nearer to pulling the threads together and eventually he too wandered up to bed.

That night Henry slept but he also dreamt and the dreams were uncomfortably vivid. In his dream Cissie Rowe stood by the seashore, but this was not England on the south coast, this was somewhere else. And behind her stood a procession of men and women and children and horses and guns, stretching out into a place that he recognized as the River Adur, though it seemed wider and deeper than when Henry had walked beside it.

Henry woke, his pyjamas soaked in sweat, but he was relieved to find that the sun was streaming through the window and it was dawn and that, despite his dreaming, his sleep had refreshed him.

*What does it matter, Henry? Just one more death, what is one more little death?* Henry wasn't sure what had called that question to mind; something in his dream had triggered a memory, together with the fury Henry had felt towards the speaker.

'It all bloody matters,' Henry said, hauling himself out of bed and striding into the little bathroom that was en suite to his bedroom. He stripped off his sodden pyjamas and dumped them into the laundry hamper, then washed thoroughly, as though using the face cloth and soap to raze the last of the dream, to scrape it from his skin.

He dressed and then sat at the small desk that Cynthia had installed beside the window and took out his journal.

*The man who spoke those words to me found himself face down in the mud. I'd hit him hard, I remember that I'd hit him hard enough for my knuckles to be scraped raw. It took him a while to get up again, or so I'm told. I'd had my fill of him, frankly. I didn't hang around long enough to see him regain his feet.*

*It sickened me then and it sickens me now, this notion that some deaths are of so little consequence. We threw men at cannon, at machine guns, sent them forward and forward until the bodies piled up and the guns fell silent because they had spent their ammunition, more often than not for the gain of a few feet of land. Often not even that.*

He paused, breathed deep and released the breath slowly. It had been ten years and yet the anger still burned just as hot and bright as it ever had. Mickey reckoned that he was afraid to release it. Lose that anger and Henry was afraid that he would lose his edge.

Cynthia knew that it went deeper than that. If Henry ceased to feel angry then he feared he might cease to feel anything at all.

The gong in the hall, announcing that breakfast was served, interrupted his reverie. Henry shrugged into his jacket, slipping the journal back into the pocket, and went downstairs, hoping that Albert would be true to form and not expect small talk at such an early hour.

\*   \*   \*

In fact, Henry and Albert didn't speak very much over breakfast, neither being the type who enjoyed early morning
conversation. Instead they read their papers and Henry caught
up with what the local press was saying about the inquiry.
He was struck by one of the headlines: 'The Final Death of
Cissie Rowe.'

He read the article with some irritation. The author talked
about the young woman's film career and how she had begun
by playing tiny parts, younger sister or second maid, and
slowly progressed through the industry. More recently she
had played the discarded lovers, young women disappointed
in love and heroines that had met sticky ends.

He noted a smaller photograph further down the page, of
Cissie Rowe caught in a candid moment, chatting to a fellow
actress. The photograph was credited to Miss S. Mars,
reminding Henry of his meeting with the young woman who
had accosted him at the studio and taken his picture. He was
discomforted to note that this image had also made its way
into the newspaper, with the caption 'Chief Inspector Johnstone
Investigates'.

Irritated, Henry nevertheless read on.

> In a career that sadly imitated real life, Miss Rowe was
> frequently depicted as the victim of violent acts. I have
> counted roughly and approximately and I believe Miss
> Rowe to have died on screen perhaps five or six times
> and, through the magic of film, five or six times she has
> walked away, gone back to her home and returned to
> delight us in yet another film. Sadly she will not get up
> and walk away this time. We are told that the police are
> investigating and that they have certain leads. Let us hope
> that the violence meted out to this quiet community and
> this graceful woman will be met by equal violence
> and determination on the part of our police force.

Henry harrumphed and put the newspapers to one side.
Albert glanced up and saw what he had been reading.

'Oh,' he said, 'that one. Purple prose incarnate.' He either had
not noticed or chose not to comment upon Henry's photograph

being in the news. He returned to his reading and Henry finished his breakfast and announced that he must leave.

'I've told Sheppard to bring the car round but that you will be doing the driving. You're all right with Cynthia's car, ain't you? It seems foolish to keep sending a driver back and forth when you might need the vehicle during the day. Let us know when you've done with it and we can arrange for collection if you can't get it back to us.'

Henry thanked him and agreed that this did indeed make more sense. It meant that he could drive back to the crime scene this morning, take another look and then drive back up to London rather than catching the train. He wasn't sure that this would be a quicker option but it did mean that he could take himself straight to the post-mortem instead of summoning a driver to pick him up from the station, and it gave him more uninterrupted time to think.

Henry always found the other people in the railway carriage something of a distraction, especially when Mickey Hitchens wasn't with him. Mickey, as his sister Cynthia had once commented, was his 'people person'. The one who was nice to other people so that Henry didn't have the bother of it. It had amused her greatly and Henry himself saw the truth in the jest.

He went up to his room to collect his belongings and then drove back along the coast road to Shoreham.

# NINE

'We've identified the boy,' Henry was told when he reported in to the police station that morning. 'We got the little toe rag down in one of the cells if you want to speak to him. His mother knows he's here, says he'll get a right pasting from her when he gets home too.'

Henry nodded briefly and requested that the boy be brought up so that he could speak to him.

The child was led into one of the side rooms, little more than a cubbyhole where records were stored and there was room only for a single wooden chair and a tiny table. Henry took the seat and the child stood opposite him. A police constable stood in the doorway to make sure he didn't make a run for it.

He was a tiny scrap of a thing, skinny and freckled, dressed in a shirt with odd buttons and a pair of shorts that were too big round the waist and kept up with a cut-down leather belt. He glared defiantly at Henry though the dirt on his face betrayed where the tears had run down.

'How old are you?' Henry asked him.

'Nowt to do with you,' the boy said. The constable swiped him round the back of the head.

The boy put his hands on his head and howled.

'I'm told that your mother knows you're here. I imagine you'll have worse from her when you get home.'

The boy stopped howling and went back to glaring.

'So, someone gave you money to tell lies to the constable. Is that about the size of it? You can tell me now or I can let them put you back in the cells.'

Henry saw the boy's lower lip trembling. In truth, Henry had no intention of sending him back downstairs and also planned to try and placate the mother's anger, but he wasn't going to tell anyone that.

'So,' he began again. 'Was it someone you knew? Was it

a stranger? What I'm assuming here is that you probably meant no harm. That you thought it was a bit of a laugh. Maybe this stranger told you that it was a joke. That was a strange kind of joke to tell a constable that a young girl might be drowning. Did you never hear about the boy who cried wolf?'

The boy immediately looked puzzled. 'Ain't got no wolves round here,' he told Henry, looking at the officer as though he was mad.

Henry sighed. 'So describe this man to me. Or was it a man?' Something in the boy's eyes told him that he had hit on the truth. 'A woman, then? A woman asked you to fetch the constable and gave you some coins for your trouble. Is that it?'

The boy nodded. 'This woman, she said there was a little girl fallen in the water. She said she knew where a doctor lived just along the bungalows and there would be a policeman nearby, because there had been a murder. We all 'eard about the murder.' He looked hopefully at Henry as though wanting details.

'Did she seem distressed, this woman?'

The boy nodded. 'Crying, she was. Said there was a little girl fallen in the water. Said the fisherman was trying to get her out. Said to get the doctor and the policeman. So I ran. And I fetched 'em. I didn't do no 'arm. It was the woman what told me.'

Henry studied the boy for a few minutes, the child squirming under his gaze.

'Stand still,' the constable ordered and raised his hand again, but he did not hit the boy this time, noting Henry's slight shake of the head.

'This woman, did you know her?'

The boy shook his head no. 'She weren't from round 'ere. I thought she must be a visitor.'

'A visitor. And yet she knew about the doctor and about the policeman.'

'Everyone knew about the policeman. Everyone knows about the murder,' the boy said reasonably.

'But not about the doctor. Dr Clark, as I understand it, had

only just arrived. He'd come down for the weekend and had
been in Shoreham for less than an hour when you ran to
find him.'

The boy shrugged.

'Describe this woman to me.'

The boy seemed to be at a loss. He shrugged again. 'Looked
like a woman, didn't she?'

'A rich woman or a poor woman? An old woman or a young
woman? Tall or short?'

'Not old like me mum. Not young like my big sister. She's
married with a little 'un. Lives just up the coast. Not tall. The
height most women are, I suppose.'

'And how was she dressed? Would you say she was a rich
woman, a well-dressed woman? Was there anybody around
who would have seen her?'

'We was on the beach, where the girls collect the flint. The
girls were there, they might have seen.'

Henry persisted in his questions for a little longer and
discovered that the woman was wearing a blue jacket
and a blue hat but the boy was clearly more interested in the
coins she had given him and the message he sought to convey
than the woman herself. Henry was left with the impression
that the child had believed this woman, the stranger. Had
believed that something was wrong and been overawed by
the opportunity to earn some coins and pass on a serious
message.

'But,' he asked, 'if you believed the message to be real and
the woman to be honest, why did you run away when you had
taken the policeman and the doctor to the scene and there was
no one there?'

'Because me mam ain't bred no fools,' the boy told him,
earning himself another slap. The constable had not looked for
Henry's approval this time. The boy did not bother to howl
this time either. 'I could see there was no one there. I could
see that woman, she'd been lying to me. I'd been fooled once,
me mam would have been mad enough at me for that, I wasn't
going to stick around, was I?' He looked at Henry as though
the action had been the most reasonable in the world and Henry,
despite himself, was inclined to agree that it probably was.

He told the constable to escort the child home and then walked back down to Cissie Rowe's bungalow.

He was pleased to see that the locks had been fitted and the windows boarded but it did make it look a sad place, neglected and unwanted all of a sudden. There were two constables on duty, one beside the door and one he could see patrolling up and down the road beyond. Henry called out to him and then told him what the boy had said about the woman, and that the girls packing flint might have noticed her. He could see them today down by the water's edge but they seemed to have abandoned their work, paddling in the shallows, stealing an hour to be children.

'Go and talk to them, they may well have noticed a woman in a blue jacket and a blue hat.'

That's if she existed, Henry thought. If the boy had not just been telling him what he thought might satisfy the policeman or what he'd been told to say, should he be questioned? But something suggested to Henry that there was in reality a woman behind this; the look in the boy's eyes when he had mentioned that possibility had indicated surprise, as though he suspected Henry of knowing too much.

It was also possible that the woman herself had been duped in some way, simply asked to pass on the message. But the nature of that message suggested local knowledge. That Dr Clark was in residence. That there even was a Dr Clark Constable Prentice had told Henry that Dr Clark travelled down on a Thursday evening to be with his family during the summer months. They did not reside in the bungalow in the winter but they might come down for the occasional weekend and had been known to have Christmas parties there. That Constable Prentice could know so much detail suggested that Dr Clark and his family were themselves very well known and their habits frequently discussed. But nevertheless, Henry thought, whoever was behind that message would have needed to know enough to make the message convincing. Once again he thought he must look to the local community with suspicious eyes. Or at the very least someone familiar with the local community.

He wandered slowly around the bungalow, examining

the living room once again but knowing he did not really have the time to spend to assess the scene properly. He and Mickey could look at the photographs later bcforc they came down again.

So what did they have? They had four young men and now this mysterious woman. They had Jimmy Cottee, who was dead, possibly by suicide, but who might or might not have been guilty of more than self-murder. Henry was inclined to doubt this. Then this Selwyn Croft, who had not yet been found though the word had gone out to the local banks that he was required and Henry expected that news to come shortly.

Then this other young man, this other admirer of Cissie Rowe and the most likely giver of the snake bracelet. If he had a car of his own then he had money. If he could give gifts of gold bracelets then he had money; even if that gold bracelet were nine carat rather than twenty-two carat gold it was still not a cheap consideration. Had Cissie threatened him in some way? Had she threatened to reveal their affair? Henry considered that to be an unlikely reason for someone wanting her dead. It was almost de rigueur, these days, for a fashionable young man to have a fling with a fashionable young actress. Very occasionally such young men even married their paramours but that still raised eyebrows in certain circles, rather in the way that his sister's marriage had raised eyebrows when she had married Albert – though those who had gained their wealth through commercial enterprise often married in less predictable ways than those who had wealth or status through ancient family connections and family name.

So who was this young man? What circles did he move in? And why would Cissie want to keep this secret? In Henry's experience young women who attracted the interest of men of a higher social status tended to be keen to advertise the fact rather than keep it from their friends. Had this urge to secrecy been impressed upon her by the young man she was seeing because his family would disapprove? In Henry's view that suggested old money rather than new. A set which regarded status as being something to keep at the head of the list of importance, a family that would turn a blind eye to a brief and inappropriate dalliance but certainly not approve should that become more serious.

And what about this Philippe? When Henry and Constable Prentice had photographed the devastation the previous day he had kept his eyes open for any hints of Philippe but had found none. Or at least none that he could recognize. Last night he had looked again at the photographs that had been on Cissie Rowe's bedroom wall but had found nothing that helped him.

He glanced at his watch thinking that he must leave soon, and the constable he had sent to speak to the flint pickers interrupted his thoughts.

'They say they saw a woman yesterday afternoon, quite late – but then neither of them have watches or timepieces so they would not know the time. She was standing just up on the road there and when some children came by, she stopped one of them and spoke to him.

'But they don't think she was wearing a blue hat or a blue jacket. In fact they don't think she was wearing a hat at all. They think she came out of one of the bungalows nearby because they think they've seen her before, but it was too far away for them to be certain.'

Henry thanked him. It was possible that they had seen this strange woman speaking to the boy who had carried the message but it was equally possible that it was just a mother speaking to her children.

'I've told them, if they remember anything else, to come and speak to whoever is on duty here.'

Henry thanked him again. 'I must leave now to go back to London,' he said.

'My sergeant and I may be down again this evening or it might be tomorrow morning. Keep the scene secure and if anyone shows an unnatural curiosity be sure to make a note of it. It's possible that whoever searched the place may not have found what they were looking for. It's possible they may try to come back.'

The constable straightened himself up and nodded sharply. 'They won't get past us,' he said. 'You can be assured of that, Inspector.'

# TEN

*Eight days before Cissie's death*

The evening of the day when Philippe had first returned to her life, they had gone out for dinner together and mostly it had been Philippe who had talked. He'd spoken about his experiences in the war, about how he had returned to the farm to find the place in ruins, nothing more than stumps of trees remaining in the orchard.

'For a little while, they had used it as a dressing station,' he had told her. 'Then the line moved again and the artillery finished the destruction of it. My parents had remained; they were killed. The troops had already left, taking their casualties with them.'

'I am so sorry, Philippe. I loved them, you know that.'

He nodded. 'I heard news of your parents' death just after that. I asked after you, but was told that you'd already gone. That your father had made you leave. I tried to find you, Cécile. I asked everywhere. Someone told me you had been killed, another that you had gone south to Marseille, someone else that you had gone to England.'

'And so I had. My father gave me what money they had and told me to leave. He said there was nothing more for me there and they would try and follow me. But of course they never did. We had nothing, Philippe, we had fled with the clothes on our backs and what my mother could cram into a tiny valise; we kept moving and moving and moving. And eventually they stayed and I moved on. There was nothing else to be done and they would have me go.'

'When did you hear that they had died?'

'It was almost a year afterwards that the news reached me. Philippe, I cried for days and then I heard your parents too were dead and I didn't believe that you had survived. And now' – she managed to smile – 'and now you are here.'

'And now I'm here. And we are together again. Cécile, I am so glad to see you. So happy, you cannot believe. Now we can begin again, just like we planned to do.'

She had smiled, hoping that he would not realize that her heart wasn't in it. Somehow, she had buried Philippe when she had buried the memories of her parents. She had been desperately sad that there had been no funeral for them, that she did not even know where their bodies lay. In her mind she had created a peaceful spot beneath the trees in her aunt's orchard and her father, mother, aunt and uncle had been laid to rest and Philippe beside them, because she had truly believed that he had not survived the war. And she picked up her life and travelled on with it. What else could she do? And in time there was nothing else she had *wanted* to do. She had created a place for herself in the world, was earning her own money, had new friends and a new name and the past had been left behind where the past belonged.

The following day she had not seen Philippe. They had made an appointment to meet this morning and now Cissie was regretting it utterly. Today she was not working, but she wished that she had been able to call in at the studio and find some task that she could take upon herself, something that would give her an excuse not to see Philippe. There were always odd jobs to be done and if not it was fun just to sit on set and watch the filming. This was her world now. But she had not been able to think of an excuse and she was also angry with herself for feeling like this. Philippe was alive; she should have been rejoicing, shouting the news out loud to the world, and of course she was glad that he had survived, only why oh why did he have to come and find her?

And why did he expect her still to be in love with him? They had been children then, cousins who by rights should not have been even thinking to have such a relationship. She knew the Church would have frowned upon it and so would their parents if they'd suspected. She'd often wondered how they had failed to suspect.

On that morning, eight days before she died, Cissie dressed carefully in a neat white blouse and dark green skirt that hugged her waist and hips and flared just a little at the hem, to accentuate the kick pleat. She had arranged to meet Philippe in Shoreham itself, away from Bungalow Town and the studio, away from the eyes of those who might gossip, but she didn't want to go.

She checked her appearance one last time in the mirror, adjusting her hat and dabbing one last time at her lipstick. Then she set out to meet Philippe, planning that today she would tell him how she felt. That of course she still loved him – but not like that. Not any more. That there was someone new in her life that she dared to hope might become serious. She knew she was foolish in hoping such a thing, though she didn't plan on telling that to Philippe.

No, her life had moved on and the past was in the past and Philippe was part of that past. Although she would always be his friend, always care about him, after all they were cousins. She glanced into the mirror again while rehearsing these lines in her head, trying for a look that was both convincing and concerned and gentle. Yes, they would always be cousins and they would always be friends but surely he must realize, they had been children, they were older now, and a relationship such as they had once hoped for, well, that was a nonsense now, wasn't it?

He must see it her way. He simply must. Cissie would tell him straight, be honest with him, and that would be that.

Having decided on this course of action she left the house, checking rather guiltily to see that she was not observed. She really didn't think she could contend with casual conversation this morning, or with enquiries as to where she might be off to.

Seeing that there was no one in sight she set off, slender fingers gripping her leather clutch bag, and the terrible weight of guilt upon her shoulders and in her heart.

# ELEVEN

Henry had stayed in London overnight and collected Mickey from Scotland Yard the morning following the post-mortems. He found him in the fingerprint bureau, in the narrow room at the top of the building overlooking the Thames.

So far nothing concrete had emerged.

Henry and Mickey drove back down to Shoreham. Mickey did the driving while Henry looked through reports that had been delivered by messenger first thing.

The first were the post-mortem records for both Cissie Rowe and Jimmy Cottee and he and Mickey were already familiar with the contents, though Henry skimmed them again just to be sure that they had missed nothing.

'It's a sad business,' Mickey commented. 'Two young lives, both wasted.'

Henry, as was his usual practice, reprised the main points as Mickey listened.

'So, we were correct in our assumption that she was concussed and then smothered. Fibres from the pillow were found in her mouth and throat and the PM report suggests that the pillow was pressed down hard. It's likely that her assailant knelt, with his knees on either side of her body, actually pinning her hands to the bed. The hands are both bruised. The powder in her throat, now that is interesting.'

'How so?'

'Not a sleeping draft, Mickey. It was cocaine.'

'Cocaine? I didn't expect that. Was she an addict?'

'The report suggests not. Perhaps a casual user. But you'll admit that it adds to the puzzle.'

'And the second report?'

'It seems,' Henry said, 'that we may have found this mysterious Philippe. And that he has a record.'

'Ah, now I'm interested. Tell me more.'

Henry scanned the pages. 'A partial fingerprint that was found at the scene matched one that related to a man called Philippe Boilieu, so it seems this Philippe must have visited Cissie at her home. The print was found on the little table, the one from which the photograph was missing. Index finger, right hand.'

'And his sheet says?'

'Well, there's quite a list. Scotland Yard are contacting the French police but on this side of the Channel we have extortion and blackmail, robbery including threats of violence. Primarily, though, it seems our man Philippe Boilieu likes to target young women who have perhaps made mistakes in their lives.'

'And what sort of mistakes are we talking about? Do they involve a presentable young Frenchman?'

'We don't know that he's presentable,' Henry argued.

'No, but we can guess. A certain degree of attractiveness is necessary to attract the average young woman. So are we talking pictures taken while in a state of undress, or compromising letters, or something in a similar vein?'

'Any or all of the above.'

'And someone like Miss Rowe, who is *almost* famous, would be a sweet target for such a man. But would he kill her?'

'That might depend on whether she threatened him. If she said she would go to the police, expose him in some way . . . I can imagine a young woman like Cissie Rowe, *almost* famous as you say, having a great deal to lose. She might risk going to the authorities when another might not.' Henry frowned. 'The thing that puzzles me is that there seems to be only the one fingerprint of his found in the bungalow.

'The bungalow was clean, but there was inevitably still some dust present. We know she can't have dusted for at least two days, so shall we say three days' worth of dust, or four just for the sake of argument. And so let's speculate that he visited her at her home perhaps four days before she died.'

Mickey laughed. 'That,' he said, 'is advanced level speculation. But all right, let's go with that thought. It's a very close and small community and the bungalows are built within spitting distance of one another, so unless he visited after dark

– in which case someone might still have heard him knocking on the door, and that might in itself have aroused suspicion – then it's possible someone might have seen him four or five days before she died, might remember seeing him.'

'I will arrange to have his pictures wired to the local police. We'll let them do the legwork on it. Local faces are more likely to elicit a positive response, I think.'

'It also occurs to me,' Mickey said, 'that the fingerprint was found on that little table and that there is a photograph missing from that same table. And everyone we speak to, who had opportunity to see it, tells us that the picture was of an older couple and a boy. Is it too much of a stretch to think that Philippe might be that boy? That this is a friend come from the past?'

'Who then took the photograph away.' Henry nodded. 'On one level that would make sense, on another it does not. Removing the photograph – and I have no doubt that you are right and Philippe Boilieu was the one who did that – would only serve to point to the perpetrator. Who else would take that picture away? It is . . . incautious, would you not say?'

'I would say only that it sounds very human,' Mickey commented. 'Repossess the photograph and you, in some way, repossess the memory. If this friendship was important to either of them, then the picture would remain so.'

'And so today,' Henry said, 'we make a re-examination of the scene and we interview Mr Selwyn Croft, assuming that our colleagues have found him.'

'Well,' Mickey said, 'if they have not they will take us from bank to bank and shout his name until he appears.' He smiled, and from his expression Henry gathered that he rather liked the idea.

'One flaw in that plan,' Henry reminded him. 'It's Saturday. The banks will all be closed.'

'Ah, so they will,' Mickey agreed reluctantly. 'Then we'll have to visit the young man in his home. I'm sure we'll try and be discreet under the circumstances.'

Their colleagues in Shoreham had indeed found the address for Mr Selwyn Croft.

Henry spent a little time in contacting the central office and arranging for photographs to be wired so that their Shoreham colleagues had pictures of the mysterious Philippe. He was assured that they would get these printed up and taken out by Monday at the latest. It might, Henry was told, be difficult to find a printer able to produce them on the Sunday but they would do their best, and Henry had to be satisfied with that.

He and Mickey walked back to Cissie Rowe's bungalow. Two constables that he did not recognize were on duty and reported that it had been a quiet night though they had had to drive off three reporters earlier that morning. One, they said, had been taking photographs with a little pocket camera but there was little anyone could do about that. From the description, Henry guessed this had been Sophie Mars. He had been relieved and surprised that the local press had not been more intrusive. The police presence on the footbridge, the easiest crossing point on to this spit of land, had probably put some of them off. Though he fully expected the story to be on the front page of some of the Sunday newspapers.

Cissie Rowe was far too photogenic and the story of her life far too romantic to be of no public interest. He wondered where her funeral would be held, there being no family to bury her, and assumed that the studio would probably take charge of this and almost certainly turn it into a big event to which the local population and the press would be drawn.

Mickey had not seen the devastation, only the photographs that Henry had taken, and he was shocked at the transformation of their crime scene.

'This was not a mere search,' he said. 'This was an act of wilful violence. Whoever did this was angry, furious even. If, as we speculate, he had only a few minutes, ten or fifteen at the most, then why waste time overturning the furniture and smashing the lamps when he could have taken what he came for and got away and we'd probably be none the wiser?'

'Perhaps he didn't find it. Perhaps the fury is because he didn't find it, but I agree with you there is an unnecessary amount of chaos being caused and the only thing I can think is that he hoped it might slow us down. Lead us to assume that there was a reason for it, other than simple malice. If there was any thought behind this violence at all, then I would say it is thought of misdirection. So, what I hope we might do is to try and read his actions. See where he actually searched, where he did not, and try and find whatever it was he was looking for. If you or I had come into a place like this, Mickey, where would we look first?'

'I'd look for loose boards. In fact, I did look for loose boards but found none. I would look beneath drawers to see if anything had been fastened there. I did that, but found nothing. I did miss one thing and that was the snake bangle. To me it was just another gee-gaw; it was you who thought to look for hallmarks.'

'I noticed it primarily because of Cynthia's. And we still don't know if it has any bearing on Cissie Rowe's death. We know only that it is an out-of-place thing.'

'But our search was logical. We are practised at this. So we should not be asking what we might look for, we should be asking what someone in a hurry looks for.' Mickey nodded as though to reaffirm his own statement. 'But of course you know that, so what you're really asking is what wouldn't we do. We wouldn't come in here and start throwing furniture about, that's for sure. There are bungalows close by where people might have heard noise.'

'We know that Dr Clark was not present. And at that time no one else was home. Mrs Clark had taken the children along the beach.'

'And on the other side?'

'The next bungalow along is empty. It's another summer let. I'm told that fewer people live here full-time now than did five years ago, and fewer still than a decade ago when the studio was operating at full strength. After the fire, production was cut right back. It's a miracle that it still continues, and there are certainly fewer theatrical types along the coast now than a few years ago.'

'So again the indications are that it is someone local, someone who can observe without being observed, without being noticed, because he is simply part of the local scene.'

'Mickey, what if this was not a search at all? What if this was simply anger, rage at Cissie or perhaps even at the person who killed her? What if we are reading this under a misapprehension?'

'It's possible,' Mickey agreed. 'So we process our scene in two ways. We look for evidence of a search and for evidence of rage. If it is rage then it's more likely there will be finger-prints. Someone committed to a thorough search is more likely to have worn gloves, or that would be my assumption anyway.'

They divided the scene and this time Sergeant Hitchens took the bedroom and Henry began in the small kitchen. A lamp had been smashed and glass shards covered the floor. The smell of paraffin was very strong in here and Henry suddenly wondered if the intent had been to set a fire but the would-be arsonist had run out of time. Henry had, after all, arrived back before the constable and that would have narrowed the window of opportunity quite considerably from the maximum of ten or fifteen minutes the perpetrator might otherwise have had.

As in a lot of the bungalows, cooking was done on a two ring burner and the fuel for that burner was paraffin. Henry realized that this too had been emptied and splashed across the walls.

He went back into the living room to inform Mickey of his discovery only to discover that his sergeant had come to a similar conclusion.

'Do you burn what you love or what you hate?' Mickey asked. 'Or what you have loved? We were right in our second guess, there was no search here. There was only anger. So my guess is we look for an angry young man.'

'An angry killer too?'

'My betting on that would be even,' Mickey said. 'It's my experience that young women who look like Cissie Rowe tend to leave a trail of broken hearts behind them, even if they have no intent to do so. Especially if there is a little bit of glamour to be had by the association. And I'm not just talking about young men here; young women can be just as drawn and just as violent in their actions, and we already have one woman implicated in sending the false message, drawing your constable away. Jealousy can also be a bitter thing.'

'It can indeed,' Henry agreed. 'As can loss.'

Sergeant Hitchens nodded. 'I don't think we can look for

just one solution here,' he said. 'The death may have one answer and this quite another. For now I suggest we close the doors and leave this place as it is. We would be better served in going to talk to this young Selwyn fellow, see what he has to say for himself. I think when we find a possible suspect for this mess we should bring them here, confront them with it, see what they have to say. I think that might be more enlightening.'

Henry agreed. They left, reminding the constable to make notes of anyone that came near, and Henry left his second, older camera with the constable. The man took it cautiously, as though afraid it might explode, and Henry talked him through the very simple controls. 'If you see anything unusual, then photograph it. If any member of the press comes by, take their picture as well. They may object but you are the law here, not them. It will be of little use in the dark, so leave it with the desk sergeant when your shift has been relieved.'

'You think that'll do any good?' Mickey asked as they walked away. 'Most like we'll get lots of pretty pictures of seagulls,' he said morosely, and Henry realized that he was a little put out that someone else had been trusted with his boss's camera, even if it was the older one.

'You're probably right,' he agreed. 'It's unlikely he'll have the skill.'

Mickey Hitchens nodded, his pride now satisfied.

# TWELVE

Selwyn Croft looked like a bank clerk, Henry thought. Even at the weekend he wore a clean white shirt with a detachable collar and the sleeves of his shirt were held up with expandable suspenders. He was still struggling into his jacket as his mother led the officers into the front parlour and twittered about tea.

Mickey thanked her and said that would be lovely, as much to get her out of the way as because he actually wanted to drink any.

Selwyn Croft's hair was slicked back with far too much grease. He had a premature widow's peak above rather a handsome face. His eyes were blue and Henry wondered if his hair was actually quite fair beneath the brilliantine.

He stood nervously on the hearth rug, his back to the unlit fire and his hands behind his back as though he wasn't quite sure what to do with them.

'You've come about Cissie – I mean, Miss Rowe? I suppose I knew someone would come and talk to me about her. I heard, I heard . . .' He broke off and Henry could see that he was genuinely upset.

'We understand that you were a good friend of Miss Rowe. Perhaps a little more than a friend?'

Selwyn Croft's cheeks coloured and it struck Henry that the young man was almost delicately pale.

'I hoped once that we might be more,' he said. 'But Cissie had other ideas. She preferred someone else.'

'Would that someone else be Jimmy Cottee?' Mickey Hitchens asked. His sergeant sounded slightly surprised, Henry thought.

Selwyn Croft shook his head vehemently. 'No, though Jimmy was dead sweet on her. And Cissie, she was kind to him, I suppose. She was never mean, not Cissie. Never mean to anyone, or cruel. But she never took Jimmy seriously.'

'Then who did she prefer?' Sergeant Hitchens asked him.

Selwyn Croft was at a loss, it seemed. He shook his head. 'I don't know who he was,' he said. 'Only that there was someone. She mentioned his name once. Geoffrey something or other, and he had a car. A blue coupé, but I couldn't tell you what make. She pointed him out one day when he was driving by, but I didn't recognize the make, only that it had a mascot on the front. It looked like a leaping horse, something like that.'

'He was driving by – where was this? And did he see you, acknowledge Cissie?'

'No, he can't have seen her, I don't think. She noticed him and she pointed to the car and said, "Oh, that's Geoffrey". And then she bit her lip as though she'd said something wrong. It was a funny habit she had, you could always tell when Cissie was unsure of herself, or when she thought she'd made a mistake. She'd bite her lip. It was kind of . . . kind of sweet.'

Henry and Mickey exchanged a look.

Mrs Croft came in with the tea tray and her son leapt forward to take it from her. He set it down on the butler's table beside the fireplace and then, his hands once more empty, went back to looking awkward.

Mrs Croft hovered, clearly uncomfortable with having two policemen in the house and not sure if she should stay to pour the tea or if she should leave. Mickey rescued her.

'No need to detain you, Mrs Croft. I'll be mother. I thank you kindly.'

'Oh,' she said. 'Oh. Then I'll leave you gentlemen alone, shall I? If you need anything I'll be . . .' She backed out of the room, casting an anxious glance at her son.

'Don't worry, Mrs Croft,' Henry said. 'Your son isn't in any trouble. He is merely helping us with our enquiries.'

'Oh, oh I see. Well, thank you. Thank you.' She disappeared into the hall and shut the door behind her.

'Did you hear that Jimmy Cottee was found hanged?' Sergeant Hitchens asked.

The pallor of the young man's face increased, so that even his lips looked grey.

'Sit down before you fall down, young man,' Mickey told him. 'I'll take it that's a no, then? You didn't hear about his death?'

Selwyn Croft shook his head. Mickey poured the tea and added extra sugar to the young man's cup. 'Get this down you, sweet tea is good for shock. So when did you last see Jimmy Cottee?'

'I–I don't know. Two weeks ago perhaps, the last time I saw Cissie. We were all down on the beach together. Jimmy was skimming stones and Cissie tried too.' Selwyn Croft smiled as though it were a pleasant memory. 'Jimmy tried to teach her, but she couldn't seem to get the knack.' His face crumpled. 'And now they're both dead. Why did Jimmy—?'

'We don't know for sure,' Mickey told him. It seemed that Selwyn Croft had made the assumption that Jimmy Cottee's death had been a suicide.

Henry said nothing to disabuse him. Mickey took that belief for a walk. 'It could have been grief, I suppose. Would you expect Jimmy to be grieving that hard?'

Selwyn shook his head and then changed his mind and nodded. 'I liked her a lot,' he said. 'But Jimmy, Jimmy thought she was like something from a magical place. Like a fairy, he told me once. He thought she was like a fairy.'

He shook his head and then looked at the policemen as though trying to explain what he had just told them. 'I'm not saying that Jimmy was simple in the head,' he said. 'I don't want you to get that impression. He wasn't simple in the head, he was just . . . simple. The way he saw the world. He just saw it like it was black and white, like Cissie could make everything special, precious. He knew she didn't love him, not like he loved her.'

'Did that upset him?'

'I don't know. It's not the kind of thing you ask, is it? But I'm sorry he's dead. I'm sorry they both are. It isn't right. Not any of it.'

There was a beat or two of silence and then Henry said, 'Did she ever speak to you about someone called Philippe? She might have mentioned that he was an old friend, that he'd returned to see her.'

Selwyn shook his head and his eyes seemed unfocused, as though he was searching his memory. 'There was a photograph,' he said. 'It was a photograph on a little table in the corner of her parlour, a photograph of an older couple and a boy of about twelve years of age. She once said that this was her aunt and uncle and her cousin Philippe. But she didn't like to talk about it. That was before she came to England, and the photograph must've been taken before the war. But I don't know anything more than that. As I say, she didn't like to speak of it. I think the memories must have been very painful.'

Henry nodded. If Selwyn had not seen her for the last two weeks, it was unlikely he knew about Philippe's visit.

'And why have you not seen her since that day on the beach? From what we have been told you and Miss Rowe were in the habit of spending regular time together. Mr Cottee too. Did that change?'

'It became plain that she preferred this Geoffrey person. A man can only take so much, give so much of himself, when it is clear that the young lady involved does not return his affections.'

'And yet it seemed you shared her time and friendship with Jimmy Cottee without too much concern.'

Selwyn allowed himself a small smile. 'Poor Jimmy,' he said. 'Inspector, I had next to no chance of capturing the heart of a girl like Cissie Rowe. But if I had next to no chance, then it must be said that Jimmy Cottee had no chance at all. She was kind to him, that was all. It was in her nature to be kind to people and I think Jimmy knew this, in his heart of hearts he must've known.'

'And this Geoffrey, Mr Croft, tell me everything you remember about him and his car. Any tiny thing that Miss Rowe might have told you about him or that you might have inferred. It is impossible to think that a man like you would not question a young lady about a rival in love.'

Selwyn Croft blushed again. 'I tried, Inspector. I really did. I felt humiliated by the whole deception.'

'Deception? A strong word, Mr Croft.'

'I'm sure it is. But I did feel that I had been deceived. That she had led me to believe that there might be some hope when all the time she was entertaining such strong feelings for another man. I told her, I said, "Cissie . . . Miss Rowe . . . we are not children. It is time that we thought seriously about the future."'

'And she said?'

Selwyn Croft closed his eyes. 'She said that I was a dear, and that she was truly fond of me but that I could surely not expect her to give up all that she had worked for. All that she had achieved. That she had no wish to marry, to settle down.'

'And yet you implied, earlier in our conversation, that you considered neither yourself nor Jimmy Cottee as having much chance with her. That you liked – not loved or were over fond – *liked* the young woman. Now, are you telling us that you proposed to Miss Rowe?'

Miserably, Selwyn Croft nodded and then he shook his head. 'I mean that I tried,' he said. 'But she knew what was coming and she stopped me before I could embarrass myself further. I have not seen her since then. I was mortified, truth be told.'

Silence fell in the small front parlour, broken only by the ticking of the mantel clock. Selwyn Croft looked down at his shoes, examining the toes, shuffling his feet on the hearth rug.

Henry waited for the question he knew Mickey was about to ask.

'And where were you on the night she died, Mr Croft? Do you have anyone to vouch for you?'

Selwyn Croft looked up sharply, met Mickey's gaze. 'I would do nothing to hurt her. Ever. I would never—'

'We have to ask everyone who knew her,' Henry told him sternly. 'There can be no exceptions. So tell us, where were you that night?'

Selwyn Croft's cheeks had flushed; they paled now as the anger drained away and the grief once more took its place. 'I was here,' he said. 'My mother plays bridge and was short a partner that evening. I played bridge with my mother and two of her friends until gone eleven. I helped to tidy up before bed and then we both retired.'

'And after that? I take it that you slept?'

'What else would I be doing! I can assure you, Inspector, that I did not leave the house that night. I had nothing to do with the death of Cissie Rowe but I am telling you, Inspector, if I should find the man who did—'

Henry raised a hand and stopped the young man from uttering the pointless threat. Instead, he took a different tack. 'Are you familiar with a young woman by the name of Sophie Mars? She takes photographs of the actors and sells them to the local newspapers.'

To his surprise, Selwyn Croft laughed. 'Oh, I know Sophie Mars,' he said. 'Her real name is Sally Morris and she works in her parents' grocer's shop. You'll find her there today, Saturday being a busy time for them.'

Henry nodded. He asked for directions to the shop and then prepared to leave. 'Thank you for your time, Mr Croft. If you think of anything that you would like to add, then please inform the constable.'

'Constable?'

'The constable who will be sent to take your formal statement. We will need a formal statement, you understand that?'

'Coming here? My mother, my mother will never cope with the shame. A policeman coming to the house. I'll come to the police station.'

Henry nodded. 'As you wish, but be sure you do. And think, Mr Croft. Anything that Miss Rowe might have mentioned about this young man with the car.'

'He wasn't young,' Selwyn blurted. 'I never said he was young.'

No, Henry thought. I just assumed it. 'I thought you didn't see him clearly.'

'I saw enough to understand that he was older than Cissie; older than me. Closer to your age, Inspector. Perhaps closer to forty than to thirty . . . not that I mean any offence,' he added anxiously.

It appeared that there was nothing more and Henry and Mickey took their leave.

'An older man,' Mickey said thoughtfully. 'That perhaps

puts a different complexion on things. Some rich young dog who fancied a fling with a pretty actress is one thing but the potential of an older, perhaps married man wanting a bit on the side is another thing entirely.'

'Perhaps a more apt subject for blackmail.'

'Perhaps so. And what about this Sophie Mars? That's the young woman with the Kodak we spotted at the studio. Is she a person of interest?'

'She's a person who takes pictures.' They had reached the car now and Henry showed his sergeant the newspaper that he had brought from his sister's house. Mickey scanned the page intently.

'She's caught you well,' he said. 'It's a fine likeness. Distinguished and purposeful.'

Henry scowled and then realized that Mickey was goading him. 'I'm more concerned with the candid shot at the top of the page,' he said. 'If she took one like this, there may well be more and she may inadvertently have captured this Philippe or even the mysterious – older – Geoffrey.'

Mickey fired the car into life. 'I like self-starters,' he commented. 'Nothing worse than wrestling with a crank handle on a cold morning. Or even on a fine autumnal one like this. So, we go and interview our Miss Sophie Mars and see what else she had captured. Henry, when did men of our age suddenly get to be termed "older"? I don't recall inviting those comparisons, do you?'

'I suspect we were born old,' Henry said. 'I don't recall ever feeling young. We talk to Sophie Mars, or Sally Morris as I suppose she will be on a Saturday in the shop, and then I'd like to return to the studio, ask a few more questions. After which—'

'After which we will find ourselves some lunch.'

'After which we discover what car dealerships are in the area and what garages specialize in the service and repair of the more exclusive cars. I think that Selwyn Croft would have made a guess as to the make had it been of a common or garden lot.'

'Agreed. Blue, and possibly with a horse mascot on the bonnet. It sounds distinctive enough to be remembered and there's also a chance it and its owner visited the studio, I suppose.'

'It was seen by our Mr Croft driving through Shoreham. I doubt that was a single occurrence. Others will have seen it and remarked upon it. People do seem to notice expensive cars.'

Mickey chuckled softly. 'Just as well your sister didn't decide to lend us the Bentley,' he said. 'Imagine what a field day the press would have had with a picture of that. Imagine the comparisons with the likes of Lord Peter Wimsey.'

'I'd rather not imagine. We have been fortunate so far. Most of the interest has been local but I doubt that will last. Our dead actress is far too photogenic for the national press to ignore for long. We can do without the distraction of journalistic interest in ourselves.'

Mickey looked sideways at his boss but did not trouble to comment on how naive that sounded. Many of their colleagues actively courted the press and found it helpful to keep a high profile. It was not something Henry Johnstone was comfortable with but Mickey himself kept good relations with the Fourth Estate – often on Henry's behalf.

Many of the senior officers in the so-called murder squad were household names; their faces were emblazoned across the nationals under headlines that suggested that even the worst of crimes would now be brought to book once the likes of Fred Wensley or Arthur Neil had become involved, and if any of those officers were paired in the headlines with forensic scientists such as Bernard Spilsbury or Sydney Smith, it guaranteed a sell-out edition.

Mickey pulled the car in to the side of the road outside the Morrises' grocery store. The shop was large, double fronted with a central door. They could see young Sophie Mars, aka Sally Morris, serving behind the counter. The smart little hat and dark blue jacket she had been wearing when they met at the studio had been replaced by a pale grey, polka dot dress, largely concealed behind a brown canvas apron. Her coppery hair was restrained by a pleated headband. She spotted Henry as he came into the shop and looked swiftly away, her attention focused on the split peas she was weighing for a customer. Henry stood quietly in line, watching as she folded the order into a brown paper cone and then crimped it closed with swift but careful fingers.

'Gentlemen, what can I do for you?'

Henry turned towards the male voice. A man he guessed must be Sally's father stood behind the other counter observing Henry and Mickey sceptically. Every other customer in the shop was female and Henry guessed he didn't look like a man who had come to purchase tea or sugar.

'If you can spare her for a few moments, I'd like a word with your daughter,' Henry said, showing the father his identification.

'You'll be in town over that woman that got killed, I suppose.' Mr Morris lowered his voice. 'I told our Sal, "You keep away from that lot. It will only lead to trouble. They're not our kind." But will she listen? Will she heck, off she goes with that camera of hers, and this is what it leads to.'

'Miss Morris is not in any trouble,' Mickey intervened. 'In fact we believe she may be of help to our inquiry. Your daughter and that camera of hers may help to capture a criminal of the worst kind, if you get my meaning.'

Henry watched as a range of emotions chased themselves across Mr Morris's broad face. Sally Morris kept on glancing their way, her hands occupied with the tasks of weighing and reaching and fetching and packaging, eyes and ears straining to work out what the policemen wanted and whether she should be worried about it.

'Sally,' – her father seemed to reach a decision – 'I'll take over Mrs Pritchard's order. You go through in the back and . . . see to things in there.'

He turned back to Henry and Sergeant Hitchens and spoke swiftly and softly, as though arranging some kind of sinister or distasteful assignation.

'If you gentlemen will go around the side of the shop, Sally will let you through the rear entrance. I don't want any daughter of mine seen being interviewed by the police, you understand.'

Henry was of the opinion that there was not a woman in

the shop who hadn't guessed who they were or that Sally
Morris, whose antics with her camera were no doubt well
known to everyone, was the subject of their visit, but he nodded
anyway and he and Mickey left. At the side of the shop ran
a narrow alley and behind that a yard. Sally Morris stood with
the rear door open, her hand resting on the latch and an anxious
look on her face.

'I meant no harm,' she said. 'I told them I'd got a picture
of the Chief Inspector that I'd taken at the studio and they
said . . . well, they paid me a bit extra for the pair of pictures.
I never meant—'

'It is of no consequence,' Henry told her. 'This is about a
related matter. If we may come inside?'

She stood back and let them into the kitchen. Gone was
the confident, smiling young journalist they had met the day
before. Instead, she looked terribly nervous and kept shooting
glances back towards the shop. Her father's voice could be
heard faintly as he chatted to his clientele. 'He's going to be
so angry,' she said. 'He keeps threatening to take my camera
away, says it's not a suitable job for a respectable girl, that
I should be learning how to run the shop ready to take over
one day.'

'I'm sure he just worries about you,' Mickey said. 'Fathers
can be over-protective at times where their daughters are
concerned. It can be a dangerous world for a young woman,
especially one intent on . . . shall we say, a less conventional
path. Like our poor Miss Rowe.'

'Oh yes,' Sally Morris said bitterly, 'he has plenty of additional ammunition to fire now, doesn't he? In my father's view
a girl of my age should be safely and respectably married,
should have brought a suitable son-in-law into the family
business and be too busy producing children to have time or
inclination for nonsense like photography. I am only twenty-
one, Inspector. I have absolutely no wish to be tied down by
so much respectability.'

She tossed her head defiantly, a gesture that somewhat lost
impact due to the restraint of the crimped band that flattened
her hair.

'Miss Morris, I think you might be of use to us,' Mickey

said. 'The photographs you have taken. Did many of them feature Miss Rowe?'

'Use to you?' She looked troubled by the idea. 'I'm not sure I understand.' Then it dawned. 'Oh, you mean I might have snapped someone who . . . you mean I might even have caught the murderer with my little camera? Oh.' She drew out a chair from beneath the kitchen table and sank into it. 'Oh, it's just like a film, isn't it?'

Mickey rolled his eyes and sighed. 'So if we could see anything you've taken in the past, say, three or four weeks now, that would be a great help.'

She got to her feet again. 'Please, gentlemen, sit down. Would you like some tea? It will only take a moment to make and I'll go and fetch my boxes. I have my own darkroom – well, it was the cupboard beneath the stairs, but it does, you know? I'll fetch everything now. This is so exciting, you just can't believe . . .'

Mickey took her vacated seat and Henry settled into one opposite. 'I don't wonder her father worries,' Mickey said. 'I'm often relieved that we had no children. Too much of a worry.'

'You'd have made an excellent father, I believe,' Henry told him.

His sergeant laughed. 'Is that something your Cynthia schooled you to say? On her list of appropriate phrases to say to new fathers or those who might be contemplating that estate?'

'No, I don't believe it is,' Henry protested, though to be fair it probably was. He smiled, recognizing that there was no malice in Mickey's observation. 'She used to make lists for me,' he said softly. 'Of appropriate things to say. She knew that I'd generally just prefer to be silent. She knew just how much that would irritate our father.'

Mickey nodded, but any response he might have made was interrupted by the return of Sally Morris. She carried three shoe boxes stacked one upon the other and, after setting them on the table, announced, 'There's more.' Then she disappeared again.

Mickey took the lid off one of the boxes. It was crammed

full of photographs and negatives, the latter encased in glassine sleeves.

'More, indeed,' Mickey said. 'I think we may be here for quite some time.'

# THIRTEEN

By the time they left Sally Morris it was well after two. Fortunately, they had been offered tea and sandwiches made with thick slices of cheese brought in from the shop and so Mickey's lunch requirements had been met.

They left with a dozen photographs and a selection of negatives depicting Cissie Rowe with a selection of young men. Most, Sally had told them, worked at the studio and she was able to put names to a few of them. Henry hoped that a further visit to the studio would name the rest.

But there was one image he could already identify. Cissie Rowe was seen sitting on the rocks close by the old fort and standing, clearly in conversation with her, was a man that Henry was certain was Philippe Boilieu. He looked somewhat different to the photograph in the police record, his hair neatly cut and his clothes of better quality, but Henry entertained no real doubts.

'So that confirms the link,' Mickey said. 'Our man Philippe and Miss Rowe's old friend are one and the same. For my money that puts him firmly in the frame.'

They called at the police station before returning to the studio and were told that further information had been sent via telegram, in response to a hunch that Henry had. Philippe Boilieu had indeed certain links to the film industry, albeit films of a particular and specialist kind, and one of his featured actresses was a girl by the name of Cécile.

'You think it's her?' Mickey asked.

'I think it's possible and, if not, that it's interesting that he should have another girl of the same name.'

'I take it we more or less discount our friend Selwyn Croft as a suspect?' Mickey said as they left the police station and made their way back to the studio.

'In all probability, yes. Though I'm hopeful he may still lead us to the mysterious Geoffrey. My guess is that he will

remember something he was told. Young women, in my experience, like to play their suitors off one against the other – even
when there is no malice intended. It seems to be part of the
accepted game.

'In the meantime, the local constabulary can spread their
net and look at the local car dealerships and garages. One way
or another, he will be found.'

'And we still have no idea as to why the unfortunate Jimmy
Cottee was so brutally killed. Of course, there is still the
possibility that he killed Miss Rowe and someone beat him
and hanged him as an act of revenge but—'

'But I don't believe that and neither do you,' Henry said.
'His injuries look more like the act of someone trying to extract
information than that of someone simply exacting vengeance.
Either he told them and they hanged him because he was of
no more use, or he failed to tell them and they hanged him
in frustration.'

'Maybe he didn't know the answers,' Mickey said. 'It's my
experience that most beatings stop when a result is obtained.
The hanging, though, that seems like such a vindictive cruelty.
A blow to the head would have finished him. There were
knives in the kitchen, a single stab wound or even a cut throat
would have finished the job.'

'And would have risked contamination with the victim's
blood.'

'True, I suppose, if the intent had been to stage a suicide.
If that was the case then hanging would be a more obvious
route to take. But surely they can't have expected that conclusion to be lasting. The post-mortem revealed the truth swiftly
enough.'

'They might not have understood that would happen. Few
people have any depth of forensic knowledge. The average
man in the street understands fingerprints and perhaps that we
can identify blood types and thus eliminate certain suspects
from our pool, but more than that? Perhaps not.'

'And none of this helps us with motive,' Mickey said
heavily. 'Not with either death. And then there is the cocaine.
Was it hers? She does not appear to have been registered as
a user with any of the local doctors. It's possible she is

registered elsewhere and, of course, a determined addict could find another source.'

'But why would they?' Henry argued. 'Addiction is a medical issue. Only the supply and manufacture or importation are criminal acts. It would be a very foolish course for anyone to put themselves in the hands of the criminal underworld when all they need to do is register their problem with their general practitioner. Even if that practitioner were not an authorized person, they would have the wherewithal and knowledge to refer any patient on.'

Mickey nodded. 'Agreed, so why did she have cocaine in her possession?'

'Was it hers or had it been brought to her home for the purpose of muddying the waters? The post-mortem suggested that she may have used at some time in the past, but there was no recent damage to the septum or the mucous membranes that might suggest recent or long-term activity. And the fact that the cocaine had been forced down the dead woman's throat is in itself odd. Why was that done? Was there a point to be made? If so, what?'

'Drug use is common in the theatrical classes,' Mickey observed. 'Three of the local doctors hereabouts are authorized persons under the Act and the local police tell me that a number of their patients are associated with the film industry here. Cissie Rowe was not among them.'

Henry was thoughtful. They were approaching the footbridge now. Two constables set to monitor the crossing were surrounded by a group of a half dozen individuals, evidently reporters, and a couple with camera equipment. They were arguing their right of passage with the constables.

Recognizing the detectives, the press men shifted their attention their way. Henry acknowledged them with a polite tip of his hat and a 'good afternoon' and then went on ahead. He walked slowly across the footbridge waiting for Mickey to catch him up. Behind him he could hear Mickey chatting to the journalists, even, it seemed, exchanging a joke. 'Soon as we have anything concrete, boys, you'll be the first, as always,' Henry heard him say, and then heard the jeers that greeted the platitude. He paused for Mickey to reach him, was aware of the click of shutters when his sergeant drew level.

'Let's hope they got our good side,' Mickey said.

'I'm not sure I have one.'

'They're just doing their job, Henry. We make use of them often enough. I thought we might ask for their help in tracking down that car.'

Henry laughed then. 'Oh, imagine the Chief Constable's delight when it turns out to belong to an Honourable.'

'We'd simply be following the evidence. Though I have to be honest and say that the thought does very much appeal.'

'I'll bet it does. Sergeant Hitchens, I sometimes suspect you of having communist leanings.'

'Now that's something not even to be said in jest.'

Henry was quiet as they completed their journey. The cocaine troubled him. While it was true that there was still illegal trading of the substances banned under the Dangerous Drugs Acts of 1920 and 1925 which had restricted the sale and distribution of opiates, cocaine and heroin to licensed individuals, the medical provision for registered addicts was sufficient for most to take the safer route and approach a doctor or pharmacist. The sale and possession of cocaine had been restricted for even longer – since, in fact, the enacting, in 1916, of a regulation in the Defence of the Realm Act of 1914 – and while Henry knew that its recreational use was still widespread, that too tended to be funnelled through either registered users requesting a little more than was needed for personal use or, in some cases, GPs taking advantage of their position and over-prescribing. No doubt it was a lucrative addition to their professional practice.

Either way, if you looked hard enough, there would be a trail to follow. Under what had become known as the British System, initiated after the Rolleston Report on drug use, criminalization was largely controlled.

He wondered what impact the latest incarnation of the Act would have when the amendment due to come into effect later in the month would essentially criminalize the possession of cannabis. That too would now require a doctor's prescription.

'Do any of Cynthia's set use drugs?' Mickey asked him.

Henry stepped down from the footbridge and on to the shingle. 'Some, I believe. Cocaine, mostly. Though I think consumption of alcohol is their most usual route to oblivion.'

'Yes, but that's not really a narcotic, is it?' Mickey said reasonably. 'Everyone likes a tot of something. Or a beer on a hot day. Or on a cold day, come to that. Speaking of which, I'd engendered hopes of a beer with my lunch. The sandwich was good, but a cheese sandwich goes down best with a pint of mild.'

'Why do you ask about Cynthia's friends?'

'Because she might have heard whispers about which doctors can be persuaded to prescribe a little extra here and there.'

'She might,' Henry agreed. 'I asked her once if she'd ever tried it.'

'And had she?'

'She told me that I'd always encouraged her to be curious about everything. And that she thought it was good advice. She also said that being curious once was enough for some things.'

'Wise woman, your sister. Your father was a doctor. Was he licensed?'

'When my father was still alive, no such license was required.'

'No, I suppose not. It was also easier to buy your daffy's over the counter.'

'Daffy's,' Henry laughed. 'I've not heard it called that in a long time. We had a couple of old ladies for neighbours when I was a very small child, used to give me sixpence to go to the pharmacist for some concoction or other. I seem to recall that they always cut their daffy's with gin.'

'So what are we asking the studio folk when we get there, apart from getting them to identify who's in the photographs?'

'We ask the same questions as before, I think. Did Cissie have enemies? Is there anyone who might not speak so highly of her? You know how suspicious I am when the dead are described as saints. Cissie Rowe was an attractive young woman who clearly attracted male admirers and it's my experience that when one woman acts like a honey pot there are others who find themselves feeling a deal less sweet.'

Henry's comments had proved to be prophetic and an hour after they had arrived at the studio the detectives had managed to put names to all but two of the people in the photographs and also discovered that not everyone held Cissie Rowe in quite such high regard.

Mrs Owens was not present in the wardrobe department that day and it seemed that the other women working there were a little less reticent in her absence.

'I know Muriel – Mrs Owens – she thought the sun shone out of her nevermind, but I can tell you she had a real temper on her, had Miss Rowe. *And* she wasn't above stealing, if you get my meaning.'

'Stealing?' Mickey settled himself more comfortably in the old armchair set in the corner of the storeroom. He had a cup of tea beside him and was attended by a rather pleasing young woman who introduced herself as Becky Stephens and who had made a point of needing to put some articles back into store while the policeman was there.

She glanced back through the open door into the wardrobe proper, where two of the other girls brushed and ironed and stitched loose buttons.

'Young men,' she said. 'She liked her young men and if they were someone else's young man, well, that didn't stop her, did it? That's stealing in my book.'

'And the victims of this stealing, how did they take this?'

'Well, she was careful about it, wasn't she? She'd tell the young men that she couldn't possibly get involved with any of them while they were involved with someone else.'

'And so they would break up with their lady friend and . . .'

'And she'd make them wait – not long, mind, any more than a week or two and young men who've already proved themselves fickle are liable to take themselves off somewhere more obliging.'

'And then she would walk out with them for a time?'

'For a time, yes. Then she'd drop them like hot potatoes and be off after the next one. Known for it, she was.'

'And yet she seems to have maintained long relationships with Jimmy Cottee and Selwyn Croft, the young bank clerk.'

Becky Stephens shrugged. 'Oh, poor Jimmy,' she said. 'He was such a lamb. Followed her around like a little lost puppy, he did. Soft as tripe. She was kind to him, I'll give her that, but never nothing more. I mean, most people won't beat a puppy, will they? You'd have to be a real mean piece to do that.'

'And Selwyn Croft?'

'Nice boy. Sweet on her and I think she liked him well enough. He was steady, like. Always there when she wanted taking out and, to be fair, I think she was fond. Then he started to get serious and she dropped him like a hot coal. She didn't want serious, not Miss Rowe.'

'Did she ever mention anyone called Geoffrey? He drove a blue car with a horse ornament on the bonnet.'

Becky Stephens looked blank. 'I don't recall anyone like that.'

'And these young men she . . . stole. And the young women she stole them from. Would you have names for them?'

'Oh.' She put her finger to her lips as though belatedly hushing her gossip. 'I'm not sure I'd like to say.'

Of course you would, Mickey thought. You just want to be coaxed. He picked up his tea and took a sip, made himself more comfortable in the old armchair and settled himself to the task.

# FOURTEEN

By four p.m. on the Saturday afternoon they were back at Cissie Rowe's bungalow and looking again at the mess and devastation.

'No one suggested that Cissie Rowe was anything more than a casual drug user,' Henry said, 'and no one can recall her wearing the snake bangle. Though something interesting did come out of that question.'

'Oh, and what would that be?'

'Well, it might fit with the claim that she steals other women's admirers and then uses and discards them. A couple of people told me that Cissie would often turn up at the studio wearing a piece of jewellery that they'd not seen her wear before. Sometimes she'd say that she had borrowed it. Sometimes that it was a present. Either way, she'd wear these items only a couple of times and then they'd disappear, be gone.'

'And she had an explanation for this?'

'That she'd either returned the piece, had it been loaned, or grown tired of it and sold it on.'

'Interesting. And what did your informants think of that?'

'Either that she was cold-hearted or that she was practical. "You can't eat gold" was one rather revealing comment.'

'Gold, is it? So she encouraged the giving of gifts before chucking her paramours aside. She's not the first young woman to have survived poverty that way and I doubt she'll be the last. Pretty young women are usually all too aware that their looks won't last and that they need to make good use of them while they may.'

'You are a cynic, Mickey.'

'No, I'm a realist.'

Henry nodded. It seemed to him that Mickey's comments echoed the conversation he had enjoyed with his sister on the promenade. Though Cynthia had always been so much more

than just a pretty face. 'What I don't understand, then, is where
the money went. If she was given gifts and then sold those
gifts, did she keep the proceeds from that here?'

Mickey pulled out his notebook and flicked back through
the pages. 'I asked the locals to track down her bank account,
if she had one. It seems she banked at the same branch of
Western and Southern that employed Selwyn Croft and that
he provided her with a reference for it, but she kept relatively
little in her account. At the time of her death she possessed
ten pounds, five shillings and eight pence and the deposits all
match the dates the studio paid her.'

'So the money from the sales of these gold trinkets . . .
that's if they were gold . . . Cynthia owns the prettiest pieces
of costume jewellery, all pastes and gilt metal, but I imagine
few people would know the difference. She saves the real
items for when Albert wants to show them off.'

'The difference being, if an obviously expensive lady like
your sister wears paste baubles, everyone just assumes they
must be the real thing because she obviously has the money
to pay for it. A woman like Cissie Rowe, the assumption would
be that these items were cheaper imitations. I made that mistake
when I first saw the snake bangle, if you recall.'

'And so, she must have made a point of demonstrating or
even stating that all that glittered was in fact gold.' Henry
frowned, thoughtful. 'What if they weren't gifts? What if that's
just what she let everyone assume?'

'So far, we just know that she stole other women's men.
It's a stretch that she also stole jewels – especially as she then
had the gall to wear them openly.'

'True, though she courted her young men openly, even when
their previous girlfriends were there to see, and it still leaves
us with the issue of what she spent the money on. Or why
there is none here.'

'Whoever killed her took it.'

'And yet left the snake bangle behind.'

'Cash is more immediately usable.'

Henry nodded. That was true. He glanced at his watch. It
was almost five and they still had to return to the police station,
report back to the central office and then write up the day's

events. The bungalow was still redolent with the smell of paraffin and Henry found that he was concerned by this.

'I want to pay another brief visit to Muriel Owens,' he said. 'I think we should go together, impress upon the lady the implications of withholding evidence. She *must* have noticed the jewellery, heard the excuses and the stories.'

Mickey nodded. 'And tomorrow we take this place apart,' he guessed, 'and Jimmy Cottee's poor little hovel too. You know, he weighs upon my mind almost more than the young woman. I can't help but feel that he would still be alive if he'd not fallen in with Miss Rowe.'

'And Miss Rowe would not be dead if she'd not fallen in with whoever killed her,' Henry said. 'You could make that statement about any of those who die by violence. No, but I know what you're saying. Jimmy Cottee seems to have been an unworldly innocent, an anomaly among those who certainly thought they knew how the world worked.'

'So let's see what Muriel Owens has to tell us about the rest of the jewellery and the stolen boyfriends.' Mickey grinned voraciously, as though relishing the idea. 'You'll let me take the lead on this? I think it's time for a less gentlemanly approach.'

Muriel Owens and her husband were about to sit down to an early dinner. They were going out, Muriel explained, so were having a bite before they went. If the officers would consider coming back?

'I'm sorry for the inconvenience,' Mickey told them, 'but I don't suppose anyone asked if the time were convenient for Miss Rowe on the night she died.'

Muriel Owens turned pink with shock but she stepped back and Henry followed Sergeant Hitchens inside.

'Inspector,' Mr Owens began, 'are such comments really necessary? Such a tone?'

'You've not been entirely honest with us,' Henry said. 'So yes, I think the tone is apt.'

'Honest?' Muriel Owens shook her head. 'I can't think what you mean.'

'Jewellery,' Mickey said flatly. 'And a penchant for breaking up relationships. Enticing young men, you might say.'

'Enticing . . . who? What?'

'It seems that the snake bangle we asked you about was not the only piece of expensive jewellery that passed through the young lady's hands. You might be telling the truth when you say you'd not seen that particular piece, but you were almost certainly aware of others of a similar type.'

'Trinkets,' Mr Owens said. 'Cissie was like a magpie, drawn to shine and glitter. She would wear things on a few occasions and then, I believe, give most of them away. I doubt they were of any value.'

Henry was watching Mrs Owens and the increased flush of her cheek told him that, whatever her husband might have been told, the truth was a trifle different.

'Trinkets, Mrs Owens?' he asked. 'Pastes and glitter? Or were they more exclusive than all that?'

'And we'll have the truth this time, if you please,' Mickey told her sternly. 'Me and my boss, we don't like to be treated like fools, especially not where murder is concerned.'

Mr Owens sat down next to his wife and took her hand. 'Muriel? What are they talking about?'

'Oh, for goodness' sakes.' She snatched her hand away. 'Cissie was a young woman. An attractive woman, and of course she would flirt a little with the young men. If they took this more seriously than she intended then how could she be held to blame? And if she accepted the occasional gift, then where was the harm?'

'Muriel!'

'It was the expectations that might follow the giving of such a gift that she should have worried about,' Mickey said bluntly. 'A woman that accepts such presents can sometimes get herself a reputation.'

Mrs Owens opened her mouth to make a sharp retort but then seemed to change her mind. 'She was young,' she said. 'And had endured a great deal in her short life. She deserved a little fun.'

'Not so young or inexperienced, Mrs Owens, and many of us have endured pain and loss of a kind that might well match those Miss Rowe endured. It behoves us to learn from the experiences, not exploit them as an excuse for—'

Henry had been about to say 'stupidity' but even *he* realized that might not be the most appropriate word.

'She may not always have judged well,' he said, hoping that would do.

'And you are suggesting that her ill judgement made her deserving of such a terrible death?' Mrs Owens was now incandescent.

'Never deserving, no. But it may well have led her down the path that made it inevitable. I'm sorry, Mrs Owens, but we have to consider that possibility.'

Muriel Owens opened her mouth and then shut it again.

'Of course we must,' her husband said quietly. 'Muriel, if you know anything that might shed light here then you have to say. You owe it to Cissie.'

'Owe it to Cissie? To have her reputation sullied? Isn't it enough that she is dead?'

'And can't be hurt by anything you might say,' Mickey said sharply. 'But what you can tell us might make all the difference to our investigation.'

'Names,' Henry said. 'Of the young men she became involved with and who may have given her gifts of jewellery. And descriptions of the pieces she wore. Mrs Owens, I'm not in the least concerned about protecting people's feelings here. Neither, Mr Owens, Mrs Owens, am I interested that you choose to make the assumption that these pieces were of little value. Information, Mrs Owens, is the oxygen of an investigation like ours. I'm sure you'd rather give it to us in the comfort of your own home than be arrested and charged with obstruction in a murder investigation.'

'Chief Inspector, really. I—'

Henry silenced Mr Owens with a look and Mickey took out his notebook.

Mrs Owens had turned deathly pale and she fanned herself with what looked like the same lace handkerchief she had used the first time they had met her. The scrap of linen surrounded by the wide border of lace.

Mickey waited, pen in hand.

'When you are ready, Mrs Owens,' Henry said.

\* \* \*

They left almost an hour later. One name had emerged which was familiar to Mickey. Evelyn Cunningham, who had lost her beau to Cissie, had also been a name coaxed out of Becky Stephens when Mickey had spoken to her earlier.

Evening light crept across the open water, shadows stretching diagonally across the strand as the sun sank below the wooden buildings of Bungalow Town. The light was violet and golden and, in Henry's eyes, marked the transition towards autumn. He both loved that particular time of year and dreaded it. Loved it for the childhood memories of playing in the woods behind the house and the sounds and smells of crushed leaves and bonfires; hated it for the later memories, for the fact that autumn presaged a change in weather. Brought dark and rain and mud and cold.

'Back to the present, if you please,' Mickey said quietly. 'You've got that look in your eye again that I'd rather not see, especially when we need you to have all your wits intact.'

'My wits are just fine, Mickey,' Henry told him. 'So, we have the local force track down these young lotharios and see what they have to say about Cissie Rowe and her liking for shiny treasures.'

'I hardly think any of them will qualify as lotharios,' Mickey chuckled to himself. 'They're just as likely to be drivers and bank clerks, if her friendship with Selwyn Croft is anything to go by.'

'And Selwyn Croft certainly could not afford to be lavish . . . perhaps Mr Owens is right, the brooches and bracelets and such were nothing more than cheap imitations and she just liked to pretend they were more. Maybe none of it is relevant.'

He felt suddenly tired and deflated.

'You need food and drink,' Mickey told him sternly. 'Your brain ceases to function, and so does your good temper, when you've not been fed.'

'You don't need to mother me, Mickey.'

'I know I don't need to,' Mickey defended, 'but some things just get to be a habit after all this time. And habits are comfortable. I hope you'd not deny me my little comforts.'

Henry managed something that was almost a laugh.

Back across the footbridge, two new constables stood on watch. 'Our friends in the press must be gone for the night.'

'Be too late for them to make the morning editions, even if anything does happen overnight,' Henry said.

'True. Anyway, it's Sunday tomorrow. The Sundays will already have been printed and be on their way out to the newsagents. They'd get nothing in before the Monday editions now, unless they struck lucky and got a brief mention on the wireless.'

They paused for a quick word with the constables and then went to make their reports to both the local police and the central office at Scotland Yard.

There was nothing new on the mysterious Geoffrey and his blue car. Several new sightings of Philippe only a couple of days before Cissie's death, but little that Henry deemed of immediate use. Those investigations could be taken care of by local constables doing further house-to-house enquiries.

They left Shoreham just after seven and drove back to Cynthia's house, knowing that even if dinner had been missed, something would have been put aside for them. 'And a beer,' Mickey said in anticipation. 'Wine with your dinner, like your sister and her husband enjoy, well, it's all very good and nice, but you need a pint at the end of a day like this. Your sister told Cook that I should have a beer with my dinner if I wished it.'

Henry laughed and shook his head. 'Anything you wanted would be just fine with Cynthia,' he said. 'And, by extension, with my brother-in-law.'

'And quite right too,' Mickey said complacently. 'You think your sister or the Honourable Albert will know of anyone called Geoffrey with a posh blue car?'

'I imagine they'll know several. But with a horse mascot? Maybe not so many. Though Albert's chauffeurs might be worth talking to. The drivers and mechanics are more likely to know of any particular marque of car that uses a horse mascot. Personally, I think it's as likely to have been bought as an addition. Mascots seem a popular thing. Cynthia told

me of friends of hers who had a Lalique fish attached to the
bonnet of their Bentley. She thought it looked a little vulgar,
I think.'

'So long as she doesn't want to spoil the lines of hers,'
Mickey said.

# FIFTEEN

Sunday morning was bright and clear but with a chill breeze coming in off the sea.

Henry and Cynthia both rose early and went out before breakfast, walking together along the promenade. Cynthia's cheeks were reddened by the sharp wind and Henry's hands felt surprisingly cold when they paused beside the rail and looked out to sea.

'So, how are you feeling this morning?' Cynthia asked him.

Henry heard the tone, the edge of concern in her voice. 'My sergeant has been gossiping behind my back again?'

'I asked him a question and he replied, honestly,' Cynthia told him. 'We both care about you, Henry, and we both know how difficult anniversaries can be.'

'I'm fine, Cyn. Truly I am.' He brushed the curls back out of his eyes and made a mental note that he must get his hair cut. It was the only unruly, uncontrolled element of either his personality or his appearance – or so people said of him. Henry knew that the rest of his facade could be characterized as austere, from his manner of dress to his pebble grey eyes.

'Your sleeves are fraying,' Cynthia observed. 'Henry, must you wear that coat day in, day out? It makes you look like an unsuccessful undertaker.'

'It's comfortable,' he told her. 'And it has deep pockets. A man needs deep pockets.'

'I can have one made for you. An identical coat. How would that be?'

Henry thought about it. 'That would be nice,' he said, knowing that this response would please his sister. 'Cynthia . . . if one of your friends or acquaintances needed to get cocaine, more than for personal use, would that be easy?'

'Down here or in London? In London I know of a half dozen physicians who might be persuaded to provide a little more than was strictly necessary. Down here, I'm not so sure.

There is an element of conservatism in Worthing compared to
the city. I could ask around, if that would help.'

'Wouldn't that arouse suspicion?'

'Oh, Henry. Everyone knows I pass information on to you.
I'm quite candid about it, so nobody minds. They find it
exciting, I suppose, the idea that a little bit of casual gossip
might help to solve a *murder*. I know you find the attitude
distasteful, Henry, but for most people, murder is a rather
exotic happening. So long as they are not directly affected, of
course.'

'And they're not afraid that it might rebound on them, this
information you might be passing on to me?'

Cynthia laughed. 'Henry, most of Albert's friends view themselves as untouchable. It never occurs to them that anything in
life might rebound. I thank the Lord that Albert is a more
cautious man, that he opens his eyes to possibilities.'

'Possibilities?'

'That life is not a menu; just because you order a certain
dish does not mean that life will oblige.'

Henry nodded, remembering the conversation he'd had with
Cynthia's husband a couple of days before. 'Albert has great
respect for your opinions,' he said.

'Oh, I know. Enough to change the odd word here and there
and make them his own.'

'Does that bother you?'

'Occasionally. But I'm a pragmatist, remember? I'm satisfied
that he takes notice of what I say. I can live without the full
credit.'

They turned and began to walk slowly back to the house.
The town was awake now, but there were still only a few
people on the streets. Most would not choose to leave home
on a Sunday morning until it was time to go to church. He
and Mickey would be long gone before then.

'I wonder how many individual habits our father fed,' he said.

'Many, I would have thought. Even in a small, country
community like ours. The vicar's wife couldn't sleep without
her powders. Our schoolmaster was dependant on morphine
– for the pain in his leg, apparently. The master of the hunt
took cocaine before he rode out . . .'

'And you know these things, how?'

'Henry, before our father decided to torture you by making you spend hours in his study grinding powders and making up pills, that was my task. I saw the scripts he wrote before he sent the medicines out. And I saw the account books. He might have taken pleasure in keeping Mother and us children short of everything from food to warm clothing, but that didn't mean the money wasn't coming in.'

They walked in silence for a while and then Henry asked, 'Do you hate him?'

'Of course I do. I always did. And while I know I wouldn't be the person I am today had our circumstances been different, I see absolutely no reason to thank him for that. Our father was mean and cruel and I was glad when he died.'

Henry nodded. Cynthia's honesty sometimes took him by surprise, but not in this case. 'I wish it could have been different, especially for you. I know that all the responsibility fell to you.'

'Oh, Henry. Don't be such an idiot. We worked our way through together. Believe me, darling, I could not have coped had I been alone. I think, in truth, that we kept one another alive, don't you?'

Breakfast was a noisy affair. It was a Sunday custom that the children should eat with their parents before church and so Albert hid behind his newspapers and Henry, Cynthia and Mickey found themselves in conversation with the younger members of the family. Melissa had settled herself beside Henry and was telling him about the books she had been reading. It seemed that she was a fan of Dickens but that she also borrowed her father's detective stories and his Jeeves and Wooster books.

'Aren't they a little old for you?' Henry enquired.

'Mummy says that if I'm capable of reading them than I should be allowed to,' she said. 'Mummy says that if there is anything I don't understand, then I should go and ask Daddy, because they're his books.'

Henry exchanged a glance with his sister and could see the laughter behind her eyes. Mischief maker, Henry thought. 'You and I must go book shopping,' he said. 'Would you like that?'

'I would like that very much.' Melissa speared a lump of sausage and looked at it thoughtfully. 'After you have finished with this murder, I'll write you a letter to remind you.'

From across the table Cynthia smiled at her daughter and Henry reflected on how alike the two female members of the household were. Somehow, he was glad of that. If Melissa grew up to be anything like Cynthia then he would be very happy.

'Do you believe in fairies, Uncle Henry?'

Henry considered. 'I'm not sure that I do. Why do you ask?'

'Well, I've been reading Mr Conan Doyle's book about the Cottingley fairies. Have you heard about it?'

Vaguely, Henry recalled that the Sherlock Holmes author had produced such a book about six years before, but he didn't know the details.

'It's about these two little girls who went out with a camera and they photographed some fairies. The pictures are in the book. I've asked Daddy if I can have a camera for my birthday and he says he will think about it.'

'And are you thinking of going out and trying to photograph fairies?' Henry asked her.

Melissa shook her head. 'I think that might be too difficult,' she said. 'I've never heard of anybody else photographing fairies and there are a lot of people with cameras. So, Uncle Henry, do you think it strange that these two little girls should go to the bottom of their garden, or into the woods near the bottom of their garden, anyway, and manage to photograph fairies just like that? I don't think I'd be that lucky.'

'And do you believe these are pictures of real fairies?' Henry asked her.

'I don't know. I think Mr Conan Doyle must be a very clever man and so perhaps that is evidence that they are really photographs of fairies because clever men should not be fooled so easily, should they? But Mummy says that just because he is clever about some things, that does not mean he is going to be clever about everything. She says that you told her that sometimes people just see what they are looking for.'

'That's true,' Henry said cautiously. He was aware that both Cynthia and Mickey were now observing him closely and that even Albert was peering around the edge of his newspaper. 'Perhaps the evidence that you should be thinking about is whether these girls knew how to create photographs that made it look as if fairies were really there. Or if perhaps they had a friend that did. Evidence can be a very tricky thing, Melissa.'

His niece considered that and ate some more of her breakfast while Henry wondered if he had given her a useful answer. Cynthia nodded at him so he decided he hadn't done too badly. Mickey just looked amused and Albert had disappeared back behind his newspaper. The boys were still talking about cricket.

Henry picked up his coffee and sipped slowly. It was very hot and the roast was rich and he knew it was probably the last decent cup he'd have all day. It seemed that Melissa hadn't quite done with him yet.

'Mummy says that the place where you're going today, the place where the poor young lady was murdered, they made a film of one of Mr Dickens's books there.'

'I didn't know that. Do you remember which one?'

Melissa looked at her mother. 'It was *Little Dorrit*,' Cynthia told him. 'I believe that they used the old fort as a setting for the Marshalsea prison. Joan Morgan played the lead role. We have some of her pictures in the albums, don't we, Melissa? I thought it might be nice – if you get the chance, that is – if perhaps you could take a few photographs of the fort and maybe the studio to add to Melissa's collection?'

Henry smiled at his sister, not fooled by the fact that she had now passed her scrapbooks on to her daughter. Cynthia, he thought, was still a little star struck for all her good sense. 'I'll see what I can do,' he promised.

Mickey and Henry left the family finishing their breakfast and set off back for Shoreham-by-Sea.

'Did you ever regret not having children?' Henry asked, and immediately wished he hadn't. It was an unusual question for him and he wasn't sure it was an appropriate one.

'I think I would have made a good father,' Mickey said. 'I'm not so sure my wife would have made a good mother. And I think it takes both. If one of you is in disagreement then it can't be much fun for the children, can it?'

'No, it can't. But I think there are men out there who have children just so that they can impose their will upon them. Some men seem to take pleasure in that.'

Mickey nodded but didn't reply. He knew who was being referenced and didn't want to encourage the melancholy that set in when Henry thought about his childhood. Henry took out his journal and began to write, his hand shaking a little as the car rumbled and jerked and bounced along the potholes. A memory had come to him, triggered by the conversation with Cynthia, and he knew that he needed to get it down or it would bother him all day.

*I recall the smell of my father's study. Chemicals and coal dust and ancient books.*

*I had to learn, he would say. I must develop the skills I would need to take over from him and he would tell his few friends and many acquaintances that he was 'training the boy'.*

*Training the boy meant standing over me while I rolled pills and worked for hours with the pestle and mortar, grinding powders, writing tiny neat labels with hands that were too frozen and stiff to wield a pen.*

*Truthfully, I can think of circumstances in which I might have enjoyed the work, but our father stood over me with a wooden rule in his hands and at any sign of failure – and his exacting standards made failure inevitable – he would smash my hands with the rule.*

*And he would laugh. 'You're useless, boy. Useless.'*

*I am past caring about this now, he is long gone. But I do care for all of those other small beings whose lives are crushed and broken by uncaring, cruel fathers. Life is tough and mean enough without our protectors becoming our torturers and taking pleasure in the fact.*

They drove straight into Bungalow Town, having arranged with the local force to have constables meet them there that morning. Henry was to remain at Cissie Rowe's bungalow while Mickey went along to Jimmy Cottee's. He would leave the car on the Old Fort Road and walk the rest of the way.

'Happy hunting.' Mickey grinned before striding off.

'Happy hunting indeed,' Henry muttered. He joined the constables on the veranda and told them that everything, and he meant everything, needed to be brought out and set on the beach. Two constables then set to searching the furniture and two more would help Henry inside.

A small crowd had gathered to watch the proceedings, including Dr Clark and his wife and children. They looked justifiably concerned and Henry tried to reassure them that everything would be put back as it had been before. For the first time he sensed hostility amongst the local people. They had been more than happy for him to investigate, eager for whoever had committed this dreadful crime to be brought to book, but did the consequences have to be paraded so very obviously for everyone to see? Somehow emptying the contents of Cissie's bungalow brought it home to everyone that she was no longer there. That she had no further need for her furniture or her pictures or her books. It was, Henry realized, almost as though her corpse had been stripped naked and laid out for all to see, the young woman's life laid utterly bare.

For the next two hours Henry worked beside the constables. The two on the beach had examined the furniture even more thoroughly than he and Mickey had done on that first day. He had given them orders that nothing need be taken apart that could not have been dismantled easily and quickly by the owner. If Cissie Rowe had hidden anything among her belongings then it would have to have been in a place accessible to her. There were two reasons that had caused him to decide that this task should be undertaken outside, on the beach, in public view. One was practical: there was very little room for manoeuvre in the bungalow and the searchers would be falling over one another. The second was more subtle. He knew how the neighbours would feel, seeing this, and he hoped that consciences would be disturbed and memories jogged as the full force of realization came home to them.

Inside the bungalow he and the constables examined the floorboards and the panelling and all the fixtures and fittings. He had also set one of them to look at the water tank again. It had been examined twice already, first by Constable Prentice

and then by Mickey Hitchens, but Henry thought it would do
no harm to look again. He also had the constable take a ladder
to peer under the eaves – though this was more for show than
anything. Had Cissie Rowe formed a habit of regularly taking
a ladder and poking around under the corrugated roof, someone
would have noticed.

Towards noon, when even Henry had stripped off his coat
and was continuing in his shirt sleeves, a message came from
the police station that a young woman called Evelyn
Cunningham, the same young woman that Cissie Rowe was
rumoured to have quarrelled with over a gentleman friend and
who had subsequently lost her job, was waiting for him at the
police station. It seemed that the police hadn't tracked her
down but friends from the studio had been in touch and told
her what questions had been asked and urged her to come
forward herself.

Henry left the search and drove back into town, glad that
Mickey had left him the car. The day was hot for September
and he would not have relished the twenty or so minutes it
would have taken to walk back.

Evelyn Cunningham was waiting for him in a small side
room off the main reception. She seemed very composed, and
had a friend with her whom Henry recognized as Violet, from
the studio. They were drinking tea and chatting though she
began to look a little anxious when Henry appeared and took
a seat opposite. This room was larger than the one in which
he had interviewed the boy and there was room for a small
table and three chairs.

'Is it all right if my friend stays?' Evelyn Cunningham asked
him, and Henry assured her that it was. 'Only I'm a bit nervous
about being here. I've never been inside a police station before,
not even to report a lost dog or anything like that.'

Henry thanked her for coming and told her that it had saved
the police a lot of time in tracking her down.

'Tracking me down? But I've done nothing.'

Henry cursed his choice of words. 'I'm sorry,' he said. 'I
put that badly. I'm very grateful that you have come to us; as
I say, it has saved us a lot of time.' He glanced at the friend,
wondering how much she knew and whether Evelyn

Cunningham would mind talking about her previous romantic involvement in front of her. He decided that if Miss Cunningham had brought the woman with her she must already have considered this. He wondered which of the several young men whose names they had obtained from Muriel Owens this particular young woman had been attached to.

'We were told that you had a disagreement with Miss Rowe. Over a young man?'

She frowned. 'She was always a flirty sort, and I told my Richard – when he *was* my Richard, you understand – I told my Richard not to take her seriously. She flirted, if you pardon the expression, with anything in trousers, if you pardon the expression. It was just her way. If the man took no notice—'

'And how often did that happen?' her friend interjected.

'Well, I suppose that's true,' Evelyn agreed. 'The truth is, I thought that Cissie Rowe was my friend and therefore she would leave my Richard alone. I was wrong about that, wasn't I? The more he ignored her the more determined she seemed to be. Anyway, it all came to a head one day at the studios. I caught her brushing a hair off his shoulder, all intimate like. I mean, what woman does that, if she's not stepping out with a man, or related to him, or something? I mean, would you come up to me and brush a hair off *my* coat?'

Henry shook his head. 'No,' he agreed. 'That would not seem proper, not if I didn't know you well.'

'I suppose Richard did know her fairly well.' The friend screwed up her nose and forehead, as though having to think about this very carefully.

'It wasn't that so much, it was the way Richard responded to her. You could see he liked being that close to her. She was standing so close you couldn't get a hand between them. I mean, if you're dancing with somebody, well, fair enough, but not when you're just supposed to be talking. If you see what I mean?'

Henry nodded. 'And so you challenged them?'

'No, not really. I took Richard's arm and we left and I just gave her a look, you know. A *look*.'

'And then what happened?'

'Well, a few days later, Richard told me that he didn't think

we should be seeing each other any more. That he thought
I was jealous and difficult. And perhaps we should take a
little break from one another. That was how he put it. Take
a little break from one another. I mean, what man comes out
with something like that? I was sure it was Cissie putting
words into his mouth.'

'And you did separate . . .?'

'And the next thing I know, only a couple of weeks later
he's collecting Cissie from studio and they are off out together.
Dancing and dinner. You don't take somebody dancing *and* to
dinner unless things are well advanced, do you? You might
take a walk first, or even go to the cinema, or take tea somewhere. But dancing and dinner, on the same night? That told
me that they had been planning this for quite some time. *Quite*
some time before we . . . separated. And then she arrives at
the studio a few days later and she's wearing a necklace. One
none of us had seen before. A gold locket, it was. Old-fashioned
looking, but still very nice.

'Well, *I* wasn't going to ask where she'd got it from, but
some of the other girls did and you can guess what she told
them.'

'That Richard had given it to her.'

'I never thought that was likely,' Violet said. 'Where would
Richard have got the money for something like that, even if
it wasn't a new thing? Even if it was bought second-hand. It
still looked pricey.'

'All I know is that in all the time we were together – and
it was a full six months, you know – he never bought me more
than chocolates, or even offered to. Not that I would have let
him. We never talked about getting engaged or anything. But
even so. After two weeks, or a little more? And it wasn't the
first or the only time.'

Henry nodded; that chimed with what they had learned the
day before. He guessed that the two women had a lot more
to say and so, taking a leaf out of Mickey's book, he sent for
more tea and settled down to listen.

Mickey Hitchens had almost finished his search and was
ready for the trek back along the beach, prepared to tell his

boss that he had found nothing, when one of the constables called him.

The young man was standing precariously on a wobbly chair and poking away at the ceiling of the railway carriage.

Metal ribs supported the roof and the constable was sliding a knife behind one of these.

'What've you found there, lad?' Mickey asked him.

'It's probably nothing, Sarge, but there's a bit of paper been jammed in between the rib and the roof. I thought it might be worth a look, but I'm having trouble getting it out. I poked it with the blade of my pocket knife and I've actually wedged it further in. I must have poked it the wrong way.'

Mickey felt in his pocket and withdrew his own pocket knife. He handed it to the young man. 'Here,' he said, 'try the blade on that. It might be a little thinner than yours.'

The constable took it, looking curiously at it. 'A German knife, Sarge?' He looked a little surprised.

'The company what made that is called Mercator and was making decent blades a long time before their countrymen decided they wanted a fight,' Mickey told him. 'I acquired that there blade in 1916 and it's been with me ever since. Its original owner having no more use for it, if you get my meaning.'

The constable must've been a child when the war ended, Mickey thought. He was no more than eighteen now. Mickey watched as he probed behind the rib once more and poked the piece of paper out. Mickey could see that whoever had slid it in there had chosen a spot where the rib had a tiny bend on it so it didn't sit quite flush to the carriage roof. In his enthusiasm the constable, instead of using the blade to fetch it out, had inadvertently pushed the scrap further into the wedge formed between the curving rib and the curving ceiling.

'So what have we got then, lad?' Mickey asked.

'Looks like a pawn ticket, sir, seems a funny thing to be putting up in a place like that. But I suppose you're not likely to lose it that way, are you? I suppose it's a kind of a safe place.'

Mickey took the knife and the pawn ticket from him and looked at both thoughtfully. 'A safe place indeed,' he said. 'Now the two big questions we have are, did Mr Cottee put it there himself and, if he didn't, did he know about it?'

The ticket was a little ragged after being poked with a knife blade and scraped out from beneath the rib. Mickey, who always kept a few spare envelopes in his pocket for just such a purpose, even when he didn't have the murder bag with him, tucked the ticket into one of them and wrote details on the outside of where it had been found and how.

'Well observed,' he said. 'What the devil made you look up there?'

The young man shrugged. 'Not sure, sir, but I had looked everywhere else and found nothing so it was just, well, the last place I could think of, I suppose.'

'Well, while you're up there, take a look at the rest. Just to be sure.'

Mickey helped him to check the remainder of the railway carriage that had been Jimmy Cottee's home but they found nothing else and finally Mickey turned back towards where his boss was supervising the search of Cissie Rowe's bungalow. Before he had put the ticket away he had noticed two things. One was that the pawnbroker was based in London and the second that the object that had been pawned was a gold brooch. At that moment Mickey would have bet a month's wages that either Cissie Rowe had put the pawn ticket in its hiding place or Jimmy Cottee had done it for her.

He was inclined towards the former option.

# SIXTEEN

Mickey Hitchens arrived back at Cissie Rowe's bungalow to find that his boss was no longer there. The search of the murdered woman's home had turned up nothing new, he was told. He asked about paperwork or receipts and was directed to a small stack of letters and bills and a few more photographs that had been gathered together. Most of these were things that Mickey had seen before. Receipts for dresses bought, a few more photographs of studio friends and two letters from Muriel Owens written when the Owenses had been on holiday.

Previously Mickey had discounted these assorted documents as being of no interest but now he looked again and noticed that two of the receipts, one for a dress and one for a winter coat, were from London shops. He took tweezers from the murder bag, carefully extracted the pawn ticket from its envelope and looked at the address. The shops that had supplied the clothes were undoubtedly more upmarket than the pawnbrokers, but in terms of distance they were no more than a few streets away.

Interesting, Mickey thought. Interesting too that he knew that the pawnbroker had previously been under observation, suspected of receiving stolen goods – though nothing had ever stuck, despite the fact that he'd been brought in for questioning on a number of occasions.

Now, Mickey thought, why would a young woman in need of a pawnbroker go all the way to London to find one? It might be that she wanted to be discreet, of course, in which case why not go to Worthing or Brighton? Her face was as likely to be recognized in the city as it was in any of the local towns.

'It looks like rain, sir. Can we start to bring things back inside? Or should we find tarpaulins and cover them down?'

Mickey looked around the empty shell of what had been Cissie Rowe's home. It seemed that everything that could be extracted from its structure had already been discovered. As good a search as possible had been done. Then he remembered that the kitchen and the bedroom were, like Jimmy Cottee's home, constructed from railway carriages; the chances were they had the same steel ribs supporting the roof.

'You can start to bring stuff back into the middle room,' he said. 'And can someone find me a chair, something to stand on?'

A chair was provided and Mickey took it through to the bedroom and began to look for likely places where something like a pawn ticket might be hidden. Standing somewhat uncertainly on a dining chair he began to poke about, watched in puzzlement by one of the constables. 'Anything I can be of help with, Sarge?' he asked, eyeing with some trepidation the rather square, rather bulky man on the rather small, rather slender chair.

'Just be ready to get out of the way should I fall off this thing,' Mickey told him, and the young man took another step back.

For several minutes Mickey poked and prodded but found nothing and then he struck lucky. Folded and flattened and tucked between rib and ceiling he found a slip of paper, and then a second. The first was another pawn ticket; the second was what appeared to be a list of jewellery, and beside the list what could possibly be initials.

Mickey felt in his pocket for another envelope and slipped the papers inside. He got down from the chair and turned back to the constable. 'You see what I was doing? Well, get up on that chair and carry on doing it. See if there's anything else. Then when you've done in here, go into the kitchen and do the same.'

He went out on to the veranda just as Henry arrived back from the police station.

'Anything?' Henry asked.

Mickey's grin was broad and wolfish. 'Oh yes,' he said. 'I rather think we have.'

It turned out to be a satisfying afternoon. Mickey was still in the middle of explaining to Henry what he'd found when a car drew up behind their own and the desk sergeant, just coming off duty, got out.

'I was on my way home, Inspector, so I said I'd bring the news across. It seems' – he paused impressively – 'that we found your car and your gentleman. The one by the name of Geoffrey. It seems that he is the Honourable Geoffrey Clifton, Esquire. And I have his address right here.'

Henry refrained from telling the sergeant that if he was an Honourable he was not also an Esquire and instead joined Mickey in congratulating the man.

'Next port of call, then,' Mickey said. 'We'll interrupt his pleasant Sunday afternoon, shall we?'

The first spots of rain were falling as they left, bruised purple clouds rolling in off the sea pursued by even darker, blackened ones driven by a suddenly freshening wind. It looked as though the mild September was losing the battle and more autumnal weather was sweeping in. By the time they had looped back past the Church of the Good Shepherd and on into Shoreham town the rain was falling heavily and the windscreen wipers proving themselves inadequate to the task. Henry stared out through thick weather, wondering if they should wait until it cleared but impatient now that they had a lead. So he drove on, keeping on the coast road and then turning inland about five miles beyond, the road narrowing and climbing on to the South Downs. The large Georgian house occupied by Geoffrey Clifton and his family – apparently the man was married – was set in a little hollow, the entrance guarded by tall stone pillars though the gates stood open. There were several cars parked on the gravel drive that swept around the front of the house but Henry parked the car as close as he could and the two of them ran up the steps and under the porch, then rang the bell. The door opened instantly and Henry guessed that the footman was there waiting for more guests to arrive. He was somewhat taken aback to be greeted by two policemen who showed their identity cards and asked to see his master.

Music was playing on a gramophone and they could hear the sound of laughter and conversation. Evidently Geoffrey Clifton was having a party, on a Sunday afternoon. And from the sound of it the merriment had already been going on for some time.

'The lady of the house has a birthday,' the footman told them. 'I'm not sure the master will want to be disturbed.'

Mickey scribbled a few words on a scrap of paper torn from his notebook and folded it carefully. 'Give him this,' he instructed. 'Then see what he says.'

They loitered in the hall, listening to the rain outside beating a tattoo on the windows. Now the rain had begun, it seemed in no hurry to let up.

A few minutes later a man appeared and gestured to them to follow him through to a smaller room off the hallway and the footman took their coats. They followed the man into what was evidently his study and he introduced himself as Geoffrey Clifton.

'Yes,' he admitted, 'I knew Cecily Rowe. I was foolish enough to become involved with the young woman, but it was a casual liaison and I ended it quickly. I heard about her murder.'

'But it did not occur to you that you might have useful information and that you should come forward?' Henry asked him.

Geoffrey Clifton looked surprised. 'No, why on earth should it? I imagine many people knew her. Have they all come forward? Frankly I did not want to be involved.'

'And yet you *are* involved,' Henry told him. 'You have been connected, romantically, with a young woman who has been murdered. Brutally murdered, I might add.'

'Romantically! I was never romantically involved. I admit she was an attractive young woman and a passing interest. But that was all. She was enjoyable company, for a time. My wife was away for several months taking the cure in Switzerland and I will admit to being bored. Miss Rowe, I suppose, alleviated the boredom for a time. It was nothing more than that, and she was aware that it could be nothing more than that.'

'*You* may have seen it that way,' Mickey told him. 'But we have reason to believe that Miss Rowe saw it quite differently.'

'Young women can be foolish.' He laughed awkwardly. 'Older men can be foolish too, I will admit that.'

'And the nature of your relationship with Miss Rowe? You can tell us about that. When did it begin? What did you do when you were with her? I imagine you would want to avoid being seen by any of your wife's friends or acquaintances. I imagine you would want to avoid any kind of scandal.'

Geoffrey Clifton sighed and, finally realizing that his unwanted guests were in no hurry to leave, took a seat behind his impressive walnut desk.

'She was a presentable enough young woman, I suppose. I took her to restaurants I knew she could never have dreamt of affording. To a couple of the London clubs I frequent and where it is possible to be . . . invisible, ignored. She was good company, and, as I say, presentable enough. But you must understand, gentlemen, it was a mere dalliance. A time filler. And to be truthful, I lost interest rapidly enough.'

'But to such a young woman it might have seemed that your interest was greater than it was. That you promised more. And I'm curious, Mr Clifton, as to what you requested in return.'

Geoffrey Clifton must have known that this question was coming but even so he flushed to beetroot red and rose to his feet, stretching to his full six feet plus in height.

Neither Henry nor Mickey was either impressed or intimidated.

'Sit down and answer the question,' Mickey Hitchens said. 'Or we'll be forced to call for back-up and have a constable come in and arrest you.'

He saw the sudden confusion in Geoffrey Clifton's eyes. 'We could do the job ourselves, of course, make nice with your guests and tell them that you are attending to some urgent business. But, frankly, why should we?'

'W–why should you?' Geoffrey Clifton stuttered.

'Why should we?' Mickey confirmed. 'My colleague here, well, he's accustomed to much more gentlemanly behaviour but me, well, as you can see, I'm just an ordinary plebeian. Of a similar class to our poor Miss Rowe and so also beneath your concern. By the same token, Mr Clifton, you are beneath mine.'

Henry stood quietly by and, when Geoffrey Clifton looked to him for support, he simply shrugged mildly.

'You'll get no sympathy from the Chief Inspector,' Mickey told him. 'Now, do we use your telephone to summon a nice constable or two and make a pretty scene for your guests to see, or do you provide us with dates and times that we can check and cross check and a list of places where you and our unfortunate murder victim might have been noticed together?'

'You might also tell us whether you made any gifts to Miss Rowe,' Henry said quietly. 'Particularly if those gifts were jewellery.'

'Jewellery?' Geoffrey Clifton sounded genuinely dumbfounded.

The study door opened and a cloud of cigarette smoke and rich, floral perfume drifted in, followed by a young woman dressed in ivory silk and carrying an extraordinarily long cheroot holder. 'Geoffrey, have you forgotten that we have guests? Oh!' She eyed the visitors curiously.

'I doubt it,' Henry told her. 'We have just been reminding Mr Clifton about them.'

'Really?' She studied Henry carefully, cautiously. 'Geoffrey, introduce me.'

'My dear, I really don't think . . . This is my wife.'

'He's a little reluctant,' Mickey told her. 'On account of us being policemen.'

Geoffrey Clifton changed colour again. He managed it with astonishing rapidity, Henry thought.

'Police officers? And they are here because?'

'My car—' Geoffrey began, but Mickey was ahead of him.

'An acquaintance of your husband thought he saw your vehicle involved in a hit-and-run accident. It would seem that he was mistaken but we have to check these things out, you understand.'

'Of course.' From her tone it was apparent that she didn't believe a word of it.

'Nice of you to lie for him, Mr Policeman, but he really doesn't deserve it, you know. I assume it's really because of that poor young actress who was killed down in Shoreham. Very sad, I'm sure, but I can assure you that my husband ceased his involvement with her several months ago.'

Henry wondered, idly, if it was possible for the redness of

Geoffrey Clifton's face to deepen any further. It had extended now to his neck and hands.

'Sit down, Geoffrey,' his wife said sternly. 'And do calm down, my dear. You'll make yourself ill.'

She picked an onyx ash tray from the desk, flicked the ash from her cigarette and then drew deeply on the elegant black and amber holder, blowing out a long stream of smoke.

She doesn't inhale, Henry thought. It's just for show.

'My husband has his dalliances,' she said. 'He usually confesses when they're over or I find out about them and he becomes embarrassed and ends them.'

'And how do you feel about that?' Henry was aware that such a direct question might not be the most appropriate but he recalled the conversation he'd had with Cynthia about Albert's little peccadilloes and was genuinely curious.

'None of your damned business,' she replied calmly.

'It is if it impacts upon our investigation. A jealous wife is capable of revenge. You must have felt put out by your husband's liaisons.'

She flicked the ash again and then sashayed over to where Henry stood. 'Confidentially,' she said, leaning her head close to his so that his senses were invaded by a *mélange* of tobacco, rose and vermouth. 'Confidentially, I enjoy his efforts to make it up to me.'

'Your husband was just about to provide us with some information,' Henry told her. 'Once he's done that, you can have him back.'

She smiled. She had a nice smile, Henry thought, and wore a deep red lipstick that emphasized the voluptuous mouth. 'Perhaps you could join us?'

'Perhaps not,' Henry said coldly.

'No.' She took a step back. 'Perhaps not. A pity, though.' She glanced back at her husband before leaving. 'I'll give your excuses to our friends,' she said. 'I'm sure they'll understand. Join us when you're ready, Geoffrey.'

She drifted out, the beaded silk emphasizing the sway of her hips, the cloud of tobacco smoke and perfume following in her wake.

'And now' – Mickey settled himself in one of the button back leather chairs and laid his hat on the arm – 'perhaps you'd be so kind as to provide us with the list we asked for. Your wife may be wise to your goings on, Mr Clifton, but I doubt you'd want them broadcast further. We can still make that telephone call. I'm sure you wouldn't want to obstruct officers in pursuit of their duties.'

It took another hour for Geoffrey Clifton to consult his private diaries – kept in a locked drawer in his desk – and provide them with the list of dates and times and locations where he had spent an evening or even a full day with Cissie Rowe.

Significantly, there were no hotels. Henry queried that. 'You are expecting us to believe that she never spent a single night in your company?'

It was now time for Geoffrey Clifton to recover a little of his smugness. 'Perhaps she wasn't that sort of girl, Inspector. Have you thought about that? Just because she was a theatrical type, an actress, it doesn't mean that she was a common whore.'

'Or even an uncommon one,' Mickey muttered as they left. 'Just very good at stringing people along, perhaps.'

'Or simply surviving,' Henry said gently. He was thinking of Cynthia, refusing to give in to Albert's blandishments until she was safely married and her legal status assured.

The footman handed them their overcoats in the hall and also gave Henry an envelope. 'The mistress said you'd be wanting this,' he said.

Henry thanked him but waited until they were in the car before looking inside. He was uncomfortably aware that Lillian Clifton was watching them as they left, perfumed and silk clad and blowing uninhaled smoke from between her cherry lips.

'So, what have you got there?' Mickey enquired as he manoeuvred the little Ford out from between its larger and more illustrious cousins. Obviously further guests had arrived while they had been occupied in the study and a range of Bentleys and Royces and De Dions now crowded the driveway.

Henry laughed, both shocked and amused. 'She had him

followed,' he said. 'Mrs Clifton hired a private detective. She's given us his card and also a selection of pictures and other information, not all concerning Cissie Rowe.'

'Who would cheat on a woman like that?' Mickey wondered aloud and, almost against his will, Henry found himself wondering the selfsame thing.

# SEVENTEEN

I t had been decided that Mickey should return to London
and follow up on the pawnbroker's tickets that had been
found in Cissie's bungalow and the railway carriage that
had been Jimmy Cottee's home. He would also interview the
private detective that Lillian Clifton had employed to keep an
eye on her husband and visit the various locations that had
been listed by Geoffrey Clifton for his assignations with the
young woman.

Or young women, as it now seemed.

Henry was to continue with the investigation on the south
coast. He dropped Mickey at the train station, intending to go
back to see Sophie Mars, the little photographer, and find out
if she had included Geoffrey Clifton in any of her candid
images. He had also retained the list of jewellery that had
been found with the pawn tickets, oddly satisfied that one of
the items listed was a snake bangle. The list had been written
on a slip of blue paper that Henry was sure had been torn
from an air mail flimsy. It was thin and could be folded easily,
hidden well.

Geoffrey Clifton had claimed never to have visited the
studio, but Henry was curious as to whether or not that was
the truth. He also planned a further visit to see the Cliftons.
On their first visit the focus had been on getting Geoffrey
Clifton to speak about his connection to Cissie Rowe but Henry
was also curious about the cocaine that had been forced down
her throat on the day she had been killed. Were the Cliftons
users of the drug? Were any of their guests? Was this the
connection or must he look elsewhere?

Of everything he had seen and discovered, this was one
thing that puzzled Henry deeply. It seemed so odd, incongruous,
somehow even wasteful. Why use what was an expensive
substance in such a way? It was unlikely, they now knew from
the post-mortem, to have contributed to Cissie's death. Had

she ingested it earlier then the effects on her body would have been clear. Cocaine broke down the walls of red blood cells, destroyed their integrity and could indeed kill, but Cissie had been half way to that state when the powder had been forced into her throat.

It carried a weight of meaning that Henry did not yet understand but which he thought must be significant – must, in some way, speak of the state of mind of her killer. If he could comprehend something of that process, he felt, he might be brought closer to discovering the identity of the man.

Or woman. Could it have been a woman? Cissie had been struck on the back of the head, probably with sufficient force to cause loss of consciousness, if only briefly.

She was small and slight and a strong woman could have carried her as easily as a man. The pillow that had been pressed against her face, smothering the breath from her lungs, would have taken little force to keep in place. The victim would still have been almost helpless, perhaps just starting to regain her senses; it would have taken relatively little effort or strength.

So yes, a woman could have done it. Possibly.

That Cissie had not been fully unconscious was certain; she had swallowed some of the cocaine and the water that followed it, though evidence of sputum and cocaine on the pillow showed that she had choked and coughed some of it back up.

Had the killer waited for her to regain her senses enough for the act of swallowing to be possible before forcing the drug down her throat and then smothering her?

Henry pondered this as he drove away from the train station in Worthing – they had spent the Sunday night at Cynthia's home – and along the coast road towards Shoreham. The day was bright and clear though a little chill and in the glimpses Henry caught of it, as the road twisted and turned along, the sea sparkled in the morning light.

Henry had seen many terrible things in his life but evidence of asphyxia always disturbed him. It was, he knew, because he had experienced the fear and dread of this for himself. Twice in his life. Once in water, and once it had been mud and flesh and dead bodies pressing down upon his chest and legs, and the fear – no, it was beyond fear – that he would not have the strength to struggle free.

The dread lived with him of it happening again and, by extension, it resurfaced when he came across deaths where the breath had been crushed out of the victims or someone had deliberately and callously deprived them of life-giving air.

He would admit these thoughts only occasionally to himself, write them in his journals. Even more occasionally he would speak about them to Cynthia or to Mickey. Cynthia because she loved him and he loved her and because she knew him better than almost anyone. Mickey because his sergeant had been there and needed no explanation.

Henry had reached Shoreham. He found himself singing softly, humming the tune to 'West End Blues'. It was not, he owned, particularly hummable but he liked the way the twelve bar blues swung so lazily and drew the melody reluctantly along. Cynthia had been playing it on the gramophone when they returned the night before. She and Albert had actually seen the maestro Louis Armstrong in action when they had visited New York that summer, though Albert was less keen than Cynthia to show his enthusiasm in public.

On impulse, Henry drove past the police station and continued out of town on the coast road. He would pay an early visit to the Cliftons, he thought. Take advantage of their post party state and press them both again on Geoffrey's relationship with Cissie Rowe. He and Mickey had taken a good look at the the private detective's reports and photographs and Mickey was due to call upon the man later that day.

It seemed that Geoffrey Clifton was inordinately fond of theatrical ladies.

In this age of technology, of cameras and telegrams, fast cars and forensic science, privacy, Henry thought, was not so easy to maintain.

It was ten thirty on Monday morning when Henry arrived at the Clifton residence but it seemed that the birthday party had not completely ended. There were still a half dozen cars in the drive and the maid who opened the door to him – the footman not being in evidence – looked decidedly frazzled. Henry wondered if the servants had managed to get any sleep.

She left him idling in the hall and disappeared through a side door. Henry caught a glimpse of a dining table and a sideboard set with chafing dishes and coffee pots. A moment later the door opened again and the maid asked Henry to go through.

Lillian Clifton sat alone at the head of a long, highly polished table. Two of her guests were helping themselves to kidneys and scrambled eggs and Henry could smell bacon and kippers. They eyed Henry suspiciously and then sat down at the furthest end of the table and ignored him conspicuously.

'Would you like some coffee, Inspector? Perhaps some breakfast? Please help yourself.'

Henry took up the offer of coffee and then sat down, placing his cup on the linen placemat. 'I'd like to see your husband,' he said.

'Difficult. He went up to London first thing. I suppose you might go to his office. That's if it's urgent.'

She sipped her coffee and then added more sugar, picking up the small brown cubes with tongs shaped like silver chicken claws. 'I'm afraid I have something of a headache,' she said.

She no longer wore the ivory silk embellished with the heavy beading but was dressed instead in a robe of blue satin embroidered with hibiscus flowers. She wore pale pink pyjamas beneath and her two guests were similarly apparelled. Henry could not recall having interviewed any woman in her night-wear before but she seemed unconcerned.

'What time did your husband leave?'

She shrugged. 'I wouldn't know. He intended to depart around eight, so I assume that's what he did. I wasn't up to see him off and we don't share a room, so I really couldn't tell you.'

'The package you gave me. The photographs . . .'

She waved a careless hand. 'I'd rather not talk about it. I thought the information might be useful. Geoffrey wouldn't have laid a hand on that young woman – at least, not in anger. Why should he? And, for the record, neither did I. I know what kind of man he is; I find it useful to have proof of that.'

'Oh?'

'Security, Inspector. I find it useful to remind him, from time to time, that he treats me abominably.' She smiled, her expression at odds with the words.

'Do you care that your husband has . . . liaisons?'

'As I told you last night, it's really none of your business. I like it when he makes it up to me.' Henry frowned and she smiled at him. 'You think I'm shallow,' she said. 'A flibbertigibbet. And you are probably right.'

'What I think about you is unimportant,' Henry told her. 'I wished to take your husband's fingerprints, for the process of elimination. Prints were found at Miss Rowe's bungalow that we have not yet identified.'

'Oh, I doubt he'd have gone there,' Lillian told him. 'That would have been far too public. Too unlike his usual habits.'

'If you'd ask him to call in at the police station in Shoreham, that would be useful.'

She got up and poured herself more coffee. 'I'm not sure when he'll be home,' she said. 'But I'll give him your message. Was there anything else? Would you like my prints? For, what did you call it, elimination purposes?'

She sat down again, moving her seat a little closer to Henry's, and smiled mischievously. 'I've never had my fingerprints taken.'

She might have been dressed in her pyjamas and robe but, Henry noted, she had still found time to apply her makeup. The bright red lipstick was gone; the colour she wore now was softer peach and she had smudged just a little grey around her eyes and added a subtle line of kohl.

'Look, Inspector, I'm sorry about the young woman. I feel no malice towards her. She was just one in a long line of pretty little things; Geoffrey has a pash for them one minute and then can't even recall their names the next. He is careless of their feelings, perhaps, but he's never deliberately cruel and most know the score. They have realistic expectations.'

'And, if their expectations become less than realistic?'

Lillian rolled her very blue, very beautiful eyes. 'Then my

solicitor writes them a letter and they quietly revise them,' she
said. 'You should try it, Inspector, a solicitor's letter is a very
powerful tool. Cheap, when you think about it, and effective.
I have never felt the need to contemplate murder.'

She drank a little more of her coffee, eyeing him thoughtfully over the rim of her cup. 'I say!' It seemed that some
connection had just been made. 'You aren't Cynthia's brother,
are you? Cynthia Garrett-Smyth?'

Henry confessed that he was.

'Well, how funny. How awfully droll.'

'My sister is a friend of yours?'

'Not in particular, but it's inevitable that we meet at the
same parties, I suppose. And I do like her, awfully. Most people
do. She's a very likeable sort.'

'I am gratified to hear it. I have another question to ask.'
He glanced at the two guests who were making such a show
of ignoring him. He could practically see how they were
straining their ears as they tried to listen.

Lillian followed his gaze. 'Oh, don't worry about them,'
she said. 'What they might think is of no consequence.
Whatever they hear will fade along with their hangovers.'

'As you wish,' Henry said. 'I wanted to ask you about drug
use, Mrs Clifton. Most specifically about cocaine.'

She looked quizzical. 'And your question is? Do I use it?
Does my husband? Do my friends and guests?'

Friends and guests, Henry thought. That's an interesting
distinction. 'All or any of those questions,' he said.

'Oh, I see. Well, it's a definite no to the first, an occasional
yes to the second and, I would think, a positive yes to the
third. Some of them, at least. They seem to find it amusing.'

'And you do not?'

'No, not especially.' She smiled at him again. 'Frankly,
Inspector, I prefer to be an observer. Audience rather than actor.'

'And where do they obtain their supply?'

She shrugged. 'How would I know? I expect they get a
prescription, like all good little addicts.'

'And are they? Addicts.'

She laughed. 'I'm not the one to be asking,' she said. 'I observe

what is before me. I admire the *mise-en-scène*, you might say.
I don't usually engage the participants in conversation.'

Henry stood. 'I must go. Please give your husband my
message.'

'Oh, yes. I'll try to remember.' She laughed at his expression. 'Now, don't even think of scolding me. I won't forget,
I was merely fashing. I'll be sure to tell him.'

Henry left, wondering if he'd achieved anything after all.

*Two days before Cissie's death*

Philippe had agreed to meet her for afternoon tea. They had
parted on bad terms and Cissie desperately regretted that.
Philippe had been her friend and he was her cousin. They
should not be enemies.

He had arrived ahead of her and already ordered. She took
her seat across the little table from him and tried to smile
cheerily.

'It's good to see you. Thank you for coming. I know it can't
be easy.'

'Easy? No. But I am here. Can I ask why you wished me
here?'

The waitress brought a second cup and more hot water for
the teapot. The three-tiered stand with tiny sandwiches and
delicate iced cakes, carefully fashioned triangles of bread and
butter and the smallest muffins Cissie had ever seen had already
been brought out.

'We may as well eat some of this,' Philippe said, 'now it
is here. I hope I have ordered the right combination for an
English tea.'

He put odd emphasis on the word 'English' and Cissie
looked at him in puzzlement.

'I meant only that now you are so intent on becoming an
English rose—'

'Oh, Philippe, I thought you might have forgiven me.'

He shook his head. 'There is nothing to forgive. I hoped
that—'

'And I'm sorry. So, so sorry. I told you that.'

'Sorry that you no longer love me or sorry that I returned?'

Her face was a picture of consternation. 'Please, Philippe. Don't.'

He looked away from her and dumped three small cubes of sugar in his tea, then helped himself to some of the sandwiches. 'What do the English see in tiny sandwiches made with slivers of cucumber and no crust?'

'I don't know. They are dainty, I suppose.'

'Dainty and without flavour. Looks without substance. A little like yourself, Cissie.'

She tried to laugh. 'I am most certainly nothing like a cucumber sandwich.'

'And you are certainly nothing like the Cécile I used to know.'

'No, you're right. I was a child then. I am no longer a child and you are no longer the young cousin that I adored. We have both changed, utterly. Life makes you change, Philippe. One cannot simply stand still and wait.'

'Not even for the one who loves you?'

'The one I thought dead and buried? Philippe, it has been so long, it's a wonder I'm not married with children.'

'And if you had been I'd have left well alone. The fact that you were still unattached, still . . . Cécile, I thought that meant that you had waited.'

'Waited? For what? For a might be? For a promise made in haste and desperation when I was not yet even seventeen? Philippe, you are unreasonable. And anyway, if you were so keen to find me, why wait? You yourself admitted it had taken little effort. If you wanted me so much, why have you taken so long? It's been eleven years. Eleven whole years. If I had even dreamt you might still be alive then I'd have come looking for you as soon as the war ended and it was safe to travel.'

'I couldn't. Things prevented me.'

'What things? Why the secrecy? Did you marry? What prevented you?'

He looked away from her again and played moodily with the food on his plate.

Cissie claimed her own sandwiches and began to eat, waiting for him to say something. Anything. This was not the way she had envisaged things.

'After I left you the last time, I made some enquiries about you.'

'Enquiries? I'm not sure I understand.'

He shook his head. 'There are rumours about you, Cécile. About your behaviour, your morals, your—'

'My morals! You question my morals?'

'I'm telling you only that there is gossip. But there are other rumours that trouble me more.'

'What rumours?'

He hesitated, seemingly less sure of himself now. 'You go to London often.'

'Well, what of it?'

'You take regular trips to a certain broker, in Whitechapel.'

She frowned but kept her calm. 'And what if I do?'

'The rumour is that you are not going there on your own account. That you . . . transport certain items on behalf of others. Others who are—'

'And who told you these lies?'

'Cécile, I told you before, I've not always earned my own living in an entirely legal or honest way. Circumstances . . .'

'And so, how have you made your way? Do I ask or do I not wish to know?' Cissie sighed. 'Philippe, I think I should be going.'

'The rumour is that you take jewellery to the city and that you also do a little trade on your own account. Cécile, I have to warn you that there are people who suspect you are doing too much trade on your own account.'

'I don't know what you mean.'

'You play a dangerous game, Cécile. I could protect you. I could—'

'You could do nothing,' she said coldly. 'Philippe, I'm leaving now and I don't wish to see you again. You understand me?'

'It was you who asked me to meet you here.'

'And it was a truly terrible idea. A ghastly thought. I regret it completely.'

He watched her leave, she could feel his gaze fixed upon her even after the door had closed behind her. It seemed that his look of accusation could pierce the very walls, follow her down the street.

What did he know? Cissie wondered. What had he found out and who had told him? Suddenly, she was very much afraid.

# EIGHTEEN

Mickey Hitchens had joined the police force in 1910, six years after Henry Johnstone. He had nearly resigned within that first year; pay was poor and they were allowed almost no time off. Somehow, he had stuck it out and things had slowly improved, though it was still a tough life for a young constable and Mickey had set his mind on getting to the detective bureau. By 1913, a constable was being paid thirty shillings a week and was even allowed one day off – though actually getting that day off could prove problematic – and Mickey was already getting noticed.

He had begun his apprenticeship in Whitechapel, at the famous Leman Street police station, and walking the streets today Mickey's feet recalled the cobbles and the slippery unevenness of the alleys and the feel of the pitch pine blocks that had been laid as a temporary repair on the corner of Leman Street itself, but never replaced.

The Whitechapel ground took in some of the poorest districts of London, the population a mix of working-class British, Jewish, German and Armenian, among others, all trying to scrape a living alongside richer streets that over-spilled from the Square Mile. He had liaised often with the City Police.

Although he had started out in L division, he had returned, after the war, to J division. He had risen swiftly through the ranks to become a detective sergeant. In his more melancholy moments – rare but still profound – Mickey acknowledged that his rise had been largely uncontested, able officers being in the minority. Few who had been recruited to replace those who'd gone off to war – and the many who had not returned – had been up to snuff. He had heard that something like seventy per cent of those substitutes had been dismissed by the early 1920s, because they had brought their office into disrepute through drunkenness or simple inefficiency. Under the leadership of the so-called Big Four – Albert Hawkins, Arthur Neil, Francis Carlin and, of course, Fred Wensley – the force had been professionalized and the dead wood excised.

Mickey had risen no further than detective sergeant, though his promotion had been urged on a number of occasions by Mr Wensley himself. But Mickey was not a political animal and neither was he an ambitious one; he was content, by and large, and knew that his experience was valued way beyond his rank. He knew, particularly, how much he was valued by Henry Johnstone.

A warehouse building on Camperdown Street had been selected for surveillance of the pawnbrokers. A notice on the shop door informed the public that the shop was closed due to a family bereavement. Camperdown was a more respectable street, but was also quite out of the way. A perfect spot, Mickey thought, for a young woman seeking not to be noticed.

'The shop's been closed for over a week,' Mickey was told by one of the local constables who'd had the task of interviewing neighbours. 'And so far today, we've seen no one going in or out. A few punters have tried the door but that's been an end to it.'

'The owner, Ted Grieves, has history for receiving,' Mickey said.

'And the neighbours reckon they did a flit. There's a rumour that Grieves has been taking too big a cut for himself and upset someone.'

'Do we know who?'

'Names have been named Josiah Bailey among them.'

'Indeed.' Interesting, Mickey thought. Josiah Bailey was a man with a finger in a great many pies. Interesting that Ted Grieves had disappeared about the same time that Cissie Rowe had been killed.

'And where are we likely to find our Mr Bailey?' Mickey asked.

'We bring him in?'

'We get him pegged and keep tabs. No need to move too precipitately.'

And then, the message came. Philippe Boilieu had been

found and it was suggested that Mickey might wish to be present at the arrest. He had been spotted by a local constable and tracked down to his lodgings in Hanbury Street.

'Hanbury,' Mickey said. 'Up near the old brewery and Brick Lane market. If he legs it, we've got a network of little alleys to cover.'

'So we hope he doesn't scarper.'

Philippe had two rooms at the rear of a terraced house. Another resident lived in the front, upstairs. The landlord kept the rooms downstairs and they had use of the kitchen and a scullery out back that also served to house the tin bath. The privy was at the end of a narrow yard.

Mickey watched the operation, two constables sent round the back of the house and two to knock on the door at the front. The landlord had been intercepted on his way home from work and pulled into an entryway between two houses almost opposite his own. Mickey could hear him protesting that he'd done nothing and knew nothing about his tenant other than that he was a foreigner and that he paid his rent.

And that he didn't want the front door knocked down when the police went in.

'He'd best hand over the keys, then,' Mickey said cheerfully. He rubbed his hands in anticipation. This Philippe fellow intrigued him and he'd been promised a go at cracking him, once they got him back to Scotland Yard – this being part of an ongoing murder investigation, the local constabulary would hand over to the central office once Philippe had been brought in.

Mickey, feeling oddly restless now he was back close to his old patch and watching proceedings in which he would once have been a very willing participant, found himself almost wishing that Philippe would resist arrest.

A constable trotted across the road to hand the key over to his colleagues.

'Keep a low profile, why don't you?' Mickey grumbled.

'Our suspect should be in the back,' the sergeant standing at his shoulder told him.

'And how do we know he's not set up surveillance in the front? In cahoots with the other tenant.'

His oppo grinned at him.

The front door swung open. Mickey watched as the constables went inside.

# NINETEEN

Henry had returned to Shoreham and went to call on Sophie Mars. She was not helping out in the shop that day and was preparing to go out with her camera. Henry explained what he was looking for.

Sophie Mars screwed up her face and thought about it. 'A blue car,' she said. 'A man in a blue car . . . doesn't ring any bells, but we can take a look if you like.'

That, Henry thought, had been the general idea.

She fetched more of her shoe boxes and set them down on the parlour table – Henry, it seemed, was now an honoured guest, no longer confined to the kitchen.

Sophie chattered happily as the two of them worked their way through her photographs. Not knowing exactly what Henry was looking for, she fished out every image that depicted a car. Any kind of car.

For half an hour Henry looked at a number of cars, none of them connected with Geoffrey Clifton. And then, 'I've found him,' he said.

'Ooh, show me. Oh yes, I remember him – or at least I remember his car. A great long bonnet on it with a horse mascot. Yes, he came to the studio to collect Cissie just a few days before . . . you know.'

'Before she was murdered.'

'Yes, that.' Sophie looked suddenly troubled. 'Do you think he . . .?'

'Miss Mars, I'm just looking for a photograph. Nothing else. And I'm sure I don't have to remind you—'

'To keep quiet? No, you don't have to remind me of that.' She glanced at him uncomfortably. 'I won't say anything. I promise you that, but if, when this is all over, you could maybe mention my name? Say how helpful I've been? And I have been helpful, you said I have.'

'Miss Mars, may I borrow this? And if you should find anything similar, be sure to let me know.'

She nodded sullenly, disappointment evident.

'And you have been helpful,' Henry assured her. 'I'll see what I can do.'

Once back in his car he took another look at the image she had taken. Geoffrey Clifton had not been the focus of her attention. He was off in the background, sitting in his car, with Cissie Rowe in the passenger seat. Behind them was the glasshouse sound stage, which gave the lie to his statement that he had never been to the studio. But what had really caught Henry's attention was that Philippe was also there. Standing off to the side, an incidental figure caught up in a group shot, he was staring at Cissie and Geoffrey Clifton with a face like thunder.

Henry spoke to Mickey Hitchens, telephoning from the police station, and they exchanged news.

'He's not said a lot so far,' Mickey told his inspector. 'We had a quick word when he was first brought in. Told him that we had questions to ask regarding Miss Rowe's death and then dropped him off in a cell to think about it. I've a mind to fetch him up sometime this evening and see what he has to say and then leave him to stew for the night.'

'His lodgings have been searched?'

'And some items of interest found. Several films of specialist interest and a number of photographs. And cash to the sum of two hundred and forty pounds.'

'And has he said anything about Miss Rowe?'

'Only that he'd heard she was dead and was very sorry for it but that it was nothing to do with him.'

'And when did he last see her?'

'He claims it was two days before she died. Then he clammed up and we stowed him in his cell.'

'So what now?'

'I asked at Mr Clifton's office and a very nice young secretary confided that he might be at the New Empire.'

'On Leicester Square? I thought that had become a cinema.'

'No, you're right, it did. This is a new incarnation, just off Wardour Street.'

'One of the places he took Cissie Rowe, perhaps. Nothing new on the pawnbroker?'

'Ted Grieves is still notable by his absence. Josiah Bailey is being kept under surveillance. It's likely he'll be brought in tomorrow, but I'll not be holding my breath. He's a man well used to our interference and concerns for his welfare. I received the photograph, by the way.'

'Good.' Henry had sent a messenger with the photograph he had borrowed from Sophie Mars. 'I doubt there's any concrete connection between them but it will be interesting to see how each of them reacts. Clifton was adamant he never visited the studio.'

'So, what else might he be lying about?' Mickey said.

What indeed? Henry thought.

Geoffrey Clifton sat with a young blonde at a table for two in a discreet corner. It was, Mickey thought, a plush kind of place if a little overblown. The walls were red and inset with murals depicting scenes of devils dancing with bright young things and a jazz band played on a small stage at the far end of the long room. Couples danced and dined and while the dance floor itself was well lit the tables were in slight shadow. It was, Mickey thought, an ideal location to meet with someone who was not your wife.

The maître d' had been reluctant to let him through, but Mickey threatened – subtly – and had been allowed to proceed, though his lack of evening dress drew many curious glances and more than a little disdain.

Now he drew up a chair, sat down at Clifton's table and laid the photograph in front of the man. Only then did he wish him a good evening.

'What the hell do you think you're doing?' Clifton demanded. 'What's the meaning of this?'

'You took a little tracking down,' Mickey said. 'But I'd not finished asking questions. You told us that you'd never been to the Shoreham Film Studio and yet there you are, large as life and twice as . . . well, never mind. I suppose you'll tell

me that you never met this young man here.' He pointed at
Philippe Boilieu. 'As you know doubt know, he was a friend
of the late Miss Rowe.'

'As indeed I don't know.'

The young woman sitting across the table reached for the
picture and looked at it hard. 'And who's she?' she demanded.
'Sitting in your car.'

'No one you need be concerned about.'

'She was a young actress,' Mickey said. 'Sadly, the young
woman is dead. She was murdered, wasn't she, Mr Clifton?'

'Are you suggesting . . .? If you are, then you'll hear
from my solicitor. You can't go around accusing respectable
people—'

'I don't know that I am,' Mickey told him. 'Accusing respectable people, that is. You had a relationship with Miss Rowe.
You've already lied to us about not visiting her at the studio.
It is of interest to me and to my boss to know what else you
might have been untruthful about.'

The blonde had latched on to just one thing.

'Murdered!' she said. 'That's terrible.' She looked accus-
ingly at Geoffrey Clifton. 'I think I'd like to go home now, if
you don't mind.'

'My dear girl, I—'

'Are you a policeman?'

'I am indeed. Sergeant Hitchens, at your service.'

'And are you going to arrest him?'

'At the moment, no. At the moment I just need to ask him
some questions.'

'Well,' she said, 'you don't need me here for that, do you?'
She gathered up her clutch purse and her gloves and flounced
away.

Geoffrey Clifton had turned bright red again. Mickey moved
into the vacated seat and pointed at the photograph. 'So, you
went to the studio.'

'And what if I did?'

'Not so much *that* you did as *when* you did,' Mickey said.
'You told us – and indeed your wife believed – that you had
broken relations with Miss Rowe some time ago. The fact is,
this picture was taken in the past ten days or so. We know that

for certain. You lied to us and you fooled your wife. Interesting, Mr Clifton.'

Mickey was aware that one of the waiters was hovering. Geoffrey Clifton waved him away. 'Maybe I did visit the studio. I could simply have forgotten. But that could have been at any time.'

'No, Mr Clifton, it could not.' He tapped the photograph. 'This young man here, his name is Philippe Boilieu, and it seems he only returned to Miss Rowe's life a matter of days ago. Two weeks at most, perhaps. And he does not look at all pleased with you. Not pleased at all.'

Geoffrey Clifton glared at him. Mickey was making assumptions here – there had only been reports of Philippe Boilieu turning up in Shoreham in the past weeks, but for all he knew that could simply have been the first time anyone had noticed him. 'You knew that your wife had hired a detective?'

'I knew. He wasn't exactly subtle. You have that in common with him.'

'How long have you known?'

'This past year, I suppose. I challenged Lillian and she admitted she had hired him. I was irritated. I made it my business to approach the man and tell him that I knew what he was doing.'

'And his reaction?'

'He told me that he didn't care. He was being paid to monitor my movements and that's what he planned to do.'

'But, on this occasion at least, you gave him the slip.'

Geoffrey Clifton shook his head. 'He can't watch me all the time. He's a one-man band, so far as I know. I think he saw my wife as a cash cow. She was willing to pay him and he was willing to take her money. On that particular day I was evidently not under surveillance.'

'And how often did you drive Miss Rowe to London? Did you take her to Whitechapel?'

'And why would I do that? What would she want there?'

'A pawnbroker's, perhaps?'

Emotions chased across Geoffrey Clifton's face but Mickey could not read them. The man was disturbed, but was that because of what Mickey said or because he was genuinely confused? 'Anything you'd like to tell me, Mr Clifton?'

'Nothing to tell. So, I kept in contact with Cissie Rowe for longer than I liked my wife to know about. I'm a man, Sergeant. Men are often easily bored. I am genuinely fond of my wife, but I also need variety, if you understand my meaning. Now, as you have completely ruined my evening, I'd ask that you leave.'

Mickey retrieved his photograph and slowly got to his feet. 'Have a think, Mr Clifton. Did Miss Rowe ever talk about this man, Philippe Boilieu? Did you speak to him?'

'Sergeant, until you showed me that photograph, I didn't even know the man existed,' Geoffrey Clifton said.

Henry had wandered back down to the crime scene to speak with the constables on duty. Their colleagues on the footbridge and positioned on the main road had kept Bungalow Town largely clear of the press and the police officers on watch outside Cissie's bungalow had endured a boring if peaceful day.

Henry wandered on. This was a curious place, he thought. A small community, strangely isolated and somewhat insular, despite being only a half mile from the town centre, just across the river.

Conversing with the residents, he heard about the tennis club and Arthur's, a club on Ferry Road where residents met to drink and chat and sometimes to dance. Regular 'shilling hops' were held at the church hall and there was even a school, just for the smallest children, presided over by Mrs Baker, who lived at La Marguerite. This short and narrow slither of land was an extraordinary spot. A village, Henry thought, filled, it was true, with performers and those involved in the technical craft of film, but linked also to the wider community. He had been talking to the Maples and the Lakers and the Pages, who fished the Adur and the coastal waters with seine nets, rowing out in groups of two or four rowing boats. The tradesmen too, like the Patchings, who sold paraffin and candles and cleaning materials from their cart, and of course the Bungalow Stores which provided for daily needs.

Even actors needed their tea and their milk and their potatoes and candles.

His walk had brought him to Jimmy Cottee's little home. It was getting dark now and most of the bungalows glowed as lamplight shone out through uncurtained windows or was filtered through muslin and chintz drapes. Jimmy Cottee's home was distressingly dark. Automatically, Henry checked the padlock and was satisfied that it had not been tampered with.

A small movement caused him to turn. Henry frowned; he was certain that he'd seen something stir between the bungalows.

'Who's there?' he called out. It was probably nothing, probably just someone out for an evening stroll, but he felt suddenly uneasy. If so, why didn't they respond?

Henry turned again, instinctively knowing that he was not alone, but he was too late. The blow fell and so did Henry, hitting the shingle hard.

# TWENTY

Mickey waited until he thought Philippe might have settled for the night and then had him brought up from the cells. He was satisfied to see that the younger man looked tired and confused.

'So, tell me about your relationship with Cissie Rowe,' Mickey said.

'What is there to tell? We had no relationship. Cécile made it clear that she had done with me. That I no longer mattered to her.'

'And how did that make you feel?'

'How do you think? I was angry, confused. Upset. She had told me that we would always be there for one another. That we would find each other after the war and we would be together.'

'So you knew her before she came to England?'

Philippe sighed. 'We grew up together. Cécile was my cousin. I hoped she would one day be my wife.'

'Are cousins allowed to marry?'

'Second cousin, then. Though she called my parents her aunt and uncle. We were related. We were also in love.'

'And you parted when?'

'In 1917, when she was almost seventeen and I was almost twenty-one. Her parents sent her away, hoping to follow, but they were killed. Cécile survived. I came and found her.'

'What took you so long?' Mickey said bluntly. 'I understand you have a record. You've broken the law both here and in your homeland. Were you in prison, lad? Is that why you failed to turn up until now?'

Philippe nodded. 'In part. In part it was because I wanted to come to her and tell her that I had been successful. That I could provide for her in a proper way.'

'And what stopped you? Were you ashamed in case she found out about your record?'

'No, not that.'

'So did you tell her?'

He shrugged slightly. 'Not all, no.'

'And why was that? I put it to you, my boy, that you spotted your one time paramour, saw her pictures in the papers and figured you were on to a good thing. Oh, maybe she wasn't famous yet, but tipped for the top, wasn't she? One of the few that could transfer easily from the silent cinema to the talkies, isn't that the way of it? You thought the time was right to . . . shall we say, re-engage.'

'I didn't think that way. It wasn't like that.'

'No? Then what way was it?'

'I loved her. I thought she might still love me.'

'And so you turned up unannounced. And was she happy about that?'

'I believed so. At first.'

'And after that?'

Philippe turned moist blue eyes on Mickey. The young man was pale and his face showed the strain of weariness and, Mickey thought, grief. 'I did not touch her, did not harm her. She told me to go and so I did. She told me not to interfere in her life and so I left. There is nothing else to say.'

Mickey changed tack. 'Your rooms were searched. Films were found. Will we find Cissie Rowe on any of them?'

Philippe stiffened but said nothing.

'Of course, someone like Miss Rowe starring in one of your two reelers would be a real coup, I suppose. I can imagine that would be something to feed your profits. Did you ask her and she refuse? Is that why you quarrelled? Is that why you killed her?'

'I didn't kill her. I could never do that. Never!' Philippe slammed his hands down hard upon the wooden table. Mickey didn't flinch.

'No use doing that, my lad. Losing your rag with me will get you nowhere. Truth might do better.'

Philippe said nothing.

'What did you argue about? Was it because she rejected you? Because she no longer loved you? Or was it because she despised what you'd become, eh, boy?'

'What I'd become?' he laughed uneasily.

Mickey, sensing that he was on to something, regarded the young man more closely. Philippe was handsome, he supposed, but in a rather coarse way, as though age had already added fleshiness that in five or ten years' time would run to flab. His eyes were very blue and his hair, previously brushed back from a central parting but now falling untidily across his forehead, was thick and dark, though now Mickey looked more closely it looked as though it might have had a little assistance to remain that way.

'And what had she become?' Mickey asked. It was a shot in the dark but he saw the change in expression and realized that he might actually have scored a point. 'Did you disapprove of her profession? Ironic, considering where most of your earnings come from. No, that's not it, is it? It's something more.' He leaned across the table and stared hard. 'Look me in the face, lad, and tell me she wasn't selling herself.'

Philippe was on his feet. He launched himself across the table and grabbed at Sergeant Hitchens, then found himself lying on his back a moment later with Mickey's fist curled tight around his own.

'Now, now, my boy. We don't have that here.' Mickey squeezed gently and twisted the wrist until Philippe squealed in pain.

The door to the interview room opened and a constable poked his head around. He eyed Philippe with professional interest and then looked at Mickey.

'I need a word, Sergeant. Urgently. It's about Inspector Johnstone.'

Moments later Mickey was racing out of Scotland Yard to where a car waited to take him to Shoreham. Henry had been found unconscious on the beach, blood pouring from a head wound. A search for the assailant was now on but no one knew how long Henry had been out cold. His attacker could be long gone.

# TWENTY-ONE

By dawn, Cynthia had taken charge. Henry had been installed in his usual room and a nurse had been hired and was in residence. Mickey didn't quite know how she'd managed that but supposed that it was one of the advantages of money. Just then he was very glad that someone had that advantage and that Henry appeared to be doing well.

The blow had been hard. He'd required stitches and the doctor had been concerned about swelling on the brain. But Henry had shown signs of regaining consciousness just after midnight and of recognizing his surroundings a little after that.

Mickey now sat on one side of the bed, the nurse on the other, both watching the man with his head swathed in what Mickey thought must be too much bandage.

Henry slept, but it was a more natural sleep now and Cynthia was satisfied enough to have gone off to bathe and change before the children woke.

'What the blazes was he doing there?' Mickey had demanded. The constables on duty outside Cissie's bungalow had become concerned that the inspector had not returned. One had gone to investigate and the other had soon been summoned by three urgent blasts on the whistle.

That had been a little after ten p.m. and Henry had spoken to them just before nine.

He had been carried to the nearest bungalow and a doctor summoned. Word had been carried to the police station and they had contacted Scotland Yard. Mickey's interrogation had been interrupted by the news.

He had then left instructions for Cynthia to be informed, and had chafed and fretted all the way to Shoreham, arriving to find that Cynthia, as usual, had everything under control.

No one knew exactly why Henry had chosen to walk down to Jimmy Cottee's railway carriage but Mickey, used to Henry's habits, guessed that he had something on his mind and simply walking the ground helped to focus his thoughts.

What was certain was that after Henry had been knocked unconscious, the lock on the carriage door had been cut through. When the constables arrived, the door had been open wide.

Mickey's head nodded and his eyes closed. He jerked himself upright in the chair and glared at the nurse as though his fatigue was her fault. Now that he knew Henry would be all right, he was finding it hard to fight sleep.

The bedroom door opened and Cynthia, scrubbed and changed, came in with a tray of tea and crumpets. She set them down beside the nurse.

'Cook and the kitchen staff aren't properly up yet. I'll get them to bring up a proper breakfast later, but this should hold you for a while.'

She came round to Mickey's side of the bed and laid a hand on his shoulder. 'Go and get some sleep,' she said. 'He'll need to talk when he wakes up and no one but you will do, you know that.'

Mickey nodded gratefully and took himself off to his usual room. Cynthia settled in his chair and took Henry's hand.

Constable Prentice had been examining the list that had been found in Cissie Rowe's bungalow and comparing the brief descriptions of the jewellery to local lists of stolen property. He'd had something of a breakthrough.

Seven of the ten items on the list tallied with items known to have been stolen in local burglaries though what they had taken to be initial letters set beside them didn't tally with anything Prentice could so far discern.

Prentice was excited by his discovery and when Mickey awoke, after a few hours' sleep, it was to a telegram giving him the news.

He checked on Henry and then telephoned Shoreham to congratulate the young constable.

'There has been a series of burglaries, sir,' Prentice told

Mickey. 'I've arranged for a messenger to bring the details to you in Worthing so you can look them over. But seven items, sir. That means something, doesn't it?'

Mickey agreed that it did indeed.

'And in every case the occupants were at home. One of them was hit over the head with a blackjack, sir. We know that because the assailant must have dropped it. We found it at the scene.'

'That's interesting, lad,' Mickey said. 'I look forward to reading the case notes.'

Prentice asked about Inspector Johnstone and was told that he was recovering.

'We've got every available man down on the beach,' he assured Mickey. 'We'll find who did this, I promise you.'

That's usually my line, Mickey thought. It seemed odd for this mere boy to be reassuring him in this way. Odd, and more than a little discomforting.

Mickey had just finished his call when another telegram arrived, informing him that there had been an early morning raid on the pawnbroker's shop.

Mickey was left with the feeling that things were at last beginning to move.

Cynthia appeared at the top of the stairs. 'He's fully awake,' she said. 'And grumpy and asking where you are.'

'I didn't realize he even knew I was here.'

Cynthia laughed. 'Of course he knew. Are you hungry? I'll bring you a tray. I don't know about you, but anxiety makes me absolutely ravenous.'

Henry was propped up against a bank of pillows. His face was almost as pale as the bandage around his head but his eyes were alert and his expression irritable. The blond curls, above the bandage, were tangled and matted with blood. Mickey caught his breath. To have survived all they had during the war and now to be attacked on a beach here in England seemed ridiculous. Both he and Henry had been wounded in the line of duty – both police duty and in France – but that made this attack no easier to take.

'So, what's going on that I should know about?' Henry Johnstone said.

\*    \*    \*

After lunch the reports arrived from Shoreham and Henry insisted on working through them with Mickey. Despite his insistence that he was fine, he kept drifting off to sleep. Mickey sat at the bedside reading through the files and bringing his boss up to speed each time he woke.

There had been seven burglaries in as many months. Each had taken place between two and four a.m. and the locations had all been fairly remote, outside the closest village by several miles. In one case the dogs had been poisoned and in another a manservant who had been woken by a slight noise had been hit over the head and severely concussed. That was the case in which the blackjack had been left behind.

'And what was taken?' Henry wanted to know. 'Mainly jewellery?'

'No, the jewellery seems to have been an afterthought. In each case the main target was the safe. Money and bonds were taken in four of the robberies, cash and sovereigns in the others. It's been theorized that the houses were targeted when the occupants were home both because there was more likely to be cash on the premises at that time and because, had the criminal failed to crack the safe, there would be someone in residence who could be threatened or coerced into opening it for them If that is indeed the case, then it must have been seen as a last resort.'

'It sounds like a viable theory.' Henry nodded. 'It also speaks of confidence and experience and of a more than competent cracksman, if they had no need of their fallback.'

'Which narrows our field. And definitely brings Josiah Bailey and his associates into the frame.'

'Josiah Bailey?' This was new to Henry.

'The pawnbroker that Cissie seems to have used has done a flit. Word is that he's in trouble with Bailey for taking too much off the top.'

'Then he'd better hope we find him first. Bailey is a brute of a man. Grieves is a fool if he thought he could get away with cheating him.'

'And he's known for planning meticulously and for employing the best when it comes to safe cracking. And for never being present when a job goes down. Keeps his distance, does Bailey.'

'And the jewellery on the list. How does that fit in?'

'Well, in every case it was out in full view. A piece taken off and dropped into a pin tray. A bracelet left on a dressing table. A brooch pinned to a coat hanging on a hall stand. Small, opportunistic thefts.'

'Always jewellery?'

'No, there's the odd pill box or table lighter or cigarette case, all small and portable and readily fenceable items.'

'And what we thought were initials on the list?'

'Nothing that I can make a connection to. They are most certainly not the names of the householders nor the names of the houses, nor even the villages closest to the scene.'

'So we need to think again. Cissie Rowe wrote that list, hid that list, considered it important. She listed items of jewellery. She added those initials or whatever they are. And, if we are right, someone went to great lengths to try and find it.'

'She wasn't tortured, not like Jimmy Cottee,' Mickey objected. 'She was murdered, but there's no evidence that anyone tried to elicit information from her. Again, not like Jimmy Cottee.'

'No.' Henry lay back against the pillows and closed his eyes. 'No, you're right, Mickey. No one did that. Perhaps no one knew that she had kept the list.'

'Why did she? How was she involved? If the assumption is true that she had possession of this jewellery, that she used the pawnbroker, Ted Grieves, to fence it, then who handed it over to her? And why? How did she make that connection?'

'And did they know she wore it first? That was a risky strategy on her part, on two counts. Someone might have recognized the piece or the individual who handed it over, trusted her as his courier, might have feared exposure. It seems to me that she played a dangerous game.'

Mickey nodded. 'A thought strikes me,' he said. He told Henry about his interrogation of Philippe Boilieu. 'I probed and prodded about what Cissie Rowe might have become, in his eyes, and came close to getting thumped for my trouble.

What if he knew about this? What if he knew that she had these, for want of a better way of phrasing it, underworld contacts? What if he knew who they were?'

'We should ask him,' Henry said.

'I should ask him. Now I know you're not at death's door, I'll take myself back up to London and put the question. You'll be staying here.'

Henry grimaced. 'I keep returning to the first thoughts we had,' he said. 'When we first viewed the body of Miss Rowe we concluded that this was a local crime. That the perpetrator had the opportunity to watch her and assess her habits. To see that she was alone, take the opportunity. But the person was also afraid that any blood on their clothing would be seen and have to be explained.'

'And you believe the same of whoever struck you down? I don't see how it can be otherwise. If they left the scene, they would have passed the constables on the footbridge or on the road.'

'They could have kept close to the river, passed under the bridge.'

'That is also true. And also speaks of local knowledge. To get away from the scene, free and clear, they must know the coastline intimately. Unless, of course, they never left Bungalow Town.'

'Unless they simply went home.'

'And if they did, then we are reliant on a wife, a mother, a brother telling us that they were absent.'

'Mickey, what do we know about the Owenses?'

'Very little. What are you thinking?'

'That we should check more deeply into their background, and the same for any others living on the beach that Cissie counted as particular friends.'

'And why did she keep those two pawn tickets? How did this scheme work? She took the item to Grieves, he gave her a ticket, just for the show of things – or perhaps she had to hand this on as proof that she had completed her task. Was she given money in exchange for the item or was she expected to give the item over for it to be sold on later?'

'Who received the money?' Henry wondered.

'And did whoever organized the gang know that someone took a little extra on the side? These items were small and random. It's a reasonable bet that such houses as they targeted were filled with such small, transportable items and yet few were taken.'

'Cash and bonds need no special arrangements for disposal. There need be no fence, no middle man, no loss of profit when the goods are traded.'

'Someone took these items on their own account,' Mickey decided. 'Small items, passed to Miss Rowe, taken to the pawn-broker's when she had the chance or reason to visit London.'

'Opportunity often provided by Mr Clifton.'

'She received the money, perhaps, or at least the ticket. It might be that some kind of notification was sent once Grieves had made the disposal and had the cash in hand.'

Henry nodded. 'And someone now wants the remaining tickets. They guessed she might have hidden them in her bungalow or in Jimmy Cottee's railway carriage.'

'But we've now chased this full circle, Henry. Miss Rowe was murdered but there seems to have been no attempt to torture, to coerce, to obtain information of any kind. Whereas Jimmy Cottee received a very different treatment before he died. That, my friend, does not add up.'

'Different reasons for their deaths? Is that possible? Of course it is, but what?'

Henry closed his eyes and it was obvious to Mickey that he needed rest.

'I'll get the next train back,' he said. 'And don't worry, you'll be kept informed. Now rest that brain of yours and allow yourself to be cared for, today at least. And if you must puzzle over something, think what those initials might mean, if they mean anything at all.'

When Mickey had left, Henry tried to sleep but his mind was too active and sleep would not come. The nurse, returning to check on him, offered a sleeping draft but Henry declined. He wanted his journal and eventually she found it for him. Cynthia looked in to see if he wanted to eat and Henry agreed to tea and a sandwich just to please her. He felt nauseous but didn't want to tell her that and when he tried to read the words swam and then fluttered before his eyes.

He managed to drink his tea and ate a little of his sandwich and then eventually he slept for a time. His dreams were of running, of chasing a man from light to shadow and then to light again and eventually into the sea. Henry felt the sea rising, to his ankles, then his knees and then his chest. He woke with a start and, to his shame, a small cry. He lay still for a moment until the panic and the sickness passed and then he struggled to swing his legs over the side of the bed and stand up.

Unsteadily he made his way to the bathroom, grateful beyond words that in his sister's house guests had their own en suite. He splashed cold water on his face and gazed at his reflection in the mirror. He'd fallen hard, his face was bruised and swollen and he had a shiner of a black eye.

Who had hit him? Had they intended to kill or just to disable? Mickey had told him that the lock had been cut on Jimmy Cottee's door. Did they know what to look for, once they'd got inside? Did they now know that it was gone?

He returned to his bed and found that he was finally hungry. He managed to eat the rest of his sandwich and drank some water from the carafe on the bedside table. Then he took up his journal once again. Henry wrote,

> *What do I recall about Josiah Bailey?*
>
> *I first encountered the man a dozen years ago when he was brought in for suspected arson and manslaughter. It took four officers to drag him through the doors and three burly constables to get him into his cell and the man, I recall, was grinning to himself the whole damned time.*
>
> *He swore he'd be out by teatime and, of course, he was. Three people came forward to provide him with an alibi and I've no doubt he'd have had a dozen more lined up if the first three failed.*
>
> *Even when we've got a conviction he's continued as though the cell door never closed and the walls were*

*paper. If he's at the back of this then we'll need to go
a roundabout way to bring him down. Take a direct
route and Bailey blocks your way faster than you can
plan it.*

# TWENTY-TWO

The police raid on the pawnbroker's shop had attracted a great deal of local attention and also interest from the press. By the time Mickey arrived, having been driven straight there from the station, it was mid-afternoon and the press corps was still very much in evidence.

There was even a newsreel camera and Mickey was reminded of what Fred Owens had told him about cameramen being routinely sent out almost on a roaming brief, to record anything of potential use. He wondered if the newsreel employees were given the same instructions.

This area close to Brick Lane market was poor – one of the few things the people there had in common, Mickey thought. The ethnic mix was Jewish, Russian and increasingly French and Belgian refugees who had never quite made it home. Mickey listened to the languages and the accents and the whispered gossip as he worked his way through the crowd. He had asked his driver to drop him off at the end of the street, seeking not to attract attention to himself. Sergeant Mickey Hitchens was a well-known figure.

He thought about Philippe Boilieu, pornographer and some-time blackmailer. He wondered if he was also a pander. During the war and in the years following there had been a dramatic influx of French and Belgian girls, many of them fleeing the fighting, traumatized and alone, coerced into service in the sex trade. Their numbers had fallen in recent years but were still of concern to the police. War makes victims of us all one way or another, Mickey thought.

He caught the eye of one of the constables manning the barricade around the pawn shop and held up his warrant card. The constable waved him through and Mickey headed into the shop, aware that his arrival had sparked interest among those who recognized him. Mickey Hitchens of the murder squad, showing up at a raid on a pawnbroker's.

Camera shutters clicked almost in unison.

'So what have we got?' Mickey asked Sergeant Finlayson, a man he'd known almost since the start of his career.

'Sweet Fanny Adams. Place has been cleared out. No stock, no paperwork. Though it looks as though the family left in a hurry. Upstairs looks like the Mary Celeste.'

'So Grieves focused on getting his business away.' Mickey glanced around. He nodded in friendly fashion at the fingerprint officer working his way along the counter and then looked more closely at the absence of prints. 'It's been wiped down,' Mickey said, astonished.

'Not just the counter, most of the shop.'

'Now, there's a thing. By Grieves or by someone that came after, I wonder?' He turned to Finlayson. 'All right to go upstairs?'

Finlayson nodded that it was and Mickey took himself off to poke around.

Outside the shop, door-to-door enquiries were under way and photographs of Cissie Rowe and Philippe Boilieu shown around. So far those of Philippe had drawn a blank but several people recalled Cissie. Well dressed compared to most of the local population and seemingly out of place, she had attracted notice.

And so had a blue car. Once it had dropped her off and left and a second time it had waited for her to return, much to the delight of the local children – and the annoyance of the driver.

Mickey, having asked that any such information should be immediately relayed to him, was interrupted in his reverie by a very eager young constable.

'I asked if the driver was a chauffeur,' he added. 'The lady said not. Said the kids were tormenting him and he got out of the car to chase them off. He was dressed like a gent, not a driver.'

Mickey felt in his pocket for the photograph of Geoffrey Clifton and followed the constable back to his informant, aware that the press corps turned eagerly in his direction as the constable led him down the street.

Mickey heard his name being called.

'Sergeant Hitchens! There been a murder, then?'

'Sergeant Hitchens! What brings you down here, then?'

Mickey waved vaguely but did not respond.

'This is the lady, sir,' the constable told him.

Mickey nodded. The informant was a young woman with a baby on her hip and another clinging to her leg. Mickey smiled at her in what he hoped was an encouraging manner. 'I understand you've seen the young lady in my picture,' he said, 'and also seen her in a blue car.'

She nodded, warily. 'I told the constable,' she said. She was clearly aware of the scrutiny of her neighbours and discomforted by it. 'She weren't from round here. If she'd been local, I'd have said nothin',' she asserted, far more loudly than a reply intended purely for Mickey's benefit.

'I'm sure you'd not grass on your neighbours, my dear,' Mickey told her. 'But this was a stranger, yes?'

There was momentary confusion in the woman's eyes. 'She came here, time to time, to the pawn shop. She's not the only toff that did. Some of them, they'd turn up in a cab, have it wait outside while they kept their heads down and shuffled in. Like they was better than the rest of us. They still got themselves into trouble and had to pawn summat, didn't they?'

'And this lady?'

'She weren't like that. That's why I noticed her at first, I suppose. She just walked up the street with her head high like she didn't care. In she went, did her business, out she came again.'

'And how many times did she arrive in the car?'

'Twice that I know about. Big car with a horse on the front. One time he just left her, the second time he waited and they drove off together.'

'And that was the time the driver got out and chased the boys off?'

'They were putting their grubby little mitts all over his paintwork and he lost his rag with them. Got out and shouted. I thought he'd be chasing them down the street but she came back out the shop and they took off.'

Mickey fished the photograph of Geoffrey Clifton out of his pocket and showed it to her. She peered at it and then nodded. 'That's the car – and that' – she prodded at the photograph – 'that's who were driving it.'

Mickey thanked her.

'I know who she is,' she said proudly. 'The young lady. I recognized her straight off. She's that Cissie Rowe, isn't she? Lovely, she is.'

Mickey smiled but made no further comment.

He could guess the pattern of things to come. The press would ask what questions Mickey had put and she would tell them, in detail. The connection between the raid on the pawnbroker's and Cissie Rowe would be made and the press, once they had sunk their teeth into the facts, would feel free to chew them over and spit out whatever gobs of narrative they deemed would sell the most papers.

Mickey sighed and then turned back towards the pawnbroker's. He was starting to think like Henry, as he had previously reminded his boss. They and their colleagues fed the beast when it suited them and hunted it down when it ceased to be complimentary. Such was the nature of things.

He wondered how his informant would feel when someone told her that Cissie Rowe was dead; it was evident from her comments that she had no idea.

Upstairs in the pawnbroker's shop, Mickey resumed his inspection. Clothes still hung in wardrobes, children's toys sat on shelves. There was some indication – empty spaces on rails and in drawers – that they had packed a few of their possessions but this was utterly different from the way that the shop had been so thoroughly cleared.

'How many lived here?'

'Ted Grieves, his wife, three children. And the mother-in-law used to stay at times. She slept in the kiddies' room.'

Two bedrooms, a living room cum kitchen. Toilet in the yard and a pot beneath the bed in case it was needed in the night – one that had not been emptied when the family had left.

It stank, Mickey thought, but the rest of the flat was relatively clean.

So, he thought, perhaps the family was sent away ahead of the shop being cleared, told by the father to pack for just a few days, so as not to arouse suspicion. They left in something of a hurry, Mickey guessed – and from the state of the pot probably at night or early in the morning.

'Did Grieves have any employees?'

'A boy who helped out with this and that. The wife, and sometimes the mother-in-law, helped to look after the shop.'

'And the boy is . . .?'

'At his mother's place in Edmonton. Seems he was sent on an errand that took him across town. He got back after midnight that same day to find that his boss had gone. He tells us that when he woke that morning the missus and kids had already left.'

'Woke? He slept on the premises?'

'Mattress behind the counter. Mrs Grieves fed him but he didn't eat with the family, and he slept in the shop.'

Mickey nodded. 'So the family left in the night while the boy slept. He was then sent off on a fool's errand and Grieves cleared the shop. Did no one notice this? I doubt he could have done this alone.'

'We have reports of a van pulled up to the yard gates, but no one took much notice. The boy left at eleven in the morning; the van was spotted late afternoon. The shop had been closed all day and a note put on the door about a family bereavement. Grieves had it put about that there'd been a death in the wife's family.'

'To provide an excuse for them going away.' Mickey nodded. 'That figures. So the family left, the boy was sent away, Grieves and at least one other – someone had to be driving the van – packed the place up and scarpered. Likely they brought the van round at the last minute so as not to draw attention. I'd bet a day's pay that we'll find it was parked up close by all day somewhere handy. Another van parked up by the market would have been ignored.'

Finlayson jerked his head in agreement. 'Question is where they went, and why. The why we can guess. Local rumour has it that he'd upset Bailey one time too often.'

'And does local rumour give a particular reason?'

'Consensus is that it was the usual reason. Grieves was skimming a bit too much off the top.'

'So, how much use did Bailey make of Grieves? Do you have a nose for that?'

'My nose is telling me that Bailey used the business to

regularize stolen goods. Grieves issues a pawn ticket for an item, the item disappears into the shop. A buyer is found, redeems the ticket, Grieves takes his cut. The amount changing hands on redemption bears no resemblance to the figure written on the ticket as having been advanced.'

'My nose tells me that yours is probably right,' Mickey said. On the tickets he had seen, the price advanced for a gold brooch and a locket with chain had seemed laughably slight. He frowned. 'Though from what we've seen our end the items Miss Rowe brought up here were trinkets. Certainly not worth the time of someone like Bailey.'

'So maybe Bailey didn't know abut these little transactions. What's not worthwhile for the likes of Bailey might represent a nice little earner for someone lower down in the pecking order.'

That chimed with Mickey's thinking and with what he'd discussed with Henry earlier and it was good to hear the same views coming from another mouth.

Which left the same question, Mickey thought. Was Bailey aware of these side deals, these little transactions, or was he kept in ignorance of them?

If that last were true, Mickey thought, then he didn't give much for the chances of the individual who'd gone behind his back. The monetary amounts might have been small but Bailey was not a man who felt he should be missing out. If all you had was a sixpence, Bailey would feel himself entitled to tuppence of it.

As he came back on to the street he noted the press men now gathered around the young woman's door. He glanced at his watch, reflecting that they would be getting close to the six o'clock deadline when the day's copy must be filed.

Let's see what they make of all this, he thought.

# TWENTY-THREE

It was almost twenty-four hours since Mickey had broken off his interrogation of Philippe Boilieu. He had, Mickey was told, been interrogated twice more but was refusing to speak to anyone but Sergeant Hitchens.

Mickey had spoken to Henry and detailed the day's events, warning him that the morning papers might be about to launch their Shoreham murder into the stratosphere. Henry had sounded better and Mickey was reassured that his boss would soon be on his feet.

He had Philippe brought up from his cell and into the interview room they had used before. Philippe looked wearier and more haggard, the hair now sweaty and matted and hanging loose around his face.

'I'm told you're ready to talk,' Mickey said. 'So sit yourself down and let's be having it. I've had a long day and my patience is wearing a little thin, if you get my meaning.'

Philippe sat. 'I have no wish to go back to prison,' he said.

'Well, I'm sorry, my lad, but that's exactly where you'll be going. The items we found in your rooms will make certain of that. I'm guessing you don't want a murder charge added to what's already lined up so, if I was you, I'd open my mouth and let the words come out.'

'I didn't kill her,' Philippe said tightly. 'I would never have hurt her. Never.'

'Even though she rejected you.'

'I would never have hurt her.'

'So, tell me. What went on between the two of you? You said you argued. What was that about, then?'

Philippe leaned back in the uncomfortable wooden chair and rubbed at his eyes. 'I followed her back to her bungalow. This was two days before she died and she had left me alone, in the café. She was angry and I thought . . . I thought that even if she no longer wanted me we should not part on such bad terms. Our families were gone. We were all that was left. So I followed her.'

'Back up a bit, my lad. You were angry with her because of what she had become, you said before. What exactly did you mean by that? What had she been telling you?'

The younger man shook his head. 'She confessed to me that sometimes she earned a little money by transporting certain items up to town. I think . . . I think she told me this because I admitted to her that I had not always earned my money honestly. That sometimes, to survive, I had stolen, I had deceived. I had made those films. Though I confess, in the end I did not tell her about the films.'

'No? But you were going to, weren't you? Going to suggest to her that it was a way of earning good money, despite the fact that it would have ruined her in the end.'

'And in the end I couldn't do it. I looked at Cécile and I remembered. We had grown up together, loved one another. Promised—' He broke off, and gestured that this was not something he wished to talk about.

Mickey had no intention of letting him off the hook. 'But the intent was there, wasn't it, boy? You'd have sold her in a heartbeat, this one time love of yours. You looked at Cissie Rowe and you could see the money rolling in.'

'It wasn't like that.'

'No? Well, we'll let that pass for a while. So she told you she'd been transporting small items up to London. On whose behalf? Did she tell you that?'

Philippe shook his head. 'She told me nothing. Only that one thing.'

'And did she tell you what she was taking?'

'Jewellery, she said. She took it to a pawn shop and got a ticket and a little cash. She waited until a message came and then she would take the ticket to the post and send it to the address she had been given.'

'And the address. Did she tell you what it was?'

'No. I did not ask. I was appalled. I did not expect that Cécile would become involved in such matters. For me, it was a matter of no choice, but for Cécile . . .'

'Choices are something I suspect many women are short

on,' Mickey said heavily. 'And you're telling me you'd put this one on some sort of pedestal. You tell me that, and yet you wanted her for your so-called speciality films. For your pornography.'

'I don't make pornography.'

'No? Tell that to the judge. And was that all she told you?'

Philippe shrugged and Mickey knew there was more but that he'd have to winkle it out. 'And so you followed her. And what happened then?'

'She walked back along the footbridge. She was across the bridge before I reached it. I could see her stepping off when I reached the Dolphin Hard at the town end. I followed, but she was at her bungalow before I had crossed the bridge.'

Mickey nodded encouragingly. The Dolphin Hard, he recalled, was the slipway close to the bridge from which the ferry was launched. 'And you went straight to her bungalow.'

'And she was inside. I opened the door and went in. She did not hear me at first. She had told me that day that she had just returned from London.'

'Two days before she died,' Mickey confirmed.

'Yes, two days. She was in her bedroom, emptying her handbag on to the bed. I said to her, "What is that, Cécile?" And she turned around to face me and I have never seen so much fury in any woman's eyes.'

'And why was she so angry? Because you had followed her?'

'No.' Philippe shook his head. 'I think it was because of what I had seen her taking from her bag.'

'And what was that?'

'Paper wrappings, like you might get from a pharmacy. The kind you might find wrapping a sleeping draft or a vermifuge. But I don't think these papers contained either of those things.'

Mickey recalled the paper wrapping on the bedside table. The one that had contained cocaine.

'I have never taken drugs,' Philippe said. 'I drink a little wine, and since I have come to England I have even learned to drink the English beer, but I do not have anything to do with narcotics. Cécile always knew how I felt about such things.'

'Nice to know you have some boundaries.' Mickey's voice was heavy with sarcasm. 'Go on,' he said, relenting a little. 'Tell me what happened next.'

'She flew at me. She said how dare I judge her, knowing how I earned my living. She said it was not for her anyway. She said it was none of my concern.'

'So, she was shouting at you?'

'Screaming at me. I tried to calm her, to say she should lower her voice, that the neighbours might hear. And I was right, Sergeant Hitchens. One of them did hear.'

'Ah,' Mickey said. 'And who might that have been?'

'I don't know. She didn't say and neither did he. He suddenly appeared in the main room and called out to see if everything was all right. "Cissie," he called. "Cissie, I heard you arguing with someone. I thought I'd come and see if everything was all right."'

'And how did she respond?'

'She was still angry. She called out to him that everything was fine and that I was just leaving. He came closer, near to the bedroom door, and she pushed me out and closed it behind her. She was angry with me and I think angry with him for coming in. I supposed she might have been embarrassed.'

'Just angry? Nothing more?'

Philippe looked puzzled. 'What more?' he asked.

'And you left then? And this neighbour, what did he do?'

'How should I know? I left, I stormed away. I didn't look back. Then . . . then I heard that she had died. That she had been killed, and I knew that this must have happened because of what she had become. I warned her. I told her that nothing good could come of being mixed up in such things and, believe me, Sergeant Hitchens, I should know. Nothing good has come to me.'

'Apart from money,' Mickey countered.

'You saw how I live? Not even so much of that.'

Mickey asked a few more questions but Philippe seemed drained now that he had said his piece and Mickey had him escorted back to his cell.

He called Henry, even though it was very late.

'And so,' Henry Johnstone said, 'we see if Cissie Rowe, or

Cécile Rolland, was registered as a user with any of the approved physicians in London. We find out whether she had her prescription filled in the days before she died.'

'Sounds to me as though her physician might have over-prescribed,' Mickey observed.

'Quite likely, but it's confirmation rather than confession we want at this stage. If she carried stolen goods to the capital and took drugs back, then the question is, did she also do this on her own account, or was it for someone else?'

'As a small-time dealer she'd have made a little side money,' Mickey said. 'There'd be few doctors willing to over-prescribe in sufficient quantity for anyone to get rich from it. Word soon gets around.'

'It does indeed. Cynthia spoke of several doctors that might be persuaded. If she knows, then others who actively seek such knowledge would have little trouble in identifying them. Mickey, what do you think about this neighbour?'

'Well, the description Philippe gave was vague, but my money is on Fred Owens.'

'Mine too. We know that Mrs Owens thinks nothing of neighbouring. Perhaps her husband is as relaxed about such things. Mickey, I want an extensive background investigation done on both of the Owenses. It might just have been a case of a concerned neighbour hearing raised voices, but I have a feeling that this is more.'

Mickey nodded, then remembered that his boss couldn't see his nod. 'That everything is local,' he said. 'Including the bastard that knocked you on the head.'

# TWENTY-FOUR

Wednesday morning's papers were full of the news that the murder of celebrated actress Cissie Rowe was in some way linked to the police raid on a notorious pawnbroker, Edward Grieves. Many of the sidebars also carried the news that the famed murder detective investigating the case had been attacked and left for dead, close by where Miss Rowe had met her end.

'Celebrated,' Cynthia said, 'notorious, famous. Darling, the press do love their adjectives, don't they? Will this interfere with your work?'

'Possibly,' Henry said. 'Though it was inevitable and I'm actually astonished that Miss Rowe's death did not make a bigger splash before. It's possible, of course, that it might aid the investigation. Those involved will imagine we are making progress where we are not and might act in such a way that they are tripped up. It's impossible to know how this will resolve itself.'

'At least you're looking better. You gave us all a scare, Henry.'

'I feel fine, Cyn. And I have work to do. Mickey is coming back to Shoreham and he'll collect your car and pick me up later.'

'Henry, are you sure? The doctor said you should rest.'

'And I have rested. But I've had enough of rest and want to be doing. I can't abide inaction, you know that.'

'Know it and sometimes fret about it. You'll be coming back here tonight?'

'Probably, but things will move faster now, I feel. We may have to return to London.'

Cynthia picked up another of the newspapers and skimmed the story. She smiled suddenly. 'Your little photographer has another credit to her name,' she said.

'My little photographer? Oh, Miss Mars. Let me see.'

Cynthia handed him the newspaper. Another picture of Cissie Rowe, in conversation with a group of young men, graced page two. Opposite was a picture of Henry himself, taken on Shoreham Beach. He was striding purposefully, unaware that his picture had been snapped.

'Well, at least she'll be making a little money out of this,' Cynthia said. 'And she is rather good, isn't she?'

Henry could see that his sister's mouth twitched with laughter and her eyes sparkled. 'Making fun at my expense, Cyn?'

'Always.' She clasped his hand, suddenly serious. 'But please be careful, Henry. Promise me you will.'

Mickey Hitchens collected Henry in the early afternoon and they drove back to Shoreham. Henry had traded his bandage for a dressing which just covered his stitches. A small patch of hair had been shaved from all around the wound and he felt dreadfully conscious of it. Worse still, it hurt to wear his hat and so he couldn't even hide the injury away.

And, though he was loath to admit it, his head still ached abominably.

'Mrs Owens has a record,' Mickey told him, 'but it was years ago when she was still a girl. She was charged with petty theft.'

'And nothing since?'

'No, but here's the thing. She grew up just off Brick Lane, not more than a few streets away from the pawnbroker's and only a few doors away from Josiah Bailey.'

'So she must have known him.'

'Inevitable. They would have been at school together at the very least.'

'And is Bailey being brought in?'

'Tonight.'

'Why wait until then?'

'Because he's out of town, not due back until late this afternoon. He'll be lifted when he gets off the train. Mrs Owens still has a sister living nearby, who's told us Mrs Owens visits about once a month but her husband goes up more often. Sometimes stays overnight at his sister-in-law's.'

'Interesting.'

'Isn't it just? On Bailey's patch, and with a direct connection to the man himself via Mrs Owens.'

'Perhaps,' Henry said. He felt the need to play devil's advocate. 'But many people would have known Bailey when they were children; it doesn't immediately link them or compel them to a life of crime.'

'No, it doesn't, but it might if your sister married into the family.'

Henry turned and stared at his sergeant. 'Muriel Owens' sister—'

'Married Josiah Bailey's cousin. Now we've nothing on either the sister or the husband, but . . .'

'But the prospect of a connection is still very much there.' Henry nodded and then wished he hadn't.

They drove round to Bungalow Town over the road bridge. Just by the Church of the Good Shepherd was a police road-block and the press and newsreel reporters were out in force. Mickey was evidently expected because the barrier was pulled aside and they drove through without pause though Henry thought it was inevitable that Cynthia's car would be featuring in the next day's papers. He didn't imagine Albert would be particularly amused.

Mickey stopped the car behind the studio. 'The Owenses are at work,' he said. 'Constable Prentice checked up for me.'

Gingerly, Henry got out of the car. Once upright, he immediately felt the headache worsen and the nausea return and was aware of Mickey eyeing him warily. 'I'm all right,' Henry told him.

'And I'm a Chinaman. You fall over and there'll be hell to pay with that sister of yours.'

They walked slowly up to the lean-to building that Mrs Owens had been working in before but were told that she was running an errand and not there. Mr Owens was sent for.

Mickey related what he had been told by Philippe about the day Cissie had returned from London and Philippe had quarrelled with her.

'He says that a neighbour intervened,' Mickey told Fred Owens.

'Well, it wasn't me. I can assure you of that.'

'The description matches you, Mr Owens.'

'Perhaps it does, but I would recall a quarrel between Cissie and a young man. I would remember going into her bungalow under those circumstances, and I can assure you I didn't.'

'Perhaps you don't like to admit to doing such a thing in front of your wife,' Henry said.

'In front of . . .' Owens turned. Muriel had just returned and was standing behind him with a quizzical expression on her face.

'Fred? What's all this about?'

'Two days before your friend was killed,' Henry said, 'she had a quarrel with a man named Philippe Boilieu. The quarrel took place in her home. Philippe reports that a neighbour came into the bungalow, having overheard the shouting, and asked Miss Rowe if everything was all right. From the description he gave, I'm very much of the opinion that this neighbour was Mr Owens, but he denies this. Did he mention anything of the kind to you, Mrs Owens?'

She looked from Henry to her husband and then shook her head. 'He *would* have mentioned it,' she said. 'I would at once have gone round to comfort poor Cissie. Your young man must be mistaken, Inspector.'

She paused and looked more closely at Henry. 'You look very unwell, Inspector. We all heard what happened to you. What an utterly dreadful thing. You really ought to be resting.'

Mr Owens smiled at his wife. He looks too smug, Henry thought. I know he's lying. The question is, why? It would be a natural thing to admit to hearing an argument and offering to intervene, to be concerned for a friend and neighbour. Why hide that?

Unless he had seen something, done something that meant he wanted to distance himself from the scene.

'Did you know that Miss Rowe used cocaine?' Henry asked, and felt Mickey look at him in surprise.

'Cissie? No, Inspector. In that you are very much mistaken. Cissie would never—'

'She travelled to London regularly, did she not?'

'Any of us might travel to London on a regular basis,' Mr Owens objected.

'Especially, I suppose, if one has family there,' Henry agreed.

Muriel Owens' cheeks flushed slightly. 'I have a sister there.'

'And sometimes your husband stays at her home when work takes him to the capital?'

She looked uncertain then. 'Sometimes, I suppose. But what does this have to do with Cissie and the dreadful allegations you are making about her?'

One of the wardrobe girls came in. 'Mrs Owens, I need—'

'Not now,' Muriel snapped.

'But Mr Noy sent me. He said—'

'Please,' Muriel said. 'Get what you need and then leave us. Can't you see we are occupied?'

The girl took something from a drawer and scooted away. The gossip will be all around the studio within the hour, Henry thought, wondering how much she had overheard.

'Miss Rowe travelled to London once or twice a month.' Henry was guessing here. 'She took with her an item or two of jewellery which she delivered to a pawn shop.'

'I told you, sometimes she was given gifts. She would tire of them and I suppose raise some little capital for herself.' Muriel Owens glared at Henry. 'Surely that isn't against any law?'

'Not if the items were hers.'

'Of course they were hers. Why else would she be wearing them?'

Why else indeed, Henry thought. He could think of only two possible reasons. One was that she gained some kind of thrill from wearing items she knew to be stolen. The other was more deliberate. That she might be taunting someone, challenging them. Showing off what someone else knew to be stolen and knowing that they would be threatened or even frightened by it.

There was also a third, related possibility. That she thought she was being in some way clever and that by taunting that individual she gained some kind of advantage over them.

'She took these items and she pawned them and brought the tickets back to her home. We found two of them: one in Cissie's bungalow and one in poor Jimmy Cottee's railway carriage. I suspect that on the night I was attacked, that is what the assailant was after. I got in his way.' *And gained a punishing headache for my troubles.* Henry could see Mickey watching him and wondered if he looked as half dead as he felt. From the expression on his sergeant's face, he guessed that he did.

'And what does this have to do with her using narcotics?' Mr Owens asked. He glanced at his wristwatch. 'Inspector, we are wasting time. I have left my work for this. If you've done with me, then I'd like to get back to it.'

'She took jewellery up and she fetched narcotics back,' Henry said. 'Not a difficult thing.'

'But a nonsensical one,' Fred Owens said. 'Gentlemen, I must go. I have work to do.'

Henry did nothing to stop him. Muriel Owens watched her husband leave. 'I don't understand,' she said. 'Cissie wasn't that kind of girl. And what on earth does this have to do with my sister?'

'More to do with your sister's husband,' Mickey said. 'And the family he comes from.'

She straightened herself up and looked Mickey in the eye. 'A family they have no dealings with,' she said. 'Now, if you will excuse me, I too will have to go.'

'What do we make of all that?' Mickey asked as they watched her walk away.

'He's rattled. She's bemused. I suspect she knows very little – or chooses to know very little. Mr Owens, though. Now I think he's in this up to his scrawny neck. And now, Mickey, I think I need to go back to the car.'

# TWENTY-FIVE

'If she was selling narcotics at the studio,' Henry said, 'someone would have known about it. We'd have heard some hint by now, I think.'

He closed his eyes and leaned back in the seat, allowing the sound of the engine to soothe and distract him.

'Unless she obtained the drugs for someone else to distribute and just took a fee. We need to chase up our colleagues, see if they've found a doctor that admits to having her on their books. And see if any progress has been made with Bailey. His train should be in by now.'

'And apply for a warrant,' Henry said. 'Or perhaps for two. I want the Owenses' house searched and I want Geoffrey Clifton's place gone over with a fine tooth comb.'

'Not going to be easy,' Mickey predicted. 'Oh, it shouldn't be difficult for the Owens place, them being only theatrical people, though frankly I think it'll be a wild goose chase. If he is guilty, then he'll not leave anything that his wife might find. Be harder to obtain an order for the Cliftons, I reckon. Pillars of the community and all that. Probably have the local magistrates along to these parties of theirs.'

'Probably so, but my money's on Geoffrey Clifton. He drives Cissie up to London to dispose of the stolen goods and then takes her to see the doctor, comes back with a little something extra to make his parties go with a swing.'

'Well, he didn't take her or fetch her back that last time. You reckon Fred Owens saw the packages? Well, so do I, but my question is, so what? She could have told him it was anything. That she wasn't sleeping and the doctor had given her powders. But why lie about hearing the argument?'

Henry was silent for a moment and Mickey glanced sideways at him to see if he'd fallen asleep. But he just looked deep in thought. A moment later he said, 'Philippe knew what she had. She could have lied to him, but what was the point? He lives on the edge of society, frequenting with criminals and those they exploit, and those who make use of their contacts and abilities. Philippe recognized what she had because he knew that she too lived on the edge of that world. Why else would she be so angry that he had caught her? My thinking is that Fred Owens saw. And that Fred Owens recognized what he was seeing. Because Fred Owens already knew. That's why he denied being in the bungalow at the time of the argument. He was already guilty so he recognized guilt.'

'All right. I'll go along with that. But guilty of what, and to what degree? And how do we prove it?'

Information awaited them at the police station in Shoreham. Josiah Bailey had been taken in for questioning but his legal council had already arrived and no one expected a swift result.

'A familiar story,' Mickey said.

But there was more. One of the fingerprints ('only a partial, mind') found at Jimmy Cottee's home had been identified. It belonged to one Billy Crane, a known associate of Bailey's.

'A thug,' Henry said. 'All brawn and very little brain.'

'Bailey doesn't employ him for his intellect. That's good, in fact that's very good. Little cracks appearing, Henry. All we have to do is jemmy them open.'

Sometimes, as Mickey would say, you just have to be content to let the fruit ripen. There was little more that could be done that day and so Mickey and Henry returned to Cynthia's house and Henry retired early to bed.

His head throbbed and he found it hard to keep his thoughts in order.

Looking around at the room his sister kept for him, Henry found himself comparing his surroundings both to his own flat in London and to the house where he and Cynthia had been children.

This bedroom was bright and cheery. Wallpaper flecked with small sprigs of flowers did nothing to make the room look small or cramped. The furniture was of excellent quality and the bed was soft. Cynthia had chosen a light blue rug for in here, laid over a paler carpet. She knew he hated dark colours and dimly lit rooms.

His own flat was small but had large windows that looked out over the river. Somehow the fact that he could gaze out on to open space and watch the river traffic made the place seem more spacious. His books were all ranged against the back wall and his furniture faced the window, looking into the light.

Neither place was anything like their father's home.

Henry took up his journal and began to write.

*And it was always our father's home. Never ours or even our mother's. We were secondary to his whims and his needs. I remember the hours spent in that dark study of his, keeping silent while I studied my schoolbooks. He liked to watch me while I worked, chastise me if I so much as raised my head or stretched my arm. I wished him dead on many an occasion, right from when I was a very little child. Even before I fully understood what 'dead' might mean.*

*And, I am deeply ashamed to say, I hated my mother for marrying him. Why had she not understood what kind of man he was? She was everything that he was not and it was as though he had captured her like some exotic insect and then trapped her in a killing jar, one to which he had added only enough poison to bring about a long and slow and painful death. Then he had settled down to watch the decline and the decay.*

*Yet should you ask anyone it would be 'Oh, Doctor Johnstone, yes, what an amiable fellow! Sad that his wife is so sickly. Just as well she married a physician.'*

'Would you like to have a child?' Cynthia had asked him when her daughter had been born and Henry had visited the new baby for the first time.

Henry had cradled Melissa, fascinated by the tiny hands and the snub little nose, and had shaken his head. 'What if I became like him?'

'You could never be like him.'

'But what if—'

'I'd shoot you first.' She'd said it with a smile, but he knew the truth of it.

'I think you would.'

*Thinking of the place where Cissie Rowe died it occurs to me that despite all of the personal items, the photographs and the clothes she kept so carefully, it would be difficult, just examining those things, to get any sense of the woman who owned them.*

*There were no books, few letters, no notebooks or personal documents apart from receipts and bills. No sense that she had settled there and made it home. It was a place to live, to alight and rest, to entertain friends, even, but not home.*

# TWENTY-SIX

Simon Monkton was a dapper little man in a bright waist-coat and rather loud dog-toothed check suit.

He had turned up at the police station in Shoreham looking for Inspector Johnstone and, on being informed that he was expected shortly, had declared that he would wait.

When Henry and Sergeant Hitchens arrived, he was perched on a bench in the reception area and swinging his legs like a schoolchild.

'You are the private detective?' Mickey sounded doubtful. 'You'd hardly blend into the background, if you don't mind me saying.'

'Which is why I employ less conspicuous personnel,' Simon Monkton told him. 'You'll be wondering what brings me here? Well, I heard you missed me at my London office and Mrs Clifton suggested that as I was coming to see her, it might be wise for me to call in to speak to both of you.'

They took him through into an interview room and Simon Monkton settled neatly on a wooden chair.

'My business with Mrs Clifton is, as I'm sure you are aware, of a personal nature. She likes to be aware of her husband's various liaisons. She is aware that they burn out quickly enough, shall we say, but she still prefers to know with what she might be contending.'

'And your associates followed Mr Clifton when he was seeing Miss Rowe?' Mickey said.

'Among others, yes. Miss Rowe lasted longer than most, I have to say, which caused Mrs Clifton some little concern, as you can imagine. They did part for a little time and then the association seems to have been rekindled about eleven months ago, after something like a three-month space.'

'And have you any idea what brought about this renewal of interest?' Henry asked.

'Well, sir, I think I might well do. In view of this turning out to be such a very serious business – I'm not used to murder creeping into my concerns, you understand. So I called upon my associates and with them I reviewed all of the documentation we had on this particular liaison. You see, as we were keeping a watch on Mr Clifton, it also happened that we kept quite a watch on Miss Rowe.'

Mr Monkton had an attaché case and he lifted it on to the table and opened it. Inside was a number of manila envelopes.

'This one, I think – ah, yes. You see here that my associate photographed Mr Clifton on a number of occasions. To be truthful, he was an easy mark. A creature of habit, one might say. My associate need only watch out for him at one of the clubs that he frequents or at his office or one of three or four restaurants he likes. But when he was with Miss Rowe there were a few little changes of habit. This being one of them.'

'The pawnbroker's,' Henry said.

'But my associates also found another anomaly. The young lady seems to have had regular appointments at a certain doctor's surgery and Mr Clifton has been known to take her to these appointments and wait for her in his car.'

With the air of a magician revealing his prestige, Simon Monkton handed a slip of paper to Henry. 'The address,' he said. 'You may recognize it. The good doctor has quite a reputation, I believe.'

They hadn't needed Simon Monkton's revelation; enquiries by their colleagues had revealed that Cissie Rowe, using her birth name of Cécile Rolland, had indeed been registered with an authorized medical man. But what had now fallen into place was that Geoffrey Clifton may have been aware of this and had on occasion accompanied her – even if he'd not gone into the surgery himself.

'We apply for the warrant now?' Mickey asked.

'No, I think we start to round up our suspects and bring them in. I think that might be the swiftest route.'

'Suspects?'

'We have Philippe. We need Fred and Muriel Owens and I think we should make our Mr Clifton as uncomfortable as we can. He's still up in London so a visit to his office by a couple of constables might be in order, don't you think? Just an invitation to help with our enquiries.'

Mickey grinned. 'I like the sound of that,' he said. 'Get that jemmy out and open up the cracks.'

It was a strange procession back to London. Mickey and Henry drove in Cynthia's car followed by two police vehicles, one containing Fred Owens and the other Muriel. They had been collected from the studio, fetched away from their work and escorted to the waiting cars in front of their fellow employees. Mrs Owens had been in tears and Henry felt a pang of sympathy for her. He was still doubtful that she had been involved in any way in Cissie Rowe's death or the criminality that led to it.

Geoffrey Clifton had been collected from his office. He was not a happy man.

Once they were back at Scotland Yard, Mickey had Philippe brought up from his cell.

'Now tell me,' Mickey said. 'Would you know this man, this neighbour, if you saw him again?'

Philippe nodded slowly. 'Yes, I think I would.'

'And tell me,' Henry asked, 'was it you who lured my constable away and vandalized my crime scene?'

Philippe shrugged. 'I had heard of Cécile's death. I was distraught. I wanted some remembrance of her and I recalled the photograph that she had on the little table. I saw the police constable and I thought that reaching it would be impossible.'

'You wanted just the photograph. You'd no thought of making off with the narcotics, I suppose?' Mickey asked.

'Of course you did,' Henry said. 'You'd not see an opportunity like that go to waste. You discovered a way of getting my constable away from the scene and you got into the bungalow, looking for the narcotics Cissie had brought from London. Did you know that when she died, cocaine was forced down her throat? She could not fight back. Her assailant knelt on her hands, poured the cocaine into her mouth and poured water after it. She was conscious enough to choke, to understand what was happening to her. And then her killer smothered the life from her. Did you know that, Philippe? Was that you?'

'No. It was not me. I could never do such a thing. I loved Cécile. I loved her.'

'And yet you returned to the bungalow intent on stealing the very thing you quarrelled over. What kind of a man are you, Philippe Boilieu?'

'A poor excuse for one, perhaps. But I never did her harm.'

Henry regarded the young man steadily and was inclined to believe him. 'And you can identify the neighbour?'

'I think so.'

It proves nothing, Henry thought. It would prove only that Mr Owens had been present, but it might serve to shake things up.

'I'm curious,' Mickey said. 'The boy that took the constable away from his duties, he said a woman had given him money to do so. What woman was that?'

Philippe smiled slightly. 'I think he fooled you, Sergeant. I gave him money to tell the constable. There was no woman.'

'Did you threaten him if he told? Even though he can't have known you.'

'I paid him money, that is all.'

'And why did you smash up her place?' Mickey wanted to know. 'Or maybe I can answer that. The stuff was nowhere to be found, was it? You knew you didn't have long and you couldn't find what you'd hoped to, so you smashed the place up. Sheer temper, was it?'

'I no longer know.'

Henry left the room briefly and when he came back he beckoned Philippe to follow him. He led the young man down the hall and into a reception area. As Philippe arrived, Fred Owens was being brought along the corridor.

'That's the man,' Philippe told Henry. 'That is indeed the man who came into Cécile's room the day we argued. I saw him there.'

Fred Owens' face was a picture of contempt. 'And that means nothing,' he said. 'Nothing at all.'

\* \* \*

A female officer had searched Muriel Owens and then waited with her in the interview room. Mrs Owens had not ceased crying or talking ever since she'd been brought from Shoreham and she continued now in clear distress. The female officer had been instructed not to reply. Henry knew how frustrating and upsetting it could be if no one paid you any mind, no matter how much you tried to attract their notice.

When he entered the room he continued the tactic, shuffling through a stack of photographs he had with him.

'Why am I here, Inspector? What are you accusing me of?'

Henry laid the photographs out on the table. 'Your friend is dead,' he said quietly. 'And I suspect that your husband, and perhaps you too, had something to do with it.'

'I?' She stared at him in horror and then looked down at the photographs of Cissie that he had laid out in front of her. She gave a little cry and covered her mouth with her hands. Shook her head.

'Your friend is dead,' Henry repeated. 'She was young and perhaps very foolish, but she did nothing to deserve this.'

'And I did nothing to bring it about. I didn't kill her. I found her. I—'

'The night I was attacked, Mrs Owens – where was your husband?'

'He was at home, with me.'

'And he never left home? Never went out to smoke or to walk?'

'Well, he may have done. He may have said that he needed a breath of air. He may—'

'And the night you and Cissie Rowe went to the theatre together. Did he go out after you'd returned? Did he want a breath of air on that occasion?'

She stared at him. 'What are you saying? What are you implying, Inspector? That my husband killed my friend? Our friend?'

Henry waited until she looked down again, her eyes drawn to the photographs.

'Someone hit her over the head and then dragged her into her bungalow. They put her on the bed and waited until she had almost regained consciousness and then, when she was aware of what was happening to her but too weak to fight, cocaine was forced down her throat and she was asphyxiated. Smothered with her own pillow. It would not have taken very long. She wasn't very big or very strong and her death would have taken little effort on the part of her attacker. It would have taken minutes, Mrs Owens. Minutes to take a life. But can you imagine what an eternity that would have seemed for poor Cissie Rowe? Can you imagine how long it must have seemed for Jimmy Cottee? Poor, simple Jimmy Cottee who loved her so much. Beaten and then hanged, strangled to death because he would not – or more likely could not – give his attackers what they wanted.'

Mrs Owens had begun to weep, to wail, to protest again. The WPC glared at Henry, regarding him as utterly inhuman.

'A fingerprint was found in Jimmy Cottee's railway carriage. A fingerprint belonging to a man by the name of Billy Crane.'

He saw her flinch.

'I see you recognize the name. He's an associate, or should I say an employee, of Josiah Bailey. A man you are very familiar with.'

'I was a child when I knew those people. I left all that behind me.'

'But perhaps it didn't entirely relinquish you. Perhaps that world drew your husband in. How often does he go to London to visit your relatives, Mrs Owens? A lot more often than you?'

'I don't understand. What could Billy Crane have been doing with Jimmy?'

'What indeed? I'd hazard that Billy Crane was employed in Jimmy Cottee's murder.'

'And Cissie's?' He sensed she was almost afraid to ask.

'No, I think your husband took care of Cissie's murder.'

'My husband . . . why?'

'So was he at home with you on that night? Did he take a walk? Did he leave you on the night I was attacked on the beach?'

'I don't know. I went to sleep. I wouldn't have known if he'd gone out.'

'Really, Mrs Owens? Would you really not have known?'

Henry left her then and joined Mickey Hitchens, who was about to go in and speak to Fred Owens.

'Any joy with Josiah Bailey?'

'Not a murmur. But I've told him and his lawyer that fingerprints were found at a murder scene and that's why he's been brought in. I've not told them which murder scene or whose fingerprints. Best to keep them guessing, I feel. You're joining me with Fred Owens?'

'Briefly. I want to give him some food for thought too. Then I'll see what I can get out of Geoffrey Clifton.'

Unlike his wife, Fred Owens had been silent on his journey and maintained that silence for almost all the time he had spent in custody. He sat staring at the narrow window set high up in the wall as though watching something of major interest, though Henry knew that there was no view to be had from this window – not even if Fred Owens had climbed upon his chair.

'Mr Owens,' Henry said, 'I've just been speaking to your wife.'

Fred Owens didn't move.

'She tells me that you went out for a walk on the night that Miss Rowe was killed. And that you also went out for a breath of air on the night that I was attacked. She reminded me too that Cissie seemed upset on the night at the theatre. That she seemed, in particular, to be ill at ease with you.'

Henry paused. 'It's my belief that you killed Cissie Rowe and that her death had something to do with the cocaine forced down her throat. Were you making a point, Mr Owens? Had she offended you in some way? Did her habit offend you?'

A slight flick of an eye, the smallest change in attention, told Henry that he was on to something – but that it wasn't that. Not offence, not contempt.

'Or were you angry with her, Mr Owens? Had she lied to you?'

That was it, Henry thought. She had deceived him in some way.

'I know you killed her,' Henry said. 'And I know you were involved in Jimmy Cottee's death.'

'No, Inspector, I did not kill her.'

'A fingerprint was found, as I've just been telling your wife. A fingerprint belonging to Billy Crane. You're familiar with Billy Crane? You're familiar, of course, with his employer. Josiah Bailey.'

'Only inasmuch as he's related to my brother-in-law.'

'A brother-in-law you visit often.' Henry let that thought hang and then nodded to Mickey. 'I'll leave you to speak with my sergeant now,' he said.

So, Henry thought as he walked back down the narrow corridor to where Geoffrey Clifton waited. It was about the drugs. Or, at least, Cissie's death was. Jimmy Cottee had been a casualty, a misunderstanding, he thought. Someone believed that Cissie had confided in the young man.

He paused suddenly and turned back to where he had left Muriel Owens as a sudden thought struck him.

He retrieved a photograph that had been taken of the list Cissie had kept and took it with him.

Mrs Owens was still crying. Someone had provided her with a decent handkerchief and a cup of tea.

She looked up anxiously as Henry appeared and he could read the dread in her eyes that he would punish her again.

This time he lay the list down on the table, but with only the initials showing. The rest he covered with another print.

'Tell me what this means.'

'Means? It's just initials. Just a list of initials.'

'And whose initials might they be?'

She looked puzzled. 'It looks like a sign-out list.'

'A sign-out list?'

'When the girls at the studio take a costume or a property, they have to sign for it. Initial the list against the article.' She looked at him expectantly.

'And whose initials might these be?'

She looked genuinely puzzled. 'Well, the C.R. would have been Cissie, and it looks as though this is in her hand. The V.A., that's Violet, I suppose, and then there's E. and M. for Ellen May, another of the young actresses we have.'

'Why would actresses sign for costumes and props?'

She was on easy ground now. 'If the film is historical then we hire our costumes from Drury's in Brighton. For contemporary films our junior performers often wear their own clothing but with little things added. Gloves, hats, perhaps a scarf or something, taken from the properties or costume department. They have to sign for them.'

Henry uncovered the rest of the page. 'And are these items taken from your costume department?'

'I wouldn't think so. No.'

Henry picked up his print and left. He was angry with himself not to have thought that C. and R. were simply Cissie's initials. He had been fixed on the idea that they had something to do with the robberies, not the next step in the journey of the stolen jewellery. What the list now suggested to him was that Cissie Rowe might not have been the only young woman carrying such items.

It was another potential piece of the puzzle.

# TWENTY-SEVEN

Geoffrey Clifton paced and smoked. He was clearly angry and about to tell the inspector so.

Henry lit a cigarette of his own and sat down. His head was throbbing again and he was feeling the effects of a long day. He was not inclined towards patience.

Geoffrey Clifton began to speak; Henry interrupted him.

'Was Miss Rowe providing you with narcotics, Mr Clifton?'

Clifton scowled. 'And why would she do that?'

'Because you asked her to. Because you offered her good money for it. Because you liked to offer your guests something in addition to your no doubt excellent cellar but without having to go to the trouble of registering for yourself. I imagine if that came out it would not enhance your reputation.'

'My reputation needs no . . . enhancement, as you put it.'

'Mr Clifton, I'm tired, and I'm not inclined to indulge you. I don't believe you had anything to do with Miss Rowe's murder, but I do believe that you made use of her. You drove her to London. You are implicated in her handling of stolen goods and you also went with her to her appointments with a doctor who was authorized to supply her with drugs. She registered her addiction. But she did not in fact have an addiction. She sold her supply to you, Mr Clifton, can we just get this out of the way? Tell me what you know and you can go on home.'

'And that will be it, I suppose. You'll stay out of my life.'

'That I can't promise, but you are low on my list of priorities. I am more concerned with murder than with deceit.'

Geoffrey Clifton considered the matter and then stubbed out his cigarette. He sat down. 'I found out that she'd been doing the same thing for someone else; I simply offered her a better deal. She told this other person that her doctor was refusing to supply, or some other excuse, and she did me the favour. I, in turn, paid her well enough to make it worth her

while and I also helped out from time to time when she needed
to come up to London.

'It was simple really. There is nothing else to tell.'

Henry considered. 'There is one more thing, Mr Clifton.
Who was this other person?'

Clifton shrugged dismissively. 'Someone at the studio. Some
cameraman or other. Owens, I believe she called him.'

'And she was happy with the arrangement? She didn't worry
that he might find out? That he might not be pleased? That
he might feel she had deceived him?'

Clifton frowned. 'She seemed content at first. I will admit
that she had grown more anxious in the past few weeks. She
said he was pressuring her again.'

Henry nodded. 'Thank you, Mr Clifton.'

# EPILOGUE

Henry sat in the quiet of his own apartment and gazed out at the river. The evening light played upon the water and the river traffic had eased – though it never completely ceased.

He picked up his journal and began to write.

*He confessed in the end that he had killed her, and that he had suggested to Bailey's men that Jimmy Cottee had kept a list of all the houses his gang had robbed and all the random items of jewellery and other trinkets that had been fenced. Knowing that Cissie was fond of the young man, Owens seems genuinely to have believed that she would have confided in Jimmy Cottee. It seems more likely that she simply hid the pawn ticket without his knowledge. No doubt she saw this as some kind of insurance.*

*No doubt, Cissie Rowe was terribly naïve.*

*Fred Owens had indeed been drawn into that other world, the world his wife had done her best to escape. He had wanted money. Simply that, and he had acted occasionally as lookout or driver. He had been indulged, if that's the right word. He had been permitted his little perks, and told how to dispose of them.*

*It had given him pleasure, I think, to involve attractive young women like Cissie in his schemes. Young women who, I suspect, reminded him of the way his wife had been in her younger, more ambitious days.*

*And then he discovered that Cissie had once had a habit. She had broken herself of it but Owens gave her a reason to continue with her prescription. Until Clifton gave her a better one.*

*He says he killed her because she deceived him. That, initially, he had no intent to kill – but no one could believe that. Cissie Rowe died a violent, terrifying and painful death and each stage of it speaks of full intent.*

Henry paused and thought of Muriel Owens.

*I'm still not convinced. What did she know? What did she suspect? Her life is ruined and I doubt she will recover either way.*

He continued to watch the river for a while, pondering on the ill logic that led him to love the deep dark water that flowed through London and yet to hate the sea. Then he turned back to his desk and picked up the letter that had arrived that day. It was from Melissa. She wrote,

> *Dear Uncle Henry,*
> *Now that you have finished with your murder, I thought it would be all right to remind you about our shopping trip. Mummy says that London has some excellent bookshops. Perhaps you would like to telephone and arrange a day.*
> *Your loving niece,*
> *Melissa.*
>
> *P.S. I have decided that Mr Conan Doyle might be mistaken in his view of fairies.*

9 781847 518088